Rally Round the Flag

Rally Round the Flag

JANE ORCUTT

Guideposts

New York, New York

Rally Round the Flag

ISBN-13: 978-0-8249-4916-7

Published by Guideposts
16 East 34th Street
New York, New York 10016
www.guideposts.org

Distributed by Ideals Publications, a Guideposts company
2630 Elm Hill Pike, Suite 100
Nashville, TN 37214

Cover Illustration by Deborah Chabrian
Interior Design by Marisa Jackson
Typeset by Müllerhaus Publishing Group | www.mullerhaus.net

Printed and bound in the United States of America
10 9 8 7 6 5 4 3 2 1

GRACE CHAPEL INN

A place where one can be
refreshed and encouraged,
a place of hope and healing,
a place where God is at home.

Acknowledgments

To Janice Burns. —Jane Orcutt

Chapter One

$\mathcal{G}$race Chapel Inn sat like a welcoming presence just up the road from the small town of Acorn Hill in southeastern Pennsylvania. Visitors often commented on how lovely the inn looked next to its namesake, Grace Chapel. But then, many visitors came to Acorn Hill to stay in Grace Chapel Inn, a charming bed-and-breakfast run by the Howard sisters.

Louise Howard Smith, Alice Howard and Jane Howard had been reared in the large Victorian home, then went their separate ways after they grew up. Their mother died giving birth to Jane, and when their father, Daniel Howard, passed away, they decided to spruce up the old house with period colors and contemporary conveniences and open their home for business.

On this second day of November, the cocoa-shaded house with green shutters was a perfect backdrop for the autumn leaves that were falling in colorful profusion. The temperature seemed to drop steadily as well. It had already forced the sisters to don sweaters while they decorated the inn's exterior for the upcoming holiday.

"Shall we try again?" Louise, the oldest of the three, asked, taking up her end of the patriotic bunting.

Alice, the middle sister, took up the other end of the fabric decoration, stretching it to its proper length. She and Louise held it against the porch railing for their younger sister's approval.

Jane studied it with a critical eye. Stationed closer to the road than the house, she had to cup her hands around her mouth to be heard. "Hold it up a little higher on your end, Alice. A little bit more. There. That's perfect."

Louise and Alice affixed the bunting to a portion of the porch rail, then moved to the next section. "It can be quite a chore to do this for all our patriotic holidays," Louise said, "but I always feel proud to decorate our home."

"Especially for Veterans Day," Alice said.

"And especially this year," Louise added.

"There's a crease in the middle," Jane called.

Louise obediently smoothed the material. "I am delighted that we have World War II veterans booked at the inn."

"I'm looking forward to the annual parade in Potterston," Alice said, referring to the larger nearby town. "I've already made sure that I won't have to work at the hospital that day." She smoothed out a wrinkle in the bunting. "Unless, of course, there's an emergency."

"Can you stretch it out a bit, Louise?" Jane called. "It's bunched up at your end."

Louise sighed, surveying the pile of bunting still to be hung. Jane had the more artistic eye, and of course each sister wanted the inn to look as nice as possible, but perhaps an eye less concerned with aesthetic perfection would have been preferable right now.

Louise could understand practicing a sonata or concerto until the performance was almost flawless; she had been trained at the conservatory long ago to seek the beauty of perfection. But it was beyond her ambition to hang all the fan-shaped dips in the bunting exactly the same distance from the ground, a goal for which Jane seemed to strive.

Alice seemed to understand her older sister's frustration. "It's all for a good cause, Louise," she said. "Think of the soldiers who will be staying here. They'll appreciate Jane's insistence on precision."

The sisters shared a small laugh. Despite their comments, they adored their younger sister and heartily admired her artistic talents. She had supervised the remodeling of their home into the lovely Victorian inn that it was today. To ensure that they felt comfortable with the changes, she had encouraged Louise's and Alice's input and solicited their help. Each sister's room reflected her individual personality, just as each of the four guest rooms possessed decorative charms of its own. Harmony existed within all three stories, testifying to the plaque by the front door that said Grace Chapel Inn was a place where God was at home.

"That one looks great, girls. Perfect." Jane held up the A-OK sign with her fingers. "Just a few more to go."

Louise smiled. She did hope the veterans appreciated the sisters' hard work.

For dinner that night, Jane, who prepared all the meals at the inn, had made boeuf Bourguignonne. She had worked as a chef in a well-known San Francisco restaurant before returning home to Acorn Hill, and she still put her culinary skills to good use, much to Louise's and Alice's delight.

"*Mmm*," Louise said, savoring a bite of the tender meat. "This is just the kind of meal to take the chill off the evening cold."

Jane passed some warm, crusty French bread. "You and Alice deserve it. You worked hard today."

"So did you," Alice said. She speared the last pearl onion on her plate with her fork and dipped it in the rich wine-flavored sauce, trying to soak up as much of the gravy as she could. "I wonder if it's going to be so cold on Friday when I go to Franklin High's football game."

"I'd forgotten all about that," Jane said. "I'm glad you reminded me, Alice, because I want to go too. It's been a very long time since Franklin has had a chance at the postseason."

"Yes, it's probably the smallest school in the region. It's hard for Franklin to compete with those big schools, but if the team wins Friday night, Franklin will go to the play-offs." Alice smiled. "It reminds me of when you were in high school, Jane. Didn't the team have a big game that year?"

Jane nodded. "When I was a senior. That one was a playoff game too. I hate to say it, but that might have been the last play-off game they've had."

"You were the captain of the cheerleaders, weren't you?" Louise asked. "I was living in Philadelphia at that time, but I remember coming home to see you cheer."

"I was cocaptain, actually." She held up two paper napkins like pom-poms. "Two bits, four bits, six bits, a dollar. All for

Franklin stand up and holler." She rose from her chair, waving the napkins. "Yay!"

Alice clapped, laughing. "Oh, how I remember those days. You always had so many friends running in and out of the house. Cheerleaders. Football players. Drama enthusiasts."

Jane sat down. "I'm sure you and Father thought I was quite a piece of work back then. I hope I didn't give you fits."

"Not at all," she said. "Father always said that you and all your activity would keep us young."

"And you and your activities still do," Louise said, smiling warmly.

"I'm afraid my cheerleading days are over," Jane said, "which is probably just as well. I'm in good health and in pretty good shape from jogging, but I am fifty. The bod's definitely getting older." She placed a hand at the small of her back in exaggerated pain.

Alice and Louise shared a smile.

"What?" Jane asked suspiciously.

"Jane, dear," Alice said, "you are twelve years younger than I."

"And fifteen years younger than I," Louise said.

"So if you think that your body's getting old, where does that leave us?" Alice finished.

Jane put a hand on each of her sister's shoulders, smiling. "Like Mary Poppins, you two are practically perfect in every way."

"*Hmm.* I notice she didn't say anything about our physical condition," Louise said to Alice.

Alice took a sip of water. "I think I prefer it that way."

Chapter Two

The next day, the sisters did a thorough inspection of all four guest rooms to make sure everything was ready for the veterans. The linens were crisp, the pillows fluffed, the floors spotless, the wood furniture gleamed, and all looked perfect.

"Patton himself would approve," Jane said cheerfully, standing with Louise and Jane in the foyer of the inn. "When do our guests arrive?"

Alice glanced at her watch. "Not for a few more hours."

"I don't understand why they're coming to town so early," Jane said. "Veterans Day is over a week away."

"Apparently, the group gets together every Veterans Day at a different place for a reunion and a vacation combined," Louise said. "The woman who called is the wife of one of the veterans. She said that a friend had recommended our inn to their group."

"I'm glad we got a good recommendation. Especially since the parade will be in Potterston, not Acorn Hill. You would think these people would want to be a little closer to the action," Jane said.

Louise smiled. "The woman mentioned that every place they'd called in Potterston was already booked. So I don't think we should let the recommendation go to our heads."

"Anyway, it's four couples, right?" Alice asked.

"Well," Louise said, struggling to remember, "they booked all four rooms, but I believe one in the group is single."

"I wonder if they will need much assistance," Alice said. "If they fought in World War II, they must be at least eighty years old."

"I hadn't thought of that," Louise said. "What will they *do* in all the time leading up to the parade? There are wonderful day trips that one can make from here, but if they are frail..."

"I guess we should be prepared to entertain them in some way," Alice said. "We always make sure our guests are comfortable and happy, but we owe a special effort to these people."

"Agreed," Louise said solemnly.

"I think I heard a car," Jane said, moving to a window to check. Louise and Alice followed, automatically straightening their skirts and touching their hair. It was not every day that they had such distinguished guests. These men were of their father's generation, and the sisters wanted to make a good impression.

"It's Melanie Brubaker," Jane said. The sisters were fond of the thirtysomething woman who was a member of Grace Chapel.

"Melanie!" Alice said, delighted. "I haven't seen her in ages. I thought maybe she had left for another church."

Melanie lifted a hand to knock, then saw that Jane was already opening the door for her. "Hi, Melanie," Jane said. "What brings you our way?"

She stepped into the house, perplexed to see all three sisters standing by the door. "Hi, Jane." She nodded at the other two. "Alice. Louise. You ladies look like you were expecting me."

Jane shut the door, and Alice smiled at Melanie. "We were expecting our next guests, who are due to check in soon. But we're delighted to see you," Alice finished smoothly. "How are you?"

"I'm fine. Working part-time keeps me busy. The family keeps me busy too, particularly with Mac traveling so much," she said.

"How are Mac and the kids?" Alice asked. "Bree is in Vera Humbert's fifth-grade class this year, isn't she?"

"Excuse me?" Melanie said, stepping closer to Alice.

"Bree's in Vera's class this year, right?" Alice said.

Melanie paused for a moment, as though pondering. "Oh." She nodded. "Yes. And Clinton is in third grade."

"I'm very glad that they're both taking piano lessons again this year," Louise said. "They're diligent musicians."

Melanie didn't respond but simply nodded. "Anyway," she said, smiling, "I stopped by to let you know that it is Grace Chapel's turn to organize a food drive for the Community Pantry. This drive coincides with Thanksgiving, and I'm heading up the committee. Would any of you be interested in helping me?"

"I'm sorry," Jane said. "I really can't. I'm helping with the Thanksgiving Day feast, so I'm already tied up coordinating that."

"And I'm particularly busy at the hospital and with a project with the ANGELs," Alice said, referring to her middle-school girls' service group.

"I would be happy to help," Louise said.

"Wonderful!" Melanie said, beaming. "What day would be good for you to meet with me so that we can plan?"

"How about Sunday?" Louise said.

Melanie looked a little lost for a moment, then nodded. "Okay. Let's meet at three o'clock at the chapel, shall we?"

"That would be fine."

"Thank you, Louise," Melanie said, backing toward the door. "I'd better get out of your way since you have guests about to arrive."

"Thank *you* for heading up the committee," Louise said.

Melanie smiled, then was gone.

"She's certainly busy," Louise said, shutting the door behind her. "She seemed a little distracted to me."

"Yes," Alice said. "It seemed as if her mind was on other things, the way she didn't respond. I hope everything is all right."

"I'm sure it is. She's probably just a bit overwhelmed. It's not easy being a working mom," Jane said, "particularly when your husband travels so much."

"That is what makes it even more special that she has taken on the food-drive project," Louise said. "She is sacrificing what little time she has available to help others celebrate Thanksgiving."

Soon after lunch, the sisters puttered off to other duties about the house, when suddenly their guests for the next week and a half arrived. The front door opened with a bang, and each sister, no matter where she was in the house, heard a booming voice. "We're here!"

"Goodness!" Alice said, moving toward the foyer from the parlor, where she had been placing vases of fresh flowers in the room.

Louise and Jane met her there, coming from upstairs and the kitchen, respectively. In the foyer they found three men and two women, each one smiling broadly. An assortment of luggage sat beside them.

A man with thick white hair stepped forward, an unlit cigar in his hand. "I was beginning to wonder if anyone was at home," he said, his voice loud but friendly. He held out his hand. "I'm Mortimer Fineman, but my friends call me Mort."

"I'm Alice Howard," Alice said, shaking his hand. "This is Louise Howard Smith and Jane Howard, my sisters."

"Nice to meet you," Jane said while Louise nodded.

"Hiya, ladies," Mort said. "This is my crew, Lars Olsdotter and his wife Zoë," he said, gesturing to a tall, still-blond, fair-complected man. Zoë was much shorter and dyed her hair approximately the same red shade as the sisters' aunt Ethel.

Lars nodded a greeting. "Hello," Zoë said, shaking hands with each of the sisters in turn. "I'm the one who made the reservations. A cousin of one of my friends stayed here with her husband last year—I can't remember their names. Anyway, when I told her we were looking for a place near Potterston, my friend steered me to you."

"We're so glad to have you," Louise said. "I remember speaking with you on the phone. Welcome."

"And this ugly mug on my left is Harvey Calabrese," Mort said, gesturing with the cigar at the remaining couple, "and fortunately for him, that is his lovely wife Penelope."

"You're the ugly one, Mort," Harvey said, laughing, as he shook hands with the sisters. His face, lined with age, wrinkled even more as he smiled, his olive complexion revealing his Mediterranean heritage. "Don't mind him, ladies. He's been carrying on like that for sixty-some-odd years now. He doesn't mean anything by it."

"He certainly does not," Penelope said in a distinctive British accent. "I must admit that I was appalled by his behavior when we first met, but he's an old softie at heart." She leaned toward Jane and winked. "Don't tell another soul about that, though," she whispered.

"I promise," Jane said, going along with the humor of the group. She looked outside. "You have four rooms reserved. Is this all of your group?"

"The kid'll be along later," Mort said.

"The kid?" Alice asked.

"Nathan Delhomme," Mort said dismissively. "He said he'd be along later in the day. The rest of us met up at the airport for the ride to Acorn Hill."

"Oh," Alice said, assuming that Nathan had earned his nickname by being the youngest in the group. "Would you like to see your rooms? Perhaps you'd like to rest before he gets here."

"Rest?" Mort laughed, turning to the group. "Did you hear that, guys? No offense...Alice, was it? But we never rest during our yearly time together. We've been getting together for Veterans Day every year since they renamed Armistice Day in 1954, and we never spend it resting."

"I beg your pardon," Alice said, feeling a smile curl at her lips. "We'd still be glad to show you to your rooms."

"Yeah, sounds like a good idea," Mort said, lifting his bag.

Louise glanced at the cigar in his hand. "I'm sorry, Mr. Fineman, but we don't allow smoking inside. You're welcome to smoke on the porch, however."

"Sure thing. I'll just set it out there right now, and it'll be waiting for me later," he said, stepping outside.

Lars smiled. "It's good to see that Mort doesn't change from year to year."

"He never does," Zoë said. "Even since Rivka died."

"His wife?" Alice asked Zoë softly.

The group nodded, saddening for just a moment. "It's been five years, and we still miss her," Zoë said.

Mort returned, clapping his hands together. "Okay, gang, let's get settled in."

While everyone grabbed a suitcase, the sisters offered to help. "Wouldn't dream of it," Harvey Calabrese said, waving them off. "You think a bunch of old duffers can't carry their own luggage?"

"Well—" Louise began.

"You were expecting maybe a bunch of old geezers and biddies, I'll bet," Mort said, winking at Louise.

"Well—" she tried again, flustered.

"Just point us to our rooms," Penelope said, smiling. "I can assure you that if anything positive can be said about this group, it is that we are quite a capable lot."

"Right this way, then," Louise said, leading the group up the stairs.

Once they arrived on the second floor, where the guest rooms were located, there was a little discussion over who would take which room. They ducked in and out of the rooms, meeting to confer briefly in the hallway. "Since these two back bedrooms share a bath, I'll take one of them," Mort said. "The rest of you pick what you want. I'm not particular."

"I'd love the Symphony Room," Penelope said, peering out of a rear room. "The climbing rose pattern on the wallpaper reminds me of the lovely flowers in my hometown."

"My English rose," Harvey said, squeezing her affectionately. "If it's roses you want, it's roses you shall have."

"And I would love the room all done up in green, with the floral border and the rosewood furniture," Zoë said. "It's so peaceful."

"That's the Garden Room," Jane said. "I think you'll like it."

"That leaves me with this room here, the one that shares a bath with Penelope and Harvey," Mort said, pointing to the Sunrise Room.

"Don't you want to have a look at it?" Penelope asked.

Mort shrugged. "A room's a room."

Penelope stepped inside. "Oh, Mort, it's lovely. It's decorated in blue, yellow and creamy white and has a darling patchwork quilt in the same colors."

Mort rolled his eyes, then smiled apologetically at Jane, Alice and Louise. "No offense, ladies, but I'm an army guy. You could have just thrown a cot in the corner and I'd have been happy.

Now, if my Rivka were here..." He faltered for a moment, then smiled even wider. "Well, she would have loved this place. And she would have scolded me not to put my shoes on your pretty furniture or that patchwork quilt, so I promise to be on my best behavior."

"I'm sure you will," Alice said, smiling back at him.

"We'll leave you all to get settled," Louise said.

"If you need anything, let us know," Jane added. "We'll head back downstairs and get out of your way."

Mort paused, then took Alice's hand. "Thank you. It's wonderful to meet such fine ladies. I'm sure we'll enjoy our stay here at Grace Chapel Inn."

"And in Acorn Hill," Penelope added. "There seems to be so much to do."

The sisters glanced at one another. Was she talking about the same Acorn Hill? They loved their town immensely, but it was somewhat short on entertainment and tourist attractions.

"No doubt she meant Potterston," Louise murmured as the sisters headed back downstairs.

"No doubt," Alice agreed.

The guests soon retired to the library, and their unbroken patter of good-natured kidding could be heard in the kitchen. Alice helped Jane prepare dinner, which was still a long time away.

"They certainly are a jolly bunch," Alice said, peeling potatoes at the kitchen table.

"Aren't they, though?" Jane commented absentmindedly, consulting a recipe book while she stirred a pot on the stove.

The doorbell rang. "I'll get it," Alice said, because Louise was busy with a piano student. The door to the library opened as she passed, and the veterans streamed out behind her.

"Maybe it's Nathan," Harvey said.

"Oh, I hope so," Zoë added.

"I've been looking forward to seeing the kid," Lars said.

There goes that nickname again. Despite the moniker, Alice decided, Nathan Delhomme seemed to be held in high regard by the others. She opened the door.

A man in his midthirties with a woman about the same age, holding a bundle, stood at the door. A suitcase and a pastel tote bag sat between them on the porch.

"Nathan!" Mort burst from behind Alice and embraced a surprised Nathan. "How ya doin', kid?"

"Pretty good, Mr. Fineman," Nathan said, breaking into a smile.

"Trisha," Mort said, turning to the young woman for a hug. Then he drew back, his arms still outstretched. "Hey, what's this?"

The woman pulled back the blanket to reveal a baby wrapped inside. "It's our daughter, Mr. Fineman. Didn't Nathan tell you? Libby's only two months old. We were afraid that she might be late and we wouldn't be able to make the holiday reunion."

"A baby!" Mort said, wide-eyed. The other veterans pushed past Alice, who stepped aside.

"Oh, look!" Zoë said, the first to flank Trisha on her other side. "Harvey, isn't she precious?"

Harvey smiled at his wife. "She certainly is, Zoë. Reminds me of our Maria when she was young."

"Now how can you remember back that far?" Zoë said, with a playful swat. "That was nearly sixty years ago!"

"I can remember," Harvey said defensively, though it was clear he knew his wife was only teasing. "Nathan, why didn't you tell us?"

"Yes," Penelope said, crowding forward for a look. "Oh, she's a perfect angel. Oh please, may I hold her?"

"Well—" Trisha said.

"What have you got to say for yourself, you young pup?" Mort asked Nathan. "Why didn't you tell us?"

He smiled, glancing from one elder to the other. "I thought it would be a good surprise."

They hooted. "A good surprise!" Mort said. "A wonderful surprise!"

Alice thought that Trisha looked tired. The baby was beginning to squirm and seemed to be working herself into an outburst.

"Come inside," she said, ushering Trisha into the home.

"Thank you," she said, wrapping the blanket more snugly around the baby. "It is a little chilly out there."

The others surrounded Nathan in the foyer, teasing him good-naturedly about such an unexpected turn of events. Alice led Trisha toward the library and gestured for her to sit in one of the room's russet-colored chairs. "May I get you anything?" she asked.

"No thanks, I'm fine," Trisha said. "I hope the baby isn't a problem. I know some bed-and-breakfasts don't allow children."

"We are delighted with anyone who shares our home," Alice assured her. "Only..."

"Uh-oh," Trisha said. "I was afraid there might be a catch."

"Oh no, no catch," Alice said. "I was just thinking that we need to find a crib and anything else baby-related you might need."

Trisha sighed. "If Nathan had thought at least to notify you that we were bringing a baby, this wouldn't be so inconvenient." She sounded defeated and exhausted.

The baby started to cry, wriggling tiny fists under the blanket. Trisha pressed her close, and tears welled in her eyes. "*Shh,* Libby. It's all right."

The baby began to cry louder, and Trisha's tears fell. "Libby, please don't cry. Mommy's tired."

"Does she need to eat? A diaper change?" Alice said. Trisha shook her head. "No, I took care of those things just before we arrived. She was so good on the plane and during the car trip."

"*Waaah!*" Libby let loose with a loud wail. Trisha looked ready to dissolve completely into tears, so Alice held out her arms.

"Why don't you let me hold her for a while?" she asked. "I've worked with babies a lot in my day. I'm a nurse at the Potterston Hospital. I'm Alice Howard, by the way, one of the owners of Grace Chapel Inn."

"Thank you, Alice," Trisha said. "You're a nurse, you say?"

Alice nodded, knowing that new mothers were often rightfully extra protective of their children, particularly their first. "Yes, I am. Sit back in the chair and catch your breath for a moment. I'd be glad to walk the baby here in the library for a while."

"She does like walking," Trisha said, handing the baby over to Alice. "Sometimes that seems to calm her down."

The baby fit snug and warm, though squirmy, in Alice's arms. She laid Libby against her shoulder and caressed her downy head. "*Shh*," she said as she started to walk slowly around the room. "It's all right, Libby," she crooned. "Your mama needs a little rest."

"Do I ever," Trisha mumbled. She leaned back in the chair and slipped out of her loafers, absentmindedly pulling her feet up under her.

The baby's cries grew softer as Alice walked around the room. "That's right, Libby," she murmured, swaying gently as she walked. "Let your mother get some rest. You've both had a long journey."

Alice glanced at Trisha. The woman looked much more relaxed now, her shoulders loosened, face softened. She evidently had found herself so comfortable that she fell fast asleep.

The library had been the study of Daniel Howard, the sisters' father. The many books in the cases against the wall testified to his scholarly interests as a preacher and his love of reading in general. Alice smiled as she looked from baby to sleeping mother. Father had been loving and always eager to help someone in need. He would not have minded this tired young woman getting some much-needed rest in his study, and neither did Alice.

"Being a baby is a lot of work," Alice whispered solemnly to Libby. "But being a new mom is even harder. You both need to catch your rest when you can."

Libby yawned and snuggled against Alice's shoulder.

Nathan Delhomme stepped through the doorway. "Trisha? Where's—"

Alice put a finger to her mouth, nodding at the sleeping woman. Nathan's face relaxed, and he smiled at his wife with tenderness. "She's been up since early this morning with the baby," he whispered. "I'm sorry about that."

"It's all right, Mr. Delhomme," Alice said, glancing down at the baby. "It looks like Libby is asleep too. Why don't we find a place to lay her down? Trisha can stay here and get a nap. She'd probably be more comfortable upstairs in bed, but I hate to wake her."

"I agree." Nathan gently took Libby from Alice. "I'll take her upstairs, if you'll show me where our room is."

Alice picked up a crocheted afghan from another chair. She draped the blanket around Trisha, who never moved. Once she and Nathan exited the library, she gently closed the door behind them. The rest of the veterans were still in the foyer.

"Is everything all right?" Zoë whispered, mindful of the sleeping baby.

"I'll take Libby upstairs to sleep," Nathan said. "I might even take a nap myself. I was up half the night with her, and Trisha was up the other half."

"We don't have a crib for Libby," Alice said, "but the bed is firm. You can put pillows around her for safety while she sleeps. While you're both resting, I'll see about borrowing what she'll need."

"Yes, get some rest," Penelope said, smiling at the baby. "Poor dears."

"We can catch up later," Mort said.

"Thanks," Nathan said, smiling wearily. "And now, Miss Howard, if you'll show me where we'll be bunking..."

While Alice led the way up the stairs, she wondered about the connection between the Delhommes and the rest of the World War II veterans. The Delhommes were part of the group, yet Nathan and Trisha were young enough to be their grandchildren.

"Here we are," she said, opening the door to the Sunset Room. Nathan didn't even glance at the creamy antiqued furniture or the Impressionist prints hanging on the rag-painted terra-cotta-colored walls. He laid Libby gently on the bed and arranged the pillows so that she couldn't fall off.

"Thanks, Miss Howard. Please let Trisha know where we are when she wakes up."

Alice smiled. "I will. And let me know if you need anything." She closed the door behind her and left the weary man and baby to rest. Downstairs again, she noticed that the veterans had retreated behind a closed door to the parlor, Louise's piano lesson apparently completed. The room had been sound-proofed for Louise's lessons, but today the sound insulation served to assure Trisha of some rest. Alice could hear only muffled chatter from the group as they renewed their friendships.

Any questions she had about the Delhommes' connection with the elderly group would have to wait.

Chapter Three

*A*lice found Louise with Jane in the kitchen. "We must borrow a baby crib and anything else the Delhommes might need for Libby," she said. "Any idea who would have them to lend?"

"I'd check with Fred Humbert. He might have heard something at his hardware store about someone having baby things to rent," Jane said.

Alice tried calling the hardware store several times and kept getting a busy signal. "Either the store's phone is out of order, or someone forgot to hang it up. It's still clear and the sun is shining, so I think I'll walk to town. I could use the exercise."

"Bundle up," Louise said. "The trees are swaying. The wind may be picking up."

Alice put on her coat and wrapped a scarf around her head. As she walked down the road to town, she noticed that the wind was, indeed, stepping up its force. Soon winter would be upon them. She thought about how the trees would look pretty again with snow on them. They looked barren now, nearly stripped of their leaves.

At the hardware store, she found Fred perched on a ladder, checking his stock of birdseed. "Hi, Alice," he said when he saw her. "I'll be right with you."

He climbed down the ladder and dusted off his hands. "I think I've got enough seed for the winter. Be sure to tell Jane, because she's always worried about feeding our feathered friends during the cold weather."

"I will. Vera tells me that you are both really busy," she said, referring to Fred's wife, one of Alice's dearest friends.

"Yes, I'm stocking winter items and storing the fall things. Vera's knee-deep in school, of course. Fifth grade is always difficult to teach this time of year. She says the kids start acting more like junior-high rather than elementary-school kids, so it's sometimes hard to keep them interested in education."

"I can imagine," Alice said, thinking of her ANGELs, who sometimes got fidgety at meetings if she didn't plan interesting activities for them.

"What can I do for you today?" he asked.

"I need to rent a crib," she said. "One of our guests brought a baby, and I'm afraid we're unprepared. Jane thought that you might know of someone who has some baby things that aren't being used."

Fred looked thoughtful, then snapped his fingers. "You know, Vera mentioned the other day that one of the teachers at her school is looking to get rid of her baby furniture. Maybe she'd rent it to you while she's waiting for it to sell. How about if I have Vera call you when she gets home? That should only be about an hour from now."

"Thank you, Fred," Alice said. "You are a lifesaver. I'll go back to the inn and wait for Vera's call. We have a full house up until the parade, and I have a feeling that we are going to be rather busy until then."

"It was great to see you, Alice," Fred said, climbing back up the ladder. "I'll be sure to tell Vera to call."

When Alice got back to Grace Chapel Inn, all was relatively quiet. She checked on Trisha Delhomme, who was still fast asleep in the library. She could hear sounds of the veterans group in the parlor, and she tapped lightly on the door.

Penelope opened it. "Hello, Miss Howard."

"Please, call me Alice," she said. "I just wanted to see if there was anything you needed. Some tea or coffee?"

"I'd like some coffee," Harvey said.

"And tea for me, if it isn't too much of a bother," Penelope said.

"Not at all."

"Is Trisha still sleeping?" Zoë asked.

"Yes, she is. And Mr. Delhomme and the baby too," Alice said.

"We've tried to hold down the ruckus," Mort said, "but we've got a lot of catching up to do."

"I'm sure the Delhommes appreciate your consideration," Alice said. "And now, I'll get you some coffee and tea."

Alice brewed and served their beverages using her mother's tea service. "Wedgwood, isn't it?" Penelope asked, accepting the Earl Grey that Alice poured. Penelope examined the side of the cup. "I do believe this is the Wildflower pattern."

Alice nodded. "Yes, it is. You know your china, Mrs. Calabrese."

"Please, call me Penelope. In fact, please call all of us by our first names. Yes, I know my china. My Wedgwood, anyway. You see, I was employed by them just before the war. They were in the process of building a new factory, but work had to be halted because of the war. It wasn't completed until the fighting was over, but by then I had already married Harvey and moved to America."

Alice set down the teapot, fascinated. "You were a war bride?"

Penelope nodded. "I met Harvey when he was stationed in England."

"Swept her right off her feet, I did," Harvey said. "I was the luckiest guy in our unit." He smiled at her. "And I still am. Who would have thought she'd leave her family for the likes of me?"

"Don't forget my country," Penelope said. "My friends thought me quite daft to run off with a Yank."

He squeezed her hand. "It's turned out pretty well, hasn't it?"

"Only because you're such a charming fellow."

Alice smiled at their banter. "If any of you need anything else, please let me know."

"The joe's great," Mort said, holding up a china cup full of coffee. "Thanks."

Alice left the room and was headed upstairs when the phone at the reception desk under the stairs rang. "Grace Chapel Inn," she answered.

"Alice, it's Vera."

"Hello, Vera. How was school today?"

"It went as well as can be expected this time of year." Vera laughed. "Come November, all the students get a little antsy about the holidays. We're trying to at least keep their attention until Thanksgiving with a special project."

"Oh? What's that?"

"We're having an essay contest about Veterans Day for the fifth graders," Vera continued. "Naturally, I'm encouraging everyone to submit something, but I'm worried that I'll only get the usual participants."

"Who's that?"

"Girls, mostly," she sighed. "For some reason, boys think it's not cool to write."

Alice chuckled. "That doesn't surprise me. Speaking of veterans, Vera, we have several World War II vets here at Grace Chapel Inn. They're staying with us until the parade at Potterston."

"Really!" Vera's voice reflected her excitement. "I've already invited some of Acorn Hill's veterans to come talk to the school about their experiences. Do you think your guests might be interested in speaking to the kids too? We don't have any veterans from that far back."

Muffled laughter emanated from the parlor. Alice could barely hear Mort and Lars arguing good-naturedly.

She smiled. "I think they'd be very interested, Vera. Would you like to come over to ask them in person?"

"I'd love to," she said. "May I come now? I want to get home in time to fix Fred's dinner."

"That'd be fine. I'll be expecting you. Let me ask you one more thing before you do. Did Fred mention to you that we have other guests who have a two-month-old baby? Fred said you know of a teacher at work who might be willing to rent us a crib and whatever else a two-month-old might need."

"Yes, he did. I got so involved in the veteran business that I forgot why I called. Kay Penderbeck's child has grown out of the baby things, and I think she's looking to part with them. If you would like, I'll give her a call before I come over to your place."

"Thanks, Vera, that would be great."

As Alice hung up the phone, Trisha came into the hallway, looking sleepy-eyed and sheepish. "I can't believe I fell asleep."

Alice smiled. "You needed your rest. Sometimes you have to get it where and when you can."

Trisha's expression turned anxious. "Is Libby okay? Where's Nathan? Is everything all right?"

"They're fine," Alice said. "They're both resting upstairs. Nathan took the baby up to your room so we wouldn't disturb you. Do you feel better?"

"A little," Trisha admitted.

Alice smiled warmly. "It's only been two months since Libby was born. Your body is adjusting to the changes and will still be adjusting for at least another four months. Be good to yourself and get as much rest as possible. While you're here, I'll do everything I can to help. So will my sisters."

"Thank you," Trisha said. "It's so hard to get everything done at home. I don't work outside the home, so I'm in charge of all the household duties—cooking, cleaning, managing the finances.... Nathan works hard, so I try to keep things running smoothly, but it's hard to get everything done when Libby requires so much attention."

"It won't always be that way," Alice said. "In a month or two she should start sleeping better during the night and napping at more regular times during the day. You'll find a way to set a schedule for yourself and keep it."

"I hope so," Trisha said. "I don't want to burden Nathan—"

"Burden me with what?"

Nathan came down the stairs, holding Libby. The baby was awake but quiet. "Do you think she's hungry?" Nathan asked, handing her to Trisha. "It's been awhile since she's eaten, hasn't it?"

Trisha nodded. "I'll take her back upstairs to nurse her."

"Would you like something to drink?" Alice asked. "I don't mind bringing it up to you."

"Thank you," Trisha said. "A glass of ice water would be nice. You've been very kind, Alice."

Alice noticed that Nathan's gaze followed his wife as she went upstairs. When he saw that Alice was watching him, he shook his head. "I know she carries a lot of weight on her shoulders," he said. "I try to help when I can, but there's still always something that needs to be done."

"Having a first child is a life-changing experience," Alice said, "in more ways than one. You'll both learn to adjust, and Libby will soon be on a more regular schedule."

"Not soon enough," Nathan said, sighing. "We were both so worn out, I almost canceled this trip. Then I decided it might be a good chance to get away."

"You were right," Alice said. "I told Trisha that my sisters and I would be glad to help you with Libby as much as possible."

"Thank you," he said. "More for Trisha's sake than mine. It's hard work for her, taking care of Libby all day."

Alice smiled. "I'll get that water I promised for her."

"I'll take it up to her. It'll give us a chance to talk." He glanced toward the parlor, where the veterans could still be heard, as he and Alice headed for the kitchen.

"I guess Trisha and I had better plan on getting sociable," Nathan said, slouching against the counter while Alice retrieved a bottle of cold water from the refrigerator.

"Don't try to tell me that you're a World War II vet like the others," she said, teasing.

"No, Gulf War. They asked Trisha and me to join them this year after my grandfather died. He was part of their group, and I guess they felt since I'm a veteran that I was eligible to take his place."

"I don't often get to say this, but thank you for your service to our country," Alice said.

Nathan didn't say anything, but Alice thought she saw him grimace. She started to say something, thought better of it, then handed him the glass of water. "Tell Trisha there's always a bottle of fresh water in the refrigerator. She's welcome to it any time."

"Thanks," he said, heading for the stairs.

Alice sat at the table, wondering if she had offended him. She knew that a lot of ex-soldiers didn't like to speak of their military service, but his attitude indicated something else concerning his past was going on.

The door to the parlor opened, and two male voices could be heard singing in fairly decent harmony. *"Don't sit under the apple tree with anyone else but me!"*

Alice smiled. She hadn't heard that song in such a long time. She could vaguely recall her mother singing it when she was a little girl. It was probably fairly new back then.

"*No no no!*"

The doorbell rang, and Alice went to answer it.

Vera Humbert stood at the front door. "Who's doing the singing?" she asked.

"The veterans," Alice said, standing back. "Come on in. Let's go back to the kitchen."

"*Praise the Lord and pass the ammunition!*"

"I don't know about the ammo," Vera said, as they walked past the parlor and into the kitchen, "but would you pass me a cup of hot tea? It's chilly outside."

"Of course," Alice said, setting the kettle on the stove to boil.

Jane entered the kitchen, holding her hands over her ears. "And you thought my Rolling Stones records were loud when I was a teenager."

Someone in the parlor struck a few polka chords on the piano, and everyone sang out together. "*Roll out the barrel. We'll have a barrel of funnnnnnn!*"

"Looks like the Rolling Stones have been topped," Alice said, pouring tea for Vera and herself. "Would you like some tea, Jane?"

Jane moved to the coffee pot. "It's going to take a significant amount of caffeine for me to get through this week," she said. "Tea won't cut it."

They heard footsteps on the stairs, and then the singing abruptly ceased. The parlor door closed, and the footsteps went back upstairs.

"Nathan must have asked them to quiet down," Alice said, sipping thoughtfully. "He and his wife Trisha have the two-month-old baby I was telling you about," she said to Vera.

"Oh, I have good news for them. Kay Penderbeck said that she would be glad to give the crib, playpen and a plastic bathtub to you. She doesn't want any money."

"But we only need them for a while," Alice said.

Vera shrugged, sipping her tea. "Can't you store them somewhere so that when you have another guest with a baby, you'll be prepared?"

"That's not a bad idea," Jane said. "We could keep them in the attic and bring them down when they're needed."

"Alice?" Vera asked.

"Sounds good to me," she said.

"Great." Vera rose. "I'll call her back right now. She said she was going to be out this way and could drop them off for you."

"That's very nice of her," Alice murmured.

Vera laughed. "I think she wants to get them out of her house to make more room."

"It will be good for the Delhommes to have the furniture for tonight," Jane said. "I know the baby took a nap in their bed, but I'm sure they'd like to have the option of a crib."

Vera drained her cup. "Would it be a good time for me to ask the veterans if they would speak to the school?"

"In honor of Veterans Day," Alice explained to Jane. "Sure, come on, Vera."

Alice tapped on the door, and Mort answered it. "Alice!" he boomed in an exaggerated tone. "We've already been scolded by

Nathan for making too much noise. Are you here to give us what-for too?"

"I only wanted to introduce you to my friend Vera Humbert."

"Hi," Vera said.

"She has something she'd like to ask all of you," Alice said.

"Come on in, ladies," Mort said, opening the door wider. "Gang, this is Vera Humbert. Vera, this is the gang," he said, then introduced them one by one.

"What can we do for you?" Harvey asked.

"I teach fifth grade at the elementary school, and I was wondering if you would have time, and the inclination, of course, to come speak to the school—the older classes—about your experiences as veterans. I think it would be so helpful for them to hear any stories you might want to share, as well as give them a chance to honor you all."

Everyone looked at each other. Harvey was the first to speak up. "Sure thing. We love to talk to the kids."

"Oh wonderful!" Vera said. "But what about the other man with your group...Nathan? Is he a veteran too?"

"He sure is," Mort said, beaming. "And his grandfather, who was our buddy, was awful proud of him."

"Nathan's a real war hero," Zoë said. "Not like these old guys here."

A round of hoots and guffaws followed. Mort turned to Vera. "We may not be war heroes, Mrs. Humbert, but we'll be glad to talk about what we do know from being in the army. So many kids only hear the bad things about military life these days. I want them to know that they should be proud of the greatest fighting outfit in the world."

"Hear hear," Lars said, raising his cup of tea.

Alice turned to Vera. "Sounds like you've got a spirited group to speak."

"This is marvelous," Vera said. "Alice, do you think I could speak to Nathan now?"

Alice remembered his uncomfortable expression when she mentioned his service. He and Trisha were probably also enjoying a little quiet time with Libby. "I think he's busy with his family right now, Vera," she said. "Would you like for me to ask him about it later?"

"Sure thing," she said. "Just let me know. The assembly is at ten in the morning on November 10, the day before Veterans Day. We're going to have our mayor, Lloyd Tynan, speak. He was a Korean War veteran. Then there's Derek Grollier, who is a decorated Vietnam veteran."

"He's now an Acorn Hill firefighter and is nearly ready to retire, I believe. Right, Vera?" Alice asked.

She nodded and continued. "As part of the Veterans Day activities, the fifth grade is participating in an essay contest: 'What Veterans Day Means to Me.' Nia and Viola have volunteered to judge the essays. They're our town librarian and bookseller," she said to the guests.

"Sounds like a great plan," Mort said. "We'll be happy to participate as speakers, Mrs. Humbert."

"Thank you. I'll let you get back to your conversation," Vera said. "It was nice to meet you all."

They echoed her sentiments, and Alice walked Vera to the

front door. "Kay should be here any minute," Vera said. "I'd stay, but I need to get home to start on dinner. Fred was complaining of a stiff back, so I want to feed him and get him into a warm tub with Epsom salts to make him feel better."

"He was up high on a ladder when I was in the store," Alice said. "Tell him I hope he feels better." At the door she paused. "How is your class this year? Is it a good group of kids?"

"They all get along just fine, but there's a certain division this year."

"How so?"

"Some of the kids are really outgoing, and some are shyer than most kids their age. As I said, they get along well, but sometimes the noisier ones overshadow the quieter ones. It can be hard to draw them out."

"You do a great job, I know," Alice said. "How many years have you been teaching now?"

Vera laughed. "Too many to count, Alice Howard, and don't you dare start. I'll be in touch later. Bye."

Vera's colleague Kay brought the baby furniture around not long after Vera left. The crib was really lovely and the playpen was collapsible; Trisha said that would be great for Libby because they could take it upstairs and down. Trisha had brought a musical mobile to keep her entertained.

Kay also brought a plastic baby tub lined with a large, thick sponge for cradling the baby's body while she was being bathed. "You can leave the tub in your bathroom. I'll bring you some extra towels for the baby," Alice said. "I know you'll want a nice soft place to lay her when you take her out of the tub and are drying her off."

"Thank you, Miss Howard. Whew! I'm glad you were able to get these things. I was afraid we were going to have to purchase them. It was difficult enough just bringing her car seat on the plane."

Alice smiled. "When I worked in the hospital nursery, one of the other nurses used to say, 'Babies mean work.'"

Trisha looked at Libby, who was lying on her back in the crib. "It's hard to believe that one day she'll grow up and start school, then become a teenager, then finally head off for college. It's hard to believe now that time will go by so fast, but my mom's told me that it will."

"Yes, it will," Alice said. "I can remember when my sister Jane was a baby. At first I thought I was going to be taking care of her forever, but then all of a sudden she was an adult."

"Oh my goodness!" Trisha said, clapping a hand to her mouth.

"What's wrong?"

Trisha giggled. "I guess I'm just punch-drunk from lack of sleep, but honestly, Miss Howard, the thought of having a brother or sister for Libby is more than I can handle right now. Nathan and I have never even talked about having another child. I suppose it would be good for Libby to grow up with a sibling."

"Don't worry," Alice said, patting her arm. "You don't have to decide anything today. Take care of *this* precious baby and your husband first. And yourself, of course. You'll know when the time is right for another one."

"I may be selfish," Trisha said, "but I hope it isn't any time soon."

Chapter Four

*T*he veterans stayed ensconced in the parlor for the rest of the afternoon and only came out when it was time to get ready for dinner. Then they all trooped upstairs, retired to their separate rooms, changed clothes and came back downstairs at almost the exact same time.

Jane was puttering at the reception desk under the stairs when she heard their footsteps. She stepped into the foyer and observed that Mort seemed to be in charge. "You run a tight ship," she said, as he made sure everyone was adequately dressed for a night out.

"Not a ship," he said, grinning. "An armored division."

"He was our sergeant," Lars said.

"And he falls right back into his old habits whenever we're together," Harvey said.

"Thank goodness," Penelope said, laughing, "because the other fifty-one weeks of the year, *I* have to be your keeper."

"Yes, dear," Harvey said, feigning meekness.

Nathan and Trisha, with the baby in arms, rushed down the stairs. "I hope we haven't held you up," Nathan said. "It takes us awhile to get ready, what with Libby here."

"She looks adorable," Penelope said, peering at the little girl wrapped in the pink blanket.

"Thank you," Trisha said, flushed. "I hope she doesn't act up."

"If she gets fussy, you'll have lots of arms to hold her," Zoë said.

"And walk her," Penelope put in. "Some of us have great-grandchildren now and are quite used to babies."

Jane smiled. "I hope you have a great first night out together. Where are you headed?"

"Zachary's," Zoë said, putting her hand in the crook of Lars's arm.

"An excellent choice," Jane said. "Zack's a great chef. He'll serve you a wonderful meal."

"Time to fall out," Mort said. "Jane," he said, clicking his heels together and saluting, "we should return around twenty-two hundred hours."

"Have a great time," she called after them as they opened the front door and began to file out.

The last to leave, Mort gave her a wink. "Don't wait up for us," he said, and she heard laughter in the distance as they headed out to their cars.

◦

The next day was Friday, the date of the Franklin High football game. While the sisters ate breakfast in the kitchen, Alice glanced outside. "There's frost outside, and I don't think it's supposed to get any warmer during the day."

"And it will only get colder after sunset," Louise added. She shook her head. "Sometimes I wonder why football isn't played during summer."

"Because everyone's watching baseball then," Jane said, setting a plate of pancakes on the table.

"How about spring?" Louise suggested.

Jane shook her head. "Basketball season."

Louise sighed. "I do not know how sports fans keep up with everything."

"Yes, and you didn't even ask about soccer, tennis, golf, hockey..."

"Curling," Alice added, smiling.

Louise cocked an eyebrow and took a sip of coffee. "I'll settle for attending Franklin High's game tonight, bundled up as much as necessary to stay warm."

"Good idea," Jane said. "And now, if you'll excuse me, I have a dining room of hungry veterans and their families to feed."

"May I help you serve?" Alice asked, rising.

Jane waved at her to sit down. "Eat your breakfast," she said. "I can handle it. I made stuffed French toast. It's all in baking dishes."

"It smells wonderful," Louise said.

"You have pancakes," Jane said, laughing. "Eat those."

She left the kitchen for the dining room, and Alice looked at Louise. "I guess she put us in our place."

"I guess so." Louise forked up a couple of pancakes from the plate and proceeded to butter them.

Jane soon rejoined them and dug into the pancakes herself. They were down to the last two when the back door opened. "Yoo-hoo!"

The sisters' aunt, Ethel Buckley, entered all smiles. The elderly woman liked to pop in on them, particularly at mealtimes, as Jane frequently noted. It was easy for her to do so, because she lived in the inn's carriage house. Ethel had been their father's half sister, and she had moved to Acorn Hill ten years ago from a nearby farm when her husband died.

"How are you girls this morning?" she asked.

"We were just discussing the football game tonight, Auntie," Louise said.

"And how cold it will be," Alice added.

Ethel smiled. "I'll be there, of course. I wouldn't miss it. Won't it be exciting if Franklin High gets to the play-offs? I don't know when this town has had the potential for so much excitement."

"Is Lloyd going to the football game too?" Jane asked. Lloyd Tynan, the town mayor, was known as Ethel's "special friend."

"He most certainly will," Ethel said, her red hair bobbing as she nodded vigorously. She craned her neck to look at the table. "What are you girls having this morning?"

"Just pancakes, Aunt Ethel," Jane said. "Why don't you pull up a chair and join us? There are two left."

"Oh, I'm sure you girls want to eat them," she said.

"I'm full," Alice said.

"I too," Louise said, patting her mouth with her napkin.

Ethel looked at Jane.

"I couldn't eat another morsel," Jane said, smiling. "Have a seat, Auntie."

"Well," Ethel said, pulling out the lone unoccupied chair. "If you're sure they'll just go to waste."

"They either go to you or to Wendell," Jane said, winking at her sisters.

"Jane Howard, don't tell me you'd feed perfectly good people food to that cat of yours!"

"Not if you eat them first," Jane said. "Go ahead. Louise, pass Aunt Ethel the syrup."

Ethel pulled the pancake plate in front of her and started buttering. "I'd hate to see you waste all your culinary skills on Wendell."

"Thank you, Auntie," Jane said gravely.

Mort appeared at the doorway. "Ladies, I hate to interrupt, but could we get a glass of milk for Trisha?"

"Sure thing," Jane said. She retrieved a glass and the milk carton from the refrigerator. "Mort, this is our aunt, Ethel Buckley. Auntie, this is Mortimer Fineman, one of our guests."

Mort smiled broadly, his eyes twinkling. "You never said anything about having an aunt, particularly one so good-looking."

"Oh." Ethel giggled, touching her hair with her hand. "Thank you."

"Do you live nearby?"

"Just over there," she said, waving her hand vaguely. "My home is the old carriage house."

"How fortunate your nieces are," he continued. "I'm sure they rely on your wisdom a great deal."

"Well..." Ethel giggled again.

"Here's your milk," Jane said.

Mort took the glass. "Thank you. I'd better get back to the group. Miss Buckley, it was a pleasure to meet you."

"It's Mrs. Buckley," Ethel said, smiling.

Mort looked crestfallen.

"I'm a widow."

"What a coincidence," Mort said with a smile returning to his face. "I'm a widower. I hope to see you around, Mrs. Buckley."

After he'd left, the sisters turned to Ethel, who was blushing and beaming like a teenager. "What a nice man."

"What a flirt!" Louise said, smiling.

"Flirt? Why, he was just being nice," Ethel said.

"He was just being an apple polisher," Jane said. "But I'm sure it's harmless enough."

"I'm sure it is too," Alice said. "Though I suspect Mort is quite the ladies' man."

"Lloyd better watch out, or you'll be swept off your feet," Jane said, a smile tugging at the corners of her mouth.

"*Tsk, tsk.* Good heavens, where *do* you get your ideas?" Ethel asked. Then she looked thoughtful for a moment. "Do you really think so?"

Now what have I done? Jane mouthed to her sisters.

"It was all harmless," Alice reassured her aunt, "and nothing for you to worry about."

Ethel ate the last bite of pancake and set down her fork. "Well, at any rate, I'd better get going. I'm supposed to meet Lloyd. He's marching in the Veterans Day parade, you know."

"I didn't know, but I'm glad to hear it," Alice said. "Vera mentioned that he was going to speak to her class."

"Yes, and that's what we want to discuss. He asked me to help him decide what he should talk about."

"Our guests are going to speak as well," Alice said. "They're World War II vets. And one of our guests served in the Gulf War."

"Do you think Nathan Delhomme will want to speak?" Louise said. "He didn't sound too enthusiastic about his military service, from what you told us."

"I don't know," Alice said. "If there's a good time to ask him, I will. I know Vera would love to have him join the others."

"It would be good for her class to hear from veterans of different wars," Jane said. "With Derek Grollier talking about the Vietnam War, that would cover four wars."

"I would like to hear such a talk myself," Louise said. "Do you think the school would mind if I sat at the back of the auditorium?"

"I want to come too," Alice said.

"Me too," Jane said.

"I already told Lloyd I'd go with him," Ethel said. "As mayor, he's certainly accustomed to public speaking, but he said this is one subject that he's never spoken about publicly and he'd like some moral support."

Alice thought for a moment. "War is something that most women our age don't understand."

"What do you mean?" Jane asked.

"Nowadays, women serve in the military as well as men, and they understand combat and being fired upon and seeing friends killed. But women our age, unless they were WACs or WAVES, haven't had any firsthand experience. Since you lived through World War II, Aunt Ethel, do you think that's true?"

Ethel nodded. "I think you're right, Alice. I was a teenager when the war was going on, and we didn't really understand what the boys were in fact going through when they faced the enemy. Seeing several of the war movies that have come out in the past few years has given me a better idea of what it was really like."

"It's odd to think that our guests in the dining room might have had experiences like that," Jane said. "How can a young man go off to a world war, fight to save his life as well as his buddies', then return home and live a normal life?"

Everyone involuntarily looked toward the dining room. They could hear laughter through the swinging door that separated that room from the kitchen. The sisters and Ethel relaxed, looking sheepishly at each other.

"It sounds like they're doing all right now," Alice said.

"It does, doesn't it?" Jane said, smiling. "Well, Auntie, you and Lloyd have your work cut out for you if you're going to figure out what to say to a group of elementary-school kids."

"Thank you for breakfast," Ethel said, dabbing her mouth with her napkin. "I'd stay to help clean up, but Lloyd is expecting me." She smiled. "Tell that nice Mr. Fineman that it was a pleasure to make his acquaintance."

"We'll do that, Auntie," Jane said.

"Best breakfast I've had since my Rivka passed away," Mort complimented Jane when she went to collect the dishes.

"Thank you," she said. "I'm glad you enjoyed it."

"It was lovely, dear," Zoë said. "The only problem is that I'm so full, I'm afraid to go try on clothes."

"Zoë and Trisha and I are headed into town to do some shopping," Penelope said. "And you know that shopping always includes trying on new outfits. Where is a good place to shop in town?"

"For clothes? Knickknacks? Antiques?" Jane asked.

The women looked at each other and burst out laughing. "Everything!"

"Our shopping motto at these yearly get-togethers is *no quarter, no mercy*," Penelope said. "We may have to spend the next year paying off the credit cards, but we definitely shop till we drop."

"Let's see," Jane said, considering. "If you truly want to shop in Acorn Hill, there's a variety of places. For clothing, there's Nellie's. Nine Lives Bookstore is a good place to get reading material."

"Go there, Zoë," Lars said. "See if that new book on World War II battleships is available."

"Gotcha," Zoë said, scribbling on a piece of paper. "Where else, Jane?"

"There's Time for Tea, which is, as you might guess, a tea shop. It not only carries a wide variety of teas, but also everything you need to serve it."

"Oh, splendid!" Penelope said. "I'd love a new tea cozy."

"There's the Acorn Antique Shop," Jane said. "You can find some wonderful things there. Besides antique furniture and lamps and things like that, the Holzmanns stock wonderful *objets d'art* and unusual gift items. There's Sylvia's Buttons, which is owned by an extremely creative artist as well as the world's best seam-stress, Sylvia Songer. Sylvia creates art quilts and has some for sale at the shop. Wild Things is a florist shop. If you get hungry—"

"And of course we will," Penelope said.

"—you should try either the Good Apple Bakery or the Coffee Shop. And," Jane said, pausing for a moment to catch her breath, "I think that about does it."

Zoë finished scribbling with a flourish. "What about sight seeing?"

Jane laughed. "Shopping isn't enough for one day?"

"I believe she's right," Penelope said. "I think we'll keep quite busy with what's already on the list."

Jane noticed that Trisha had stayed silent throughout the discussion. "Don't any of the stores I mentioned interest you?" Jane asked.

Trisha glanced down. "I probably should stay here and take care of Libby."

"Why?" Mort boomed. "Don't you trust us old geezers to take care of her?"

"It's not that," Trisha said. "I just think I'll get tired. I don't want to hold up Penelope and Zoë."

Penelope frowned. "But we can—"

"She might want to take it easy today," Nathan said. He turned Trisha's way. "Right, Trisha?"

She nodded, bending over to tuck the blanket closer around the baby.

The light mood evaporated, and an uncomfortable silence settled in its place. "Are you sure, Trisha?" Zoë asked softly.

Trisha nodded. "I—I think I'll go lay Libby down in the play-pen upstairs. She's acting drowsy, like she's ready for a nap."

"I'll go with you," Nathan said.

"You'll be back, though, right?" Mort asked him. "We're getting ready to play gin rummy, and we need a fourth."

"Sure thing," Nathan said, smiling.

After the young couple left, everyone looked at each other. Jane hurried to gather all the used breakfast dishes, silverware and cups. As she was ferrying the last of the items through the swinging door to the kitchen, she overheard Penelope say, "...looks so tired. I wish there was something we could do."

"Now, now," Zoë said. "I remember how it felt to be a young mother and—"

The door swung shut, and Jane took the dishes to the counter to be rinsed before she ran them through the dishwasher. She, too, wished there was something someone could do to help Trisha Delhomme.

Zoë and Penelope returned from their shopping excursion early that afternoon with seven bags between them. Louise was finishing up a piano lesson when they came in the front door, blown in by a gusty wind.

"My goodness," Penelope said, unwrapping a rose-colored scarf from her head. "It is quite windy out there."

"*Brrr.* And the temperature's dropped quite a bit too," Zoë said. "I would love to have walked around your lovely town, but I'm glad we had the rental car."

"I'm sorry to hear that," Louise said. "We're supposed to attend a football game tonight. Our local high school has a chance to go to the play-offs."

"Better layer your clothes," Zoë said.

"*Lots* of layers," Penelope said, shuddering, rubbing her arms even though she still wore her coat. "Oh, how I hate cold weather!"

Zoë smiled. "No wonder. You're accustomed to living in sunny Southern California. Lars and I like it cold."

"They live in Minnesota," Penelope said to Louise. "The poor dears."

Louise smiled. "I will certainly take your advice and wear my heaviest clothing. Meanwhile, what treasures did you find in town?"

"We'd be glad to show you, but we need to find Trisha first. Have you seen her?"

"I think she's in the parlor with the men," Louise said.

"How'd that sweet little baby do?" Zoë asked, smiling.

"As far as I know, fine. I didn't hear a peep out of her."

"Come on, Zoë," Penelope said, scooping up her bags. "Let's find Trisha. You come too, Louise."

Not normally much of a shopper, but intrigued by the sheer volume of their purchases, Louise followed them to the parlor. Sounds of a spirited gin rummy game could be heard through the door. When the women entered, they saw all four men seated around a card table, with various stacks of poker chips in front of each of them.

Penelope set down her bags and put her hands on her hips. "That doesn't look like gin rummy to me."

"It's Texas Hold'em," Mort said, an unlit cigar between his teeth. Louise gave him a reproving look, and he shrugged, eyes twinkling. "It's not lit, Louise. I've been a good boy."

"I made sure of that," Nathan said, smiling. He raked in a large stack of red, white and blue chips.

Chin in hand, Trisha sat in the corner beside the playpen. Libby was fast asleep on her back. Trisha blinked her eyes as though she was trying hard to stay awake. She looked like she wanted to crawl into the playpen with her daughter to nap.

Zoë and Penelope exchanged a glance, then went straight over to Trisha. "We brought you a present," Zoë said in a singsong.

Trisha sat upright. "What? Oh, hi, ladies. Did you have fun?"

"We would have had more fun if you'd been with us," Zoë said.

"We insist that you come with us on our next excursion," Penelope said.

"But in the meantime"—Zoë withdrew a box from a shopping bag—"look what we brought you."

Trisha smiled shyly. "You didn't have to do that." She opened the box, pushed back the tissue paper and lifted a lovely ceramic figurine music box of a woman in a full skirt holding a baby.

"Wind it up," Penelope said.

Trisha did, and the strains of "I'll Be Loving You Always" issued forth. The mother with the baby twirled slowly. Trisha's eyes filled with tears. "This is so beautiful," she said, "this is…" She sniffled. "Why can't I stop crying?"

Zoë handed her a handkerchief. "It's okay, honey. It's the hormones."

"Yes, dear," Penelope said, kneeling beside her. "It happens to every new mom. Just have yourself a good cry when you feel like it."

"And meantime, let these lunks over there"—Zoë gestured at the men, absorbed in their poker game—"take care of Libby next time. You're going out with us for some female fun."

Trisha wiped her eyes with the handkerchief, then blew her nose. "Thank you, but I c—can't." She glanced at Nathan to make sure he wasn't listening, then lowered her voice. "Nathan's so proud that he wouldn't want to admit this, but what with Libby and trying to save for a house, we're tight on cash. We had just barely enough for this trip."

Penelope wrapped an arm around her. "Don't worry about it. Let Zoë and me spoil you, okay?"

"Well..."

"It's a date. Louise, you're our witness. Trisha, we won't be gone so long that you'll start to feel guilty about leaving Libby. But it will do you a world of good just to get away for a few hours."

"That does sound nice," Trisha said.

"Great," Penelope said, then shivered. "And tomorrow, I'll wear a heavier coat."

The weather only got colder as the afternoon wore on. Louise consulted with Alice and Jane just before dinner. "Do you think we should go to the game?"

"Why not?" Jane asked. "I thought you wanted to go."

"Would it be terrible if I didn't? I am not much of a sports fan, for one thing, and someone should stay here in case our guests need anything."

"Does the cold have anything to do with your change of heart?" Jane asked.

"Yes, it does," Louise said. "The idea of curling up with a good book in front of a roaring fire in the living room sounds rather more enticing than sitting in those cold stands."

"I'm still willing to go to the game," Alice assured Jane.

"Good," she said. "Louise, you're probably right. Someone does need to stay here. And Alice, I'll pack some hot chocolate, and we'll take lots of blankets."

"Did I hear that Sylvia wants to go too?" Alice asked.

"Yes, and I told her we'd pick her up around seven o'clock."

Alice smiled. "She was a cheerleader, too, wasn't she?"

"Yep, she graduated four or five years after me," Jane said, reflecting. "I wish we had been on the same pep squad. I wish we had been friends."

"You're certainly friends now," Alice said, "and I'm glad she's going with us."

It seemed as though everyone in Acorn Hill, Potterston and the other surrounding towns turned out for the game that night. The onlookers sat together in clumps, trying to keep warm with blankets, hats and thick mittens. Lloyd Tynan even brought a battery-operated foot warmer, which he shared with Ethel. As everyone waited for the game to begin, frosty breath hung in a cloud above the stands. The Franklin High band played standing up so that they could stamp their feet to keep warm. The visiting Washington Wildcat fans on the other side of the field looked like they were struggling to keep warm too.

"It must be twenty degrees out here," Jane said, unfolding another stadium blanket. She huddled under the blankets between Sylvia and Alice.

"Y–yes," Sylvia said, shivering. "Look at the p–poor cheerleaders."

"Thank goodness they're wearing thick tights," Jane said. "I remember a few cold football games, though not as cold as this one, when we only wore panty hose under those short wool skirts."

"I think our jumps were extra high during those late-fall games," Sylvia said, smiling in remembrance. "We tried to move around as much as possible just to stay warm."

"The Franklin cheerleaders look like they're doing the same thing," Alice said, nodding at the group of girls jumping and cheering in front of the stands.

"Look! Here comes the Franklin Patriot," Sylvia said.

The high school's mascot, a student dressed in a patriot costume, complete with a tricorn hat, vest and knickers, ran onto the field. The mascot ran among the cheerleaders, and the band started playing the school's fight song. The football team ran between the goalposts onto the field, breaking through a large paper rally banner that the spirit club had made.

"Franklin, Franklin, fight so good and true," everyone in the stands sang. "Franklin, Franklin, we're behind *you*!"

The song warmed Jane, and suddenly she was taken back over thirty years, when she was on the field, jumping, fist punching the air. Her cheeks flushed with excitement as they finished the song. Everyone clapped and cheered, and the football team warmed up on the sidelines, preparing to begin the game. Though she wanted to keep standing, it was much warmer huddling with Alice and Sylvia under the thick blankets.

"Anybody want some hot chocolate?" she asked. "I've got some here in a thermos."

"I'll take some," Sylvia said. "Do you have any marshmallows?"

Jane laughed. "If I did, they'd be ice cubes by now. Sorry, no marshmallows."

"I'll take some, too, please," Alice said.

A man called down from a higher bleacher. "Got any extra for me?"

Jane laughed. "Isn't the concession stand open?"

"Are you kidding? They had enough good sense to stay home where it's warm," he said, laughing.

Jane poured the cocoa for Sylvia and Alice, who accepted it gratefully, letting the steam warm their faces and the cups warm their hands. "Even through mittens, I can feel this," Alice said.

"Here comes the kickoff," Sylvia said, nearly upsetting her cocoa in her enthusiasm. "Oh, Jane, this is so exciting. I'm as nervous as I used to get when I was on the cheer team."

Jane identified completely. "Remember some of those cheers? 'Choo choo. Bang bang—'"

"'Gotta get my boomerang,'" Sylvia finished, her eyes shining. "Oh, Jane, remember this one? 'H-e-l-l-o, that's the way we say hello—'"

"'Hello! Hey, hey, hello!'" Jane said. "Those were certainly fun times, Sylvia."

"I hate to complain," Alice put in, "but it's *cold* times now, and with you two attempting arm movements, you're pulling the blankets away from my end."

"Sorry," Jane said. She looked at Sylvia. "Alice always did act way too much like an older sister."

Sylvia and Jane giggled, feeling like teenagers again as Franklin High kicked off.

Chapter Five

*L*ouise headed for the living room, clutching a biography of Beethoven. Viola Reed, the owner of Nine Lives Bookstore, had recommended it to her, and she had been looking forward to reading it for quite some time. Tonight was the perfect opportunity. Jane and Alice were at the football game, and the guests seemed content in the parlor.

She stacked wood in the fireplace and waited for the kindling to ignite before deciding on a place to sit. Mother's rocker, which sat in a corner? No, she didn't feel like dragging it close to the fireplace. The burgundy sofa with its throw pillows? No, she would probably fall asleep if she lay down.

Ah. The overstuffed chair would do wonderfully. Made of the same burgundy upholstery as the sofa, it was just perfect for curling up in and close enough to the fireplace for her to feel its warmth. Just to be certain she stayed warm, however, she lifted the cream-and-gold knitted throw from the sofa to wrap up in.

Settled in, she let the cares of the day slide away as she opened the book. "Chapter one," she murmured, contented.

"Louise?"

Louise turned toward the door. Penelope stood there, smiling apologetically. "I wanted to ask for some tea and coffee," she said, "but I don't want to disturb you. I don't mind making it myself if you'll tell me where it is."

"I don't mind at all," Louise said, laying aside her book to head for the kitchen. After brewing a pot of decaf tea and one of coffee and setting it on the Wedgwood Wildflower service, she carried it into the parlor. Baby Libby slept peacefully in her playpen, and everyone else—including Nathan and Trisha—was involved in a spirited game of Trivial Pursuit.

Mort asked Harvey a sports question, then roared with delight when Harvey couldn't answer. He spied Louise setting the tea service nearby and smiled. "I knew you were a great gal," Mort said. The unlit cigar, now chewed to a stub, dangled from his lips. "I don't suppose you have anything to nosh on, do you?"

She thought for a moment. "I think Jane left some crudités in the kitchen."

The cigar stub nearly fell out of Mort's mouth. "Some *huh*?"

"Raw vegetables, Mort," Lars said, giving him a light tap on his arm. "Come on. It's time to ask the next question."

"I'll bring you something to eat," Louise assured them.

In the refrigerator, she found a vegetable tray, complete with dip, that Jane had made up before leaving for the game. She peeled back the plastic wrap and took it into the parlor. Zoë looked up long enough to thank her as Louise set it nearby, but the rest of them were engrossed in the board game.

Louise slipped back to the living room, sighing. She settled into the chair and picked up the book but couldn't get her mind off the vegetable tray. The green pepper slices had looked enticing, along with the baby carrots. Maybe Jane had set aside enough for the sisters. She frequently did.

Louise tossed back the throw, cast a loving look at the fireplace, then headed back to the kitchen. Ah! There were some baby carrots left. And just enough of a green pepper for her. She sliced it up on a cutting board, arranged the slices and the baby carrots on a plate, then cleaned up the mess. She took the bounty back to the living room and set it beside the chair, preparing to settle in again.

Oh no. She'd forgotten to get something to drink. Decaf coffee? Tea?

"Tea," she said to herself. She made her way, once again, toward the kitchen. "And this is it. A large cup of tea and no more interruptions!"

Once she'd brewed the tea, she took the cup back to the living room, made herself comfortable in the chair, and proceeded to wrap herself in the throw again. She lifted the book and—

"Louise?"

Louise smothered a groan and turned. "Yes?"

Zoë stood there, all smiles. "We were about to sing some old songs, World War II tunes and such, and we wondered if you would accompany us on the piano. That is, if you'd like to."

Louise glanced at her book, the snack tray and her cup of tea. Then she smiled. "I'd love to, Zoë. As a matter of fact, I have a songbook of old tunes in the piano bench. It's been a long time since I've opened it." She rose. "I'll bring my tea with me."

"Oh, good!" Zoë said, clapping her hands. "I can plunk out

some tunes, but nothing very complicated. A good pianist might actually make us sound good. Look, everybody," she said as they entered the parlor. "Louise is going to play for us."

"That's wonderful," Lars said.

"Splendid," Penelope said, smiling.

Mort winked. "Like I said, you're quite a gal."

Louise retrieved her *Old Tunes from Olden Times* songbook from inside the piano bench. "This has just about everything from World War I through World War II," she said. "What would you like to start with?"

"Oh, 'Swinging on a Star,' please," Zoë said, looking over her shoulder.

"Very well." Louise turned to the appropriate page and set the music book on the rack. She played a few introductory measures, then everyone launched right in. They sang their way through the verses about mules, pigs, fish and monkeys, belting out the final lines about being better off swinging on a star, then collapsed into laughter.

"That was so much fun," Penelope said, holding her sides.

"It was, wasn't it?" Trisha said, smiling. She glanced over at Libby, who slept peacefully through the noise.

"That's one good thing about the youngest of babies," Penelope said, squeezing the younger woman's hand. "They sleep through nearly anything."

"Including our caterwauling," Harvey said. "How about another one?"

"What next?" Louise asked.

They sang their way through "Shoo Shoo Baby," "Vict'ry Polka," "I'll Be Seeing You" and at least a dozen others.

"How about 'Yankee Doodle Dandy'?" someone suggested.

"Oh yes," Penelope said, pinching Harvey's cheek. "I can still remember hearing that song and thinking about my Harvey."

Louise smiled and struck up the tune. Penelope sang heartily with the others, resting her head on Harvey's shoulder by the end of the song.

Almost before the last note sounded, Harvey spoke up. "If you're going to play that one for Penelope, then you need to play 'White Cliffs of Dover' for me."

"Oh, Harvey," Penelope said, settling her head against his shoulder again.

The others sang the somber song about bluebirds returning to the famous cliffs. Louise noticed that Penelope didn't sing but let tears pool in her eyes. When the song ended and the others fell silent, she raised her head, dabbing at her eyes with a handkerchief.

"Thank you, everyone," she said. "That brings back memories."

"That's why we get together each year for Veterans Day," Zoë said, putting her hand on her friend's shoulder. "To remember."

"We don't ever want to forget the past," Trisha said softly, putting a hand on Penelope's other shoulder. "We always want to honor those who've lived through a war, and especially our soldiers." She looked up at her husband. "Right, Nathan?"

He frowned and jammed his hands into the pockets of his

pants. "Uh, yeah, Trisha," he said, his gaze dropping to the floor. "Listen, I, uh, think I'll head for bed. It's been a lot of fun, y'all. Trisha, do you want me to take Libby?"

"I'll take her," Trisha said, a puzzled look on her face. "Are you sure you—"

"Good night, everybody," Nathan said, giving a halfhearted wave before leaving the room.

"Is there something wrong, Trisha?" Zoë asked.

Trisha shook her head, tears in her eyes. "I don't know. He acts this way every time the war is mentioned. He's been even more agitated since we agreed to join you all. But he insisted that we come. He said he wanted to march in the parade for Gerry Vickers."

Louise noticed that the others bowed their heads slightly, their expressions somber. It would not be polite to inquire further. "Perhaps we should call it a night," she said instead.

"It was lovely," Penelope said, shaking Louise's hand. "Thank you so much, dear. Your playing really does make us sound better."

"I think you sound lovely," Louise said. "It's rare to find people who enjoy music so much."

"Music was a huge part of our lives," Zoë said. "Back then, we didn't have television or computers. We only had the radio for amusement, so we listened to it all the time."

"Everyone knew all the tunes and words," Penelope added.

Louise left the songbook on the piano stand. "I'll leave this out and will be glad to play for you again, if you would like."

"Isn't she a great gal?" Mort said, smiling. "Say, Louise, can I ask you a question?"

"Certainly, Mort."

He settled the cigar stub between his teeth and grinned. "What's the story with your aunt?"

"Story?" Louise asked.

"You know. Is she engaged? Seeing any special fella?"

Louise tried not to smile, but the corners of her mouth twitched. Mortimer Fineman *was* interested in Ethel. "I'm afraid," she said as soberly as she could, "that Aunt Ethel is a special friend of Lloyd Tynan, our town mayor."

"Too bad," Mort said, but his smile never wavered. "Well, you can't win 'em all!"

Though it was nearly eleven o'clock, Louise headed for the living room. She wanted to wait up for Alice and Jane, and perhaps she could read at least a few pages of the Beethoven biography before they returned. She stoked the fire until the embers came to life, then settled into the overstuffed chair. Relaxing, she popped a baby carrot into her mouth and opened the book to page one.

"Louise? Louise?" Jane called.

Louise shut the book. Perhaps there would be time to read in bed before she fell asleep. "In here, Jane."

"They won, they *won*!" Jane bounded into the room and bent over the back of the chair, throwing her arms around Louise.

"What—?" Louise laughingly disengaged herself from her sister's embrace.

"Franklin High won the game," Alice said, standing behind

Jane. "They kicked a field goal in the last thirty seconds and won the game."

"They're going to the play-offs!" Jane said, bouncing on her toes. *"They're going to the play-offs!"*

"Calm down, Jane," Louise said. "I'm excited for the team, but aren't you a little too wound up?" She looked at Alice, who shrugged.

"She's been like this all night," Alice said. "She and Sylvia would have performed with the Franklin High cheerleaders if they'd been asked."

"I would *love* to try a cheer or two again," Jane said. "Sylvia and I had such fun remembering the stunts we used to perform. Oh, if only we could do them again."

"Don't we know several of the cheerleaders?" Louise asked.

Jane nodded. "Several of the youth group girls are on the pep squad."

"Maybe you and Sylvia could ask them to help you start a not-too-peppy squad," Louise said.

"Very funny," Jane replied, sending a throw pillow Louise's way.

"When is the next game?" Louise asked, having deftly caught the pillow.

"Thanksgiving," Alice said. "We'll have to attend, of course, but that will make for a busy holiday, with the Thanksgiving feast at Grace Chapel."

"I wonder how Melanie is coming with her food drive," Louise said.

"I'm sure she'll let you know when you have your meeting," Alice said.

Jane thrust her arms to the right, then the left, as though she were carrying pom-poms. "Two bits, four bits, six bits, a dollar. All for Franklin, stand up and holler!"

"*Jane*, please do not 'holler,' dear," Alice said. "I'm sure our guests have already gone to bed. And you do remember that we have a baby under our roof?"

Jane nodded, then straightened the hem of her pullover sweater, pretending to be wounded. "I can't help being excited. I would think you'd be too."

"I'm very happy for the team and the school," Alice said, "but I'm also very cold, very tired and very much in need of a warm bath before bed. Louise, did you have a quiet night?"

Louise glanced at the unread book and thought about the World War II sing-along. "Quiet enough, I guess." She yawned. "But like you, I'm tired. I think I'll head for bed."

"I couldn't possibly sleep," Jane said, twirling. "I think I'll go bake some brownies—or maybe some cookies. 'Night you two." She quickly left the room, heading for the kitchen.

Louise and Alice exchanged a glance, then smiled. Alice said, "I really do love when she acts so young, but sometimes it's a little too much."

"I was wishing that I had half her energy," Louise said.

"Did you really read the entire time we were gone?"

Louise shook her head. "Our guests wanted to sing, so they asked me to play the piano."

"How fun," Alice said. "I wish I had been here to hear them."

"They all have lovely singing voices," Louise said. "Nathan

and Trisha sang along too, though neither of them was even alive during World War II."

"How was Libby?" Alice asked.

"She slept through the entire thing." Louise paused. "Maybe it's not my place to say, but I'm worried about Nathan."

"Why?" Alice asked.

Louise described how anguished he had looked when the subject of honoring veterans came up. "Then Trisha mentioned something curious. She said that Nathan had sworn this year to march in honor of Gerry Vickers."

"Who's he?"

Louise shrugged. "No one said. But they all seemed to know who he was. They all became quiet when his name was mentioned."

"If he said that he was marching in honor of the man, perhaps he is dead."

"Perhaps." Louise smiled. "You'll never guess what Mort Fineman asked me."

"What?"

"He asked me what the 'story' was about Aunt Ethel."

"He wanted to know if she was dating anyone?"

Louise nodded.

"What did you tell him?" Alice smiled.

"Why, the truth. That she was a special friend to Lloyd Tynan."

"And what was Mort Fineman's response?"

Louise grinned, pretended to fan a cigar stub between her fingers like Groucho Marx and arched her eyebrows. "He said, 'You can't win 'em all!'"

She and Alice were still laughing quietly as they left the room.

⌒

Saturday morning, Zoë and Penelope talked Trisha into joining them on what they called "a whirlwind tour" of Acorn Hill.
While Louise helped Jane collect the empty breakfast dishes,
they sat around the table and coaxed the younger woman into a
shopping excursion.

"It'll be good for you to get out and walk around," Zoë said.
"You should get lots of exercise postpartum."

"Yes," Penelope said. "We'll do a bit of window shopping,
then we'll pop into the Good Apple Bakery and have a delicious
high-calorie treat."

"It does sound like fun," Trisha admitted. "Nathan, do you
feel up to caring for Libby while I'm gone?"

"Sure thing," he said, no trace of last night's anguish apparent
on his face. He lifted Libby from her playpen and rubbed his face
in her terry sleeper–covered tummy. "Daddy'll be your playmate
for the day, right, precious?"

She cooed in response, and he smiled.

Louise noticed that whenever Nathan looked at his daughter,
it seemed as though the weight of the world lifted from his shoulders. It was obvious that he loved her dearly.

Penelope and Zoë left with Trisha in tow. The vets settled
in the parlor with Libby for a game of gin rummy. When they
assured Louise that they didn't need anything, she retired to her

room to prepare for tomorrow's meeting about the Thanksgiving food drive.

Louise loved the traditional décor of her room. Jane's room was contemporary, and Alice's folksy, but her own was decorated with Victorian-style floral wallpaper that never failed to calm her.

She settled in at her delicate lady's writing desk. She wanted to make notes about the food drive. Though Melanie Brubaker was heading up the drive, Louise had a few ideas that she wanted to commit to paper before the meeting.

Louise knew that they could collect canned goods at the area churches as they usually did, but this was the Thanksgiving drive and should be something special. Perhaps they could solicit businesses to donate specific items? It couldn't hurt to ask. She made a list of various Acorn Hill proprietors who might be amenable to donating food. She made another list of potential financial donors. Perhaps she and Melanie could divide the list and start canvassing the town Monday.

Satisfied with her ideas, she worked until she had a complete list to show Melanie at their meeting the next afternoon.

Chapter Six

*L*ouise rose early, as was her custom on Sunday, so that she could eat breakfast and head over to church well before the service would begin. As the chapel's organist, she wanted to warm up on the instrument and make sure that it was working properly. It wasn't exactly reliable as the organ was nearly one hundred years old. Even with maintenance, it had a tendency to wheeze during the middle of a song.

The congregation didn't seem to mind, however, and neither did Louise. She had learned to play on the organ many years ago and had even been the chapel's organist when she was in high school. Hezekiah Watkins had been her mentor, and though the dear man had long gone on to his heavenly reward, his love of the old instrument had buried itself deep in her heart. She was grateful to share her talent with the congregation and pass along Hezekiah's legacy.

Some Sundays, she ate breakfast even earlier than Jane and Alice, and today was one of those mornings. She toasted an English muffin and spread it with jam. She was just sitting down at the table when Mort Fineman entered.

"I'm sorry to bother you," he said. He took the cigar stub out of his flannel shirt pocket and palmed it in a thoughtful manner.

"That's quite all right, Mort. What can I do for you?"

He looked serious. "All my friends will be attending Grace Chapel today."

"That's wonderful," Louise said. "We'll be delighted to have them. How about you?"

"Oh no, ma'am. You see, I'm Jewish."

"Will you be all right here by yourself?" she asked. "Would you like one of my sisters to stay here?"

"I'll be fine," he said. "But I do want to ask a favor of you."

"What is it?"

Mort rolled the cigar stub between two fingers, looking hesitant. "Your sister Alice told me that you play the organ at Grace Chapel."

"That's right."

"I know it's the day of the service, and you probably have your music program set and all...," he said, trailing off.

"But...," she prompted.

He drew a deep breath. "It would mean a lot to me—and a lot to my friends—if you could play 'Bringing in the Sheaves.' Are you familiar with it?"

"Yes, I am, although I'm afraid I haven't played it in a long time."

Mort looked earnest. "It would mean so much to us if you could work it in. Please, Louise?"

"It is a standard hymn," she said, considering. "The chapel members probably would enjoy hearing it. I suppose I could replace the closing hymn with it. That is, if Rev. Thompson doesn't mind."

"Surely he won't, if he knows how much it would mean to several old veterans," Mort said.

"No, I think not," Louise said. She smiled. "Very well, Mort. I'll play it for your friends."

"Please let it be a surprise," he said. "Don't tell them ahead of the service that I asked you to play it."

"I won't breathe a word."

Mort put the cigar between his teeth, smiled and turned to go, but Louise called him back. "Mort?"

"Yes, ma'am?"

"I should have thought to tell you that there is a synagogue in Potterston with a wonderful rabbi. Perhaps you wanted to go to service on the Sabbath," she said. "But I don't mean to pry."

Mort removed the cigar from his mouth. "You're not prying, Louise. I know you and your sisters are religious people and that your father was a pastor. It's probably in your blood to be concerned about others, particularly their spiritual state."

"Well, I..."

"The truth is, I don't always observe the Sabbath when I'm out of town." He glanced down at his feet. "Okay, I don't always observe the Sabbath when I'm at home either."

Louise smiled gently. "Despite what you think about religious concerns being 'in our blood,' as you say, my sisters and I feel that people's relationships with their chosen religious institution is their own business. But since you've mentioned it, is there a reason you don't visit your temple on a regular basis?"

Mort shrugged. "There didn't seem to be any reason to go once Rivka died. I guess I went mainly for her."

"My husband died several years ago too," Louise said softly. "I didn't blame God for his death, but I did find it difficult to be in places where Eliot and I had been seen as a couple. I didn't feel as welcome, somehow, even though I know now that was strictly my imagination."

"I don't blame God for my wife's death either. But it just doesn't seem the same to attend without her." He smiled. "I'm getting more used to the idea, though, and may actually go back pretty soon. Meanwhile, if you'll play 'Bringing in the Sheaves' for my friends, I'd appreciate it."

"As long as the pastor approves, I'll give it my best effort," she said.

After Mort left, Louise finished her breakfast and was rinsing off her dishes when Jane and Alice appeared in the kitchen. "I'm heading over to the chapel to get the organ ready," Louise said. She shivered, drying her hands. "It's so chilly today. I hope the cold weather doesn't affect the organ."

"You'll make it sound fine," Jane said. "You always do."

"Thank you, dear. I'll see you two at church."

As Louise walked to Grace Chapel, the strong wind nearly bowled her over. She was glad that she had only to go a short distance to reach the church. As she approached the door, she was met by Grace Chapel's pastor, Rev. Kenneth Thompson.

"Good morning, Louise," he said, holding the door open for her.

"Good morning, Pastor Ken. Whew!" she said, as he closed the door behind her. "The wind is quite fierce this morning."

"It certainly is. I'm hoping I can enlist someone to help people in this morning. I ran into Jane yesterday and she said that your guests will be attending."

"Yes," Louise said, "two of the men are World War II veterans, here to visit with their wives. The other two are a couple with a baby. The husband is a Gulf War veteran. Then there is one more World War II vet, who won't be attending services because he is Jewish. But he did have a request that I must ask you about. He asked if I would play 'Bringing in the Sheaves.' He said it would mean a lot to his friends."

"An interesting request," Rev. Thompson said.

Louise nodded. "I told him that I could play it in place of the final hymn, if that was all right with you."

"That would be fine," he said. "I'll be delighted to announce it. What is his name?"

"Mortimer Fineman," Louise said, then paused. "But Mort said that he wanted the hymn to be a surprise for his friends."

Rev. Thompson smiled. "Well, then, I won't ruin the surprise."

Louise smiled. "Thank you, Pastor Ken."

They went their separate ways, and Louise went back to the organ so that she could limber up her fingers and rehearse. She played "Bringing in the Sheaves" twice, feeling quite comfortable with the hymn after the second run-through.

Soon the chapel members filed into the sanctuary. Louise played and glanced over her shoulder to see friends and family finding their seats. Just as she began to think that their guests weren't going to make it after all, Harvey and Penelope looked up and smiled as they passed her. They were followed by Zoë and Lars, then Nathan, Trisha and Libby. The group filled up one of the back pews.

The service proceeded as normal. Louise was delighted that the old organ seemed to be holding up with very little wheezing. Near the end of the service, Rev. Thompson spoke.

"We have some special guests worshipping with us this Sunday before Veterans Day," Rev. Thompson said. "Would those veterans who are staying at Grace Chapel Inn please rise? We want to honor you."

The men stood, and the congregation applauded. The wives smiled, while Lars looked embarrassed. Harvey Calabrese waved. Nathan Delhomme, Louise noticed, frowned.

"Now," continued the pastor, "would our own veterans stand and join our visiting military men?"

Several men and one woman rose to their feet, and the church again resounded with applause.

"Thank you, one and all, for your sacrifices for your country," Rev. Thompson said. "And now we will sing a hymn specifically requested by another veteran."

Rev. Thompson invited the congregation to stand, then nodded at Louise.

As she played the opening chords, she glanced in the mirror that she always placed above the organ so that she could see the congregation. She saw Harvey and Lars turn to one another with questioning expressions.

"Sowing in the morning, sowing seeds of kindness..."

Harvey nudged Lars, and their shoulders began to shake with laughter.

"Bringing in the sheaves, bringing in the sheaves, we shall come rejoicing, bringing in the sheaves."

What could be so funny? Louise nearly missed a note but quickly recovered as she kept an eye on Lars and Harvey. She could tell that they were singing, but their necks were turning red. Zoë gave her husband a gentle poke in the side. That only seemed to make him laugh harder.

Thankfully they reached the final verse and then the chorus, one last time.

"Bringing in the sheaves, bringing in the sheaves, we shall come rejoicing, bringing in the sheaves."

Louise played the final "amen" not a moment too soon. Rev. Thompson raised his hands to offer a benediction and a prayer. Harvey and Lars were still trying to restrain themselves, so Zoë and Penelope quickly stepped between them.

At last the service was over. Louise played the recessional, which seemed to take forever. She could not wait to find out the source of Lars and Harvey's mirth. She had never suspected that the significance of the song would be humorous.

Finally, most of the members left the sanctuary. The Grace Chapel Inn guests lingered at the back row, waiting for Louise.

"I am so sorry," Zoë said. "These two *boys* obviously have forgotten how to act in church."

"Yes, Harvey," Penelope said, giving her husband a reproving look. "I really am quite ashamed of you."

"I'm sorry, ladies," Harvey said. "Louise, I truly am sorry. I hope the pastor didn't see us. Do you think he did?"

"I don't know," Louise said truthfully. "I had my eye on you two. May I ask what was so funny?"

Harvey looked at Lars, who looked at Harvey. They both laughed out loud. "Mort Fineman put you up to this, didn't he?"

"He made a special request that I play the hymn for you, yes," Louise said, bewildered. "Why?"

"We were on patrol in France," Lars said, "at the head of our unit."

"We were scared, green kids who had barely been in France two days. We hadn't seen any action yet, but we were certain there was a Nazi waiting for us behind every boulder or tree," Harvey said. "We crested a hill and suddenly, out of nowhere it seemed, there was a flock of sheep. They must have lost their way during the fighting, but they were keeping our unit from getting through."

"So Mort—Sarge—yelled at Harve and me to round up those sheep and get them out of the way."

"But Lars and I were city boys. We'd never seen a sheep up close in our lives. I think we were almost as scared of them as we were of the Nazis."

"Sarge could see our hesitation," Lars said, starting to chuckle, "so he said, 'Music is supposed to calm animals. Why don't you two boys try singing to them? Maybe that'll get them to move.'"

"'But Sarge,' I said," Harvey recounted, spreading his hands wide as he reenacted the conversation, "'what should we sing?'

"'How should I know what sheep like?' he answered. 'Isn't there some song about sheep that you sing in your church?'

"Lars and I scratched our heads," Harvey went on. "We couldn't think of any such song. 'You got us,' we said. Sarge got all exasperated and said, 'Ain't there some song about bringing in the sheep? Seems like I've heard that tune somewhere before.'"

Lars laughed. "It dawned on us then what song he was talking about, but neither Harvey nor I wanted to contradict him. We both knew it was *sheaves*, not *sheep*, but we sure didn't want to correct our sergeant."

"So we sang it as 'bringing in the sheep.' Years later, of course, we made sure to inform Sarge at the first reunion."

"And we've all had a good laugh about it since," Lars said.

"Somebody always brings it up every time we get together, and this year Sarge has found a new way to remind us. We're sorry you were brought into this, Louise."

Louise felt a smile tugging at her lips. Who would have thought the irrepressible Mort could be such a good actor? She had honestly believed that there was some spiritual reason why Lars and Harvey would enjoy hearing the song.

"Well, he certainly pulled the *wool* over my eyes," she said with a twinkle in her eye.

Harvey and Lars started to chuckle, but Zoë hushed them both. "We're in a church. Show a little respect."

The men instantly sobered, but once they were outside, they let loose with a round of loud, nonstop laughter.

Mort was waiting for them at the front door when they returned. Louise trailed behind the veterans and wives, not wanting to spoil the counterattack. "So?" Mort asked when they stepped through the doorway. "What did you think?"

As planned in advance, Harvey and Lars had composed their expressions into long faces. Zoë shook her head. Penelope shot him a reproving look. "Mortimer Fineman, how *could* you?" she asked.

Mort's face fell. "What? Did somebody get angry? I hope it wasn't Louise." He caught her eye. "I just asked you to play that song so that they—"

Lars and Harvey could stand it no longer and broke into laughter. "You really got us," Harvey said.

"Yeah, Sarge. You really had us going."

Mort's face lit up. "Then I didn't make you angry, Louise?" He looked to her for confirmation.

She shook her head. "It was nice to play that old hymn again, even if you did suggest it for a practical joke."

"And what a joke it was," Zoë said, smiling. "Mort, you old fox, you certainly got them this year."

Mort put his arm around Lars and Harvey. "If a sergeant can't have a little fun with his men, I don't know what this world is coming to."

Louise left them to their laughter and slipped away to the kitchen. Jane had already fixed lunch, and she and Alice were just about to sit down. Louise explained what had happened with the final hymn, and Jane and Alice both smiled. When she repeated her earlier line about having the wool pulled over her eyes, they laughed.

"So I guess you're feeling a little sheepish," Alice said.

"Don't let it *bahhhh-ther* you," Jane said, her eyes twinkling.

Louise groaned. "If you promise not to make any more puns, I'll eat my lunch and go up to my room for a rest. I have a three o'clock meeting with Melanie Brubaker about the food drive."

"That's right," Jane said. "And I'm glad you mentioned it, Louise, because I need to get together with Craig Tracy about the Thanksgiving feast sometime soon too."

"The holiday will be here before we know it," Louise mused.

Jane smiled mischievously. "Yes, it will, but there's no need to look like a lost lamb about it."

Louise groaned and pretended to wad up her napkin and throw it at her sister.

Promptly at three o'clock, Louise arrived at the chapel. There was no sign of Melanie Brubaker. Louise checked the Assembly Room, then when she didn't find Melanie there, she looked in the vesting room. She went upstairs and drifted to the back of the sanctuary to make certain she had put away her sheet music. The morning had been so out of the ordinary with the veterans visiting that she couldn't remember if she'd tidied up. If she waited at the organ, she might catch Melanie when she arrived.

"Hello, Louise," Rev. Thompson said, walking down the aisle toward her. He had changed into casual attire, khaki trousers and a pullover sweater. "What are you doing here?"

"Putting my music away, but I'm also waiting on Melanie Brubaker."

"Melanie?" He frowned.

"We were supposed to meet to discuss the Thanksgiving food drive."

Rev. Thompson's frown deepened. "She didn't say anything about it to me. In fact, let me check my Palm Pilot. I think I remember her scheduling time here for another day."

He took his PDA out of his pocket and consulted it. "Yes, she scheduled time for tomorrow at three in the afternoon."

"Tomorrow?" Louise said, bewildered. "She asked me what day would be good to meet, and I said Sunday. She said she would meet me here." She sighed, shaking her head. "We must have had a miscommunication. I'll get in touch with her at home. Thank you, Pastor Ken."

"You're welcome, Louise. Sorry you had to go out in the cold for nothing," he said.

Louise trudged back to the inn, bracing herself against the wind. Thank goodness she had wrapped a long scarf around her neck. The air had a decided bite to it.

Inside the inn was warm and comforting. The veterans were nowhere to be seen...or heard. She found Jane in the kitchen, stirring something on the stove. Louise sat at the table, unwinding the scarf from her neck. "That smells wonderful, Jane. What are you cooking?"

"The sauce for chicken tetrazzini," Jane said, pausing to sample a bit. She wrinkled her nose. "Needs a little more white wine."

"Isn't that a lot for just the three of us?"

Jane shook her head. "I invited our guests, along with Lloyd and Aunt Ethel, to join us for dinner tonight. Is your meeting with Melanie over already? That didn't last very long."

Louise sighed. "Apparently Melanie thought that we were meeting tomorrow at three, not today. It's a good thing Pastor Ken was at the chapel to tell me he had scheduled it for her on his PDA, or I'd still be waiting for her."

"That's strange. I heard you suggest Sunday. She said that would be fine."

Louise sighed. "I'm glad you agree. I thought maybe I made the mistake, although I was quite certain that we had agreed on Sunday."

"I guess you'll just have to meet tomorrow then."

"Unfortunately, I can't make it," Louise said. "I have a piano lesson at a quarter after three." She rose reluctantly. "I'd better call Melanie so that we can reschedule." She walked to the doorway, then turned back, reminded by the silence. "By the way, where are our guests? They're unusually quiet."

"They went for a Sunday drive, as Mort called it," Jane said. "The Delhommes are upstairs napping. I think Libby didn't sleep well last night so they're trying to catch up on their rest."

"I may do that myself, after I phone Melanie," Louise said. "What time is dinner?"

Jane added a pinch of something to her sauce, her concentration moving from the conversation to her cooking. "Uh, dinner? Six thirty."

Louise went to the telephone under the stairs and dialed Melanie's house. She didn't get an answer, and apparently the Brubakers didn't have an answering machine. Louise replaced the receiver and headed upstairs for the comfort of her room and a much-needed Sunday afternoon rest. It had already been a long day.

After the veterans returned from their drive, they quietly congregated in the library. Nathan and Trisha joined them, with Libby, and even the baby seemed to realize the need for silence.

At six thirty, Alice rapped on the door to call them all to dinner. When she entered, she saw that they were all seated at various chairs in the room, each person reading a book. Even Trisha read while Libby snoozed on her shoulder.

"You all look so peaceful, I hate to disturb you," Alice said.

"Whew. Please do," Mort said, clapping his book shut. "I'm starving."

"Oh, I do hate to stop here," Penelope said, placing a crocheted bookmark in her book. "It's such a good mystery, and I can hardly wait for the culprit to be revealed."

"Same here," Zoë said, "although I'm reading a romance novel."

Lars laughed. "You *know* how that will end. The boy will get the girl and they'll live happily ever after."

"I know that," Zoë said, "but it's how they manage to get together that's worth reading."

Alice smiled. "I didn't realize you were such enthusiastic readers."

"Some of us are, some of us aren't," Mort said, shrugging. "It's a compromise we men made with our wives years ago. We could play cards, sing, shop and sightsee as much as we wanted, but Sundays are always reserved for church for the churchgoing and reading for everybody."

"It's our day of quiet," Zoë said.

Mort rubbed his hands together. "But now it's time to eat, folks. What's in the chow line, Alice, do you know?"

"If you mean what has Jane prepared for us, I forgot to ask, but it smells wonderful," Alice said, laughing. "Right this way to the dining room, everyone."

The group filed out, chattering as they went. As they were entering the dining room from the hall, Ethel and Lloyd entered from the kitchen. Right behind Ethel and Lloyd were Louise and Jane.

Just as Alice was about to make the introductions, Ethel and Zoë caught sight of each other. They stopped and stared at each other's red hair.

All conversation stopped. Louise caught Alice's gaze, and they shared a smile. "Well, well," Mort said, grinning. "It looks like we have twin matchsticks."

Ethel touched her hair, then recovered quickly. "I like that shade," she said to Zoë, sticking out her hand. "I'm Ethel Buckley, the girls' aunt."

"And I'm Zoë Olsdotter. I like *your* hair too," she said, smiling.

Ethel leaned closer. "Titian Dreams?" she whispered, naming the red dye she used.

Zoë nodded. She and Ethel laughed out loud.

That got everyone moving again, and they took their places, with Jane directing the seating arrangements. "Let me sit near the door," Trisha said, "so that I can take Libby out quickly if she gets fussy."

"Nonsense," Ethel said, glancing up from a conversation with Zoë. "I'd be glad to help you if that little angel starts to complain. You need a nice, warm meal. I remember how it was as a new mother."

"How many children did you have, Mrs. Buckley?" Trisha asked.

"Three," she said. "I don't see them often because they don't live here in town."

"But they're wonderful children," Lloyd said, stepping forward to introduce himself.

Mort smiled. "So this is the famous mayor of Acorn Hill."

"Lloyd Tynan," he said, offering his hand. Mort shook it, then Lloyd moved to each inn guest, making sure to meet them all.

"It's an honor to meet you veterans and your lovely wives," he said. "On behalf of Acorn Hill, we're honored that you're staying in our town."

"We're delighted to be here," Zoë said.

"We're even more honored that you've agreed to speak at the elementary school," Lloyd said. "I know we'll all benefit from what you have to say."

"I hear you're a fellow veteran," Mort said.

"I served in the Korean War," Lloyd said proudly. "I look forward to speaking after you and marching with you in the parade in Potterston."

"Same here," Harvey said. He looked at Jane. "I sure smell something good from the kitchen."

"Thank you," she said. "Take a seat, everybody, and we'll start serving."

They all found their places, which Jane had indicated. Harvey tucked a corner of his napkin into the front of his shirt. "I need maximum coverage," he said to Ethel, who looked at him with puzzlement. Harvey spread the napkin across his chest, shrugging. "I come from an Italian family, what can I say? Mama taught us kids to do this so we wouldn't slop sauce all over ourselves."

After saying grace, Alice and Louise followed Jane to the kitchen, where they served up the delicious creamed-chicken dish. "This looks wonderful and smells even better," Alice said, sniffing appreciatively.

"I do think it's one of my better versions," Jane said. "I keep adding a little of this and cutting back on a little of that. Someday I'll get it perfect."

"I have a feeling it's pretty close to perfect right now," Alice said.

The sisters served each guest, and Jane brought in a basket of tiny baking-soda biscuits and chilled plates of spinach-and-orange salad. "It's something with a little tang to contrast with the cream sauce," she said.

Zoë sighed. "This is heavenly, Jane."

"Thank you. Another biscuit?" she asked, passing the basket. When it returned, only crumbs remained. In between bites of Jane's delicious fare, everyone chatted companionably.

"So, Mr. Delhomme," Lloyd said at the first lull in the conversation. "I hear you're a Gulf War veteran, is that right?"

Nathan glanced up, his expression frozen. "That's right, sir," he said in a low voice. He ducked his head and found renewed interest in his dinner.

Lloyd, who had finished his meal, leaned forward, obviously primed for conversation. "I've never talked to anyone who served over there. What was the desert like?"

Nathan's jaw tightened. "I imagine that war was pretty much the same as any other."

"He's just being modest," Harvey said, wiping his mouth with the corner of his napkin, which was still tucked into his shirt. "He's a hero. Tell them, Nathan."

"There's nothing to tell," he mumbled.

"Go on," Mort said.

Libby started to cry, and Nathan grabbed her from Trisha's arms. "I'll take her for a while," he said. "She probably needs a diaper change."

"Wait, Mr. Delhomme," Ethel said, "I'll—"

Nathan rushed from the room. They could hear his footsteps on the staircase. Trisha turned back to the group. "He doesn't like to talk about the war," she said. "Please don't think him rude."

"Is it impolite to ask what he did that made him a hero?" Ethel asked.

"The kid was a fighter pilot, and he got shot down over the desert," Mort said.

"My goodness!" Ethel said. "How did he survive?"

Trisha rose, pressing her hands against the table. Alice noticed that her fingertips were white. "Excuse me, but since I know Nathan doesn't like to talk about it, I'm sure he would appreciate it if you didn't talk about it in his absence."

"He's a heroic kid," Mort said. "What's the harm? Jackson Delhomme was mighty proud of him. So are we."

Trisha opened her mouth as if to say something, then she reconsidered. "I'd better go find Nathan and see how Libby is doing."

She left the room, and everyone looked at one another. Jane cleared her throat and rose. "Who's ready for dessert?"

Chapter Seven

*A*fter several unsuccessful attempts to reach Melanie on Sunday evening, Louise decided to call her first thing in the morning before the woman left for work. Melanie answered on the third ring, immediately recognizing Louise's voice. "Oh, Louise," she said, "I'm looking forward to our meeting this afternoon."

"That's why I am calling," Louise said. "I tried to get you yesterday but there was no answer. I'm afraid that we seem to have had some sort of misunderstanding. I thought you agreed to meet yesterday afternoon, not today. Pastor Ken set me straight when I waited for you at the chapel. He had it recorded in his PDA that you scheduled time for us to meet this afternoon, and I'm afraid I can't make it. I'm giving a piano lesson."

"Sunday? Oh, Louise, I'm so sorry. I hope you didn't wait too long. I must have misunderstood. I thought you said Monday."

"It's all right, and no, I did not wait too long at the chapel. Is there another time we can meet?"

"It needs to be soon," Melanie said. "If you can't make it this afternoon, can you meet tomorrow? Oh, wait, no, I can't do that either. I don't have anybody to watch the kids. I suppose I could take them to Grace Chapel with me."

"I can make it tomorrow, and I would be glad to come to your house. Would that be easier for you?"

"It certainly would. Thank you, Louise. What a relief! How about three o'clock?"

"I will be there," she said.

"See you then," Melanie said.

As Louise hung up the phone in the reception area, Alice came down the hall from the kitchen.

"Did you have any luck with Melanie?" Alice asked.

"We're meeting tomorrow afternoon. She said she misunderstood me."

Alice shook her head. "That's odd, don't you think?"

"Yes. I don't know how that could have happened. The rest of us understood," Louise said. "I guess we're going to have a quiet morning here. I saw everyone troop out while I was on the phone."

"Everyone's gone, except for Nathan. He's seemed moody ever since breakfast. Ever since last night, as a matter of fact."

"Do you think the discussion of his being a hero upset him?" Louise asked.

"I don't know why, but apparently it did. He's upstairs and has been ever since the others left. I heard Trisha pleading with him to go, but he refused."

"Maybe he doesn't feel well," Louise said.

Alice shook her head. "I already asked. He said no, and I didn't want to pry further. I'm worried about him, Louise. I know that having a new baby can be stressful to a couple, but I think it's something more."

"I agree. But what can we do?"

"Nothing. Unless he asks for help." Alice checked her watch. "I'd better hurry off to work. I want to get there a little early, because Mondays are always so busy."

As Alice drove to work, she thought about Nathan. Why would anyone not be proud to be considered a hero? And what exactly had he done that earned him that honor?

At Potterston Hospital, she got out of her car in the parking lot and walked briskly toward the building. As she clutched her coat closer to ward off the chill, one of the hospital's doctors, Chad Uhel, fell in step with her.

"Hi, Alice. The days are certainly getting shorter and colder," he said.

"They are indeed." She didn't know Dr. Uhel very well, so she racked her mind for conversation while they walked together. Someone had said that his first job in health care was as a medic during the Vietnam War and—

"Dr. Uhel," she said.

"*Hmm?*"

"Is it true you were an army doctor?"

"I wasn't a doctor, just a medic, but that experience helped me decide to go to medical school," he said. "Why do you ask?"

She described Nathan's behavior without divulging his name or that he was an inn guest, of course, then finished with, "Do you have any insight as to why he might be reluctant to talk about his experiences during the Gulf War?"

Dr. Uhel thought for a moment. "It could be posttraumatic stress disorder," he said. "Maybe something bad happened and he doesn't want to relive it."

"But supposedly he was a hero. How can that be bad?"

The doctor stopped just outside the hospital door. "Heroes often have bad things happen to them—or see bad things that they can't banish from their memories. I'm sure you've dealt with people who were involved in fatal accidents or who have seen loved ones killed and who have had a difficult time in the aftermath."

"Yes," Alice murmured. "They frequently need counseling to get on with their lives."

The doctor opened the door and held it for her. "I have a feeling that may be the problem with your friend. Of course, I'm no psychiatrist, just an internist. But I'd still recommend that he undergo some counseling. I did so myself, after the war."

"And then you became a doctor?"

He smiled. "I certainly did. I took the bad medical experiences I witnessed in Vietnam and used them as my motivation to get through med school and learn how to better heal hurting people."

"Thank you, Dr. Uhel," Alice said, smiling. "You've been a wonderful help."

As she walked to her station, Alice thought about Nathan. She wasn't sure that she would ever approach him about such a personal matter, but now she knew that if the opportunity arose, she would at least be forearmed with knowledge.

That afternoon, Jane was in the kitchen preparing dinner. She had the radio tuned to an oldies station, and she danced around the room as she fixed polenta lasagna. "One-two-cha-cha-cha, three-four-cha-cha-cha," she mumbled as she mixed the cornmeal and water to make polenta. The radio tune was before her time, but it had a catchy beat. "One-two, three-four—"

"Hi, Ms. Howard," a teenage voice said at the back door. "I hope we're not intruding."

Jane looked up to see Candace Brighton and Sophie Alvarez, two girls from the church's youth group. They were also cheerleaders at Franklin High, and they were wearing their cheerleading uniforms. They looked like carbon copies of each other with ponytails, white shoes and red wool skirts and tops with a large white *F* on the front.

"Hi, girls," Jane said, dusting stray cornmeal from her hands. "Come on in."

"We ran into Mrs. Buckley outside, and she said it would be okay to come in through the back door," Sophie said.

"It's fine," Jane assured them. "Have a seat. Did you just get out of school?"

Candace nodded as they took chairs at the table. "Sophie drove us straight over here after practice. We can't stay very long, though."

"What can I do for you?" Jane sat as well.

Candace and Sophie looked at each other. "We were looking through some of the really old yearbooks and we saw that you and Ms. Songer used to be cheerleaders at Franklin High," Candace explained.

The "really old" jolted Jane, but she kept her face expression-less as she answered, "Yes, though Ms. Songer cheered after I graduated."

"Well, you know that the football team hasn't been in a play-off for a long, long time. We thought it'd be fun to do some old-time cheers," Candace said.

"And we were hoping maybe you and Ms. Songer could show us a few you used to do back in your day," Sophie finished.

Jane sat back. "I suppose we could." She looked at the girls. "But was what we did then really so different from the cheers now?"

"Our cheerleading sponsor, Mrs. Thrush, said that the sport has changed a lot over the years," Sophie said.

"Yeah, when was that, Ms. Howard, the fifties?" Candace asked.

Jane blinked. "I was born in the fifties, ladies."

"Oh. Sorry," Candace said, looking at Sophie. They broke into giggles. Then Candace asked, "Do you think Ms. Songer would be interested? We're going to see her next, but we won't bother her if you think she wouldn't."

"I think Sylvia will like the idea as much as I do," Jane said. Hadn't she and Sylvia both been reminiscing fondly about their high school days? They'd show these young pups a thing or two about cheerleading.

"Before you go, though," Jane said, "I just made some choco-late chip cookies. Would you girls like some?"

"Oh, thanks!" Sophie said, her eyes twinkling.

"Sweet!" Candace said.

Jane frowned. "Yes, of course they're sweet."

"No, I mean—" Candace giggled. "It's kind of a teen thing."

Jane set a plate of cookies in front of the girls, along with two glasses of cold milk. "I really shouldn't eat any," Sophie said, glancing down at her figure, which looked fit and trim to Jane.

"Suit yourself," Jane said, pouring herself a glass of milk and taking a large cookie. "*Mmm*. These are still warm."

Sophie took a cookie and bit into it with gusto.

Finishing one cookie and taking another, Candace said to Jane, "Did you hear about the Patriot mascot?"

"No, did something happen to him?" Jane asked.

"Alvin's fine," Sophie said, washing down the rest of her cookie with a gulp of milk. "But he won't be able to be the mascot at the game with Billings High. His parents have grounded him until he gets his GPA back where it should be. When they saw some of his grades last week, they said his clowning days were over."

"It's kind of cool, though," Candace said, "because they're going to hold tryouts for a substitute mascot. You know, somebody to fill in for Alvin."

"Will Alvin be back next year?" Jane asked.

Candace shook her head. "He's a senior. It's too bad he can't perform at the game. He's really disappointed."

"But it's a good chance for somebody else," Sophie said. "Whoever wins the tryout, if the school likes them during the game, they'll probably be asked to be the mascot next year."

"When are the tryouts?" Jane asked.

Candace nearly shot milk through her nose. "*You* aren't thinking about the job, are you, Ms. Howard?"

"No," Jane said, smiling.

"I'm not sure," Sophie said. "Mrs. Thrush wants to make sure that everyone has a chance to rehearse a little, since it's such short notice."

"Sophie, we've got to talk to Ms. Songer about the costume too," Candace said.

Sophie nodded, her dark ponytail bobbing. "Right."

"Costume?" Jane asked. She knew she sounded nosy, but she was drawn into their conversation.

"Yeah, the cheer squad took a vote, and we decided that the Patriot costume is all raggedy and needs to be replaced," Sophie said. "We're going to ask Ms. Songer if she would consider making us a new one."

"Yeah," Candace said. "We want our mascot to look really good for the game against Billings."

"We'll have the best football team *and* the best spirit squad," Sophie said, her eyes shining. "I hope Ms. Songer will agree to do it."

"A new Patriot costume *would* be really fly," Jane said.

The girls looked at one another, bewildered. "Uh, *fly?*"

Jane realized that she must have committed a slang faux pas. "Fly, you know, like *phat? Swell?*" She searched her memory. "What did you say earlier, *sweet?*"

Neither girl responded but stared at her blankly.

"All right, I give up," Jane said, exasperated. "What *do* you say?"

Candace laid her hand over Jane's. "Thanks for the cookies, Ms. Howard. Sophie and I need to head over to Ms. Songer's before she closes for the day. We'll call you later about helping us with our cheers."

"Okay, girls," Jane said. "Good luck at Sylvia's."

They both thanked her again for the cookies and milk, then headed for the back door. On the way out, they sneaked a glance back at her, then put their heads together and giggled.

Feeling old and out of touch, Jane shook her head. She collected the cookie plate and empty glasses, carrying them to the counter. Alice entered. "Was that Aunt Ethel at the door?"

Jane laughed. "No, someone who *really* made me feel old." She explained about Candace and Sophie asking her and Sylvia to help with some new cheers and a new costume for the Patriot mascot.

"I'm sure she'll do it," Alice said. "Sylvia's so creative and talented."

"It certainly would be an improvement over the old one," Jane said. "The guy who performed as the Patriot was definitely talented, but the outfit needed some updating. It was looking a little threadbare."

"Yes, it did look a little worse for wear," Alice said.

"Did you hear that the mascot will have to be replaced for the play-off game with Billings?" Jane asked.

"No, why?"

Jane explained about the boy's grades and his being grounded, then added, "The girls said that they're going to hold tryouts for a replacement mascot. If the school likes the new mascot, he can keep the job next year, providing he's not a senior, of course."

"That's too bad for Alvin," Alice said.

"Yes, particularly if Franklin beats Billings and moves on to another play-off game and maybe even a state championship after that."

"Oh, Jane, wouldn't a championship game be fun?" Alice asked. "That would do so much for everyone's morale, not just the students."

Jane passed the plate of cookies to Alice, who accepted one with thanks and immediately started nibbling at it. "Do you ever wish you were back in high school?" Jane asked.

Alice chewed thoughtfully for a moment, then swallowed. "No, not really. It was lots of fun when I was there, but there was a lot of pressure too. It's a difficult age to be. My generation was lucky that it didn't have the pressures that today's generation does: drugs, sex—"

"Rock and roll," Jane added mischievously.

"We had rock and roll," Alice said. "In fact, we had Elvis."

Jane laughed. "I remember your listening to him on the radio and my dancing to the music. I must have been about six years old then."

Alice smiled. "Was it really that long ago? It seems like only yesterday."

Jane glanced at the door that Sophie and Candace had walked through. She smiled. "In some ways, it was."

Alice headed toward the stairs, preparing to change out of her nurse's uniform. The phone rang at the desk. "Grace Chapel Inn," she said.

"Alice? This is Frieda Thrush at Franklin High. I'm the cheerleading sponsor."

"Yes, Frieda. How are you?"

"A little harried," she said. "I'm in charge of Career Day, which is tomorrow, and I've had a couple of last-minute cancellations, which has left me woefully short of speakers. One of the cheer-leaders reminded me that you and your sisters have interesting careers. I wonder if any or all of you would be interested in speaking to some of our juniors and seniors tomorrow at ten o'clock."

Before Alice had a chance to speak, Frieda said, "I'm begging here. I have Lloyd Tynan on the schedule, and a lawyer, and Nia the librarian and Viola the bookstore owner. Everyone else seems to be busy."

Alice smiled. "I know that all three of us would be delighted to help. And I can answer affirmatively for myself. But I'll have to check with Jane and Louise. I'm afraid I don't know what their plans are for tomorrow. May I call you back?"

"That would be fine. But let me know as soon as possible, please. And do you know anyone else who might be interested?"

Alice thought for a moment. "You might try Sylvia Songer."

"Sylvia, of course! Why didn't I think of her? Thank you, Alice. Call me as soon as you can."

Frieda hung up the receiver so quickly, presumably to phone Sylvia, that Alice never got a chance to say good-bye. Before heading back upstairs, she checked with Jane, who laughed and said that her dance card was wide open tomorrow morning and she would love a chance to see old Franklin High again.

"Good," Alice said. "Now all I need to do is find Louise."

"Find Louise for what?" their older sister asked as she entered the kitchen.

Alice explained the last-minute invitation from Frieda Thrush. "What a pity," Louise said. "Normally I would love to help out, but I have a piano teachers' guild meeting tomorrow morning in Potterston that I can't miss."

Jane smiled at Alice. "Looks like it's you and me. Maybe we can have lunch in Potterston when we're finished speaking."

"Sounds good. I'll call Frieda to tell her you and I can make it."

Alice dialed from the extension in the kitchen. Frieda answered on the first ring and was more than enthusiastic when Alice explained that two Howard sisters could help out. "Wonderful! Sylvia said that she could help too," Frieda said. "Oh, I know this is going to come together after all." She thanked Alice again, gave her directions about where to go, then hung up nearly as rapidly as she had the first time.

When Alice hung up her own receiver, Jane asked, "Did I hear that Sylvia is coming too?"

Alice nodded.

"Why don't we see if she'd like to ride with us?" Jane asked. "Is that all right with you, Alice?"

"I think it's a great idea. I hope she can go to lunch with us as well."

"And maybe we can practice some cheers," Jane said, cupping her hands around her mouth to make a megaphone. "Hey, gang! Are the Billy Goats going to win this game?"

"Well, no!" Alice yelled back. Louise looked confused, so Alice told her about Jane and Sylvia's invitation from the Franklin High cheer squad to help them create a special routine.

Jane took two dish towels in hand as substitutes for pompoms. "P-P-P-A-T. R-R-I-O-T. P-A-T. R-I-O-T. Patriots, Patriots, Patriots, are *the best. Yay, Pats!*"

"Yay!" Alice and Louise cheered, waving their hands.

Flushed, Jane lowered the dish towels, smiling.

Chapter Eight

The next morning, Alice and Jane headed out in Alice's blue Toyota to pick up their friend. When Sylvia came out to the curb, Jane jumped out of the front seat and got into the back with Sylvia.

"You don't mind, do you, Alice?" Jane asked. "Sylvia and I can talk better back here."

Alice glanced at the empty seat beside her. "I suppose not."

"Oh, good. Sylvia, I've been trying to remember some old cheers. Listen to this," Jane said, launching into a routine.

"I remember that one!" Sylvia squealed. "How about this one?"

Alice shook her head. With the two women in the backseat chanting, she felt like a chauffeur to teens again. Memories were coming back to her, too, and what she remembered was driving Jane and her friends around before her younger sister was old enough to get her own license.

By the time they got to the school, Alice's ears ached. She'd heard more rah-rahs in the last thirty minutes than she thought she'd ever heard in her life. She also noticed that Jane's and Sylvia's voices had increased in incremental pitches as they reminisced. Alice parked the car, and they all headed into the high school building.

As they opened the door, Sylvia sniffed the air. "Smell, Jane. Doesn't it bring back memories?"

Jane sniffed. "It certainly does."

Alice wondered what all the fuss was about. "I don't smell anything."

"You don't?" Sylvia and Jane said in unison.

"How about the smell of cafeteria rolls baking?" Jane asked.

"Or old gym clothes?" Sylvia added.

Alice sniffed again, then shrugged. "Nope, I'm afraid not, though I'm glad to be missing the latter."

Jane and Sylvia sighed as though she was hopeless.

Alice struggled to smother a smile.

"Alice! Jane! Sylvia!"

Alice turned to see Nia Komonos, Acorn Hill's librarian, and Viola Reed, the owner of Nine Lives Bookstore. They had evidently arrived only a few moments ago and were walking toward them from the parking lot. Alice held the door open, waiting for them to catch up.

"Shouldn't we hurry?" Sylvia asked.

"I agree," Jane said, looking worried. "We don't want to be late."

Alice squelched her irritation with the middle-aged teens. "Why don't you two go on ahead and let Frieda Thrush know that we're here? I'll wait for Nia and Viola."

Looking grateful, Jane and Sylvia hurried down the hall. Alice had to wait only a few moments before the other two women caught up with her.

"They went ahead to let Frieda know we've arrived," she said by way of explanation to Viola and Nia.

Huffing and puffing because she was heavyset, Viola put her hand over her heart to catch her breath. "At least one of you was kind enough to wait," she said when she could speak again.

Nia rubbed her gloved hands together. "I'm looking forward to this opportunity to talk to the high schoolers. I want to stress to them how important it is to work hard to fulfill their dreams."

"Let's go to the auditorium," Alice said, taking Viola's arm. "Are you all right?"

"I'm fine." She tossed the end of a brightly colored knitted scarf over her shoulder. "Let's get this over with."

Frieda Thrush met them and pointed them toward the stage. "We're just about to start," she said as they entered behind the curtain. Jane and Sylvia were already seated in the row of chairs set up for the speakers, and the conversations of the waiting students buzzed on the other side of the curtain.

Frieda pointed out the prearranged seats for Alice, Viola and Nia, then addressed them all in a soft tone. "I'm so glad you could all make it," she said. "Each of you will have five minutes to discuss your career, then we'll have a question-and-answer session with the students. I know that you all have already given of your valuable time, but I hope you can stay to answer any questions. That's the part of these career days that the students seem to get the most from."

They all murmured that they could stay. Frieda smiled, then stepped around the curtain to begin the presentation.

Each guest was introduced, then they spoke and answered questions. The students applauded, and Frieda again thanked each speaker and invited any students who might have additional questions to come up to the stage. The majority of the crowd dispersed, but a few approached the speakers for more information.

Alice fielded several nursing questions, then found herself alone. She drifted over to Viola and Nia, who were deep in discussion with a female student. The girl held up several books, one at a time, her voice animated.

"I really liked this one," she said, all smiles. "The author really—"

She broke off when she saw Alice. "Please don't let me interrupt," Alice said.

"Th—that's all right," the girl said. She ducked her head and clutched the books to her chest, as if she was afraid to be seen with them.

"Alice, this is Carole Keith," Nia said. "She is one of Franklin High's most avid readers and comes to the Acorn Hill library quite often."

"*And* to Nine Lives," Viola added.

"How do you do, Carole?" Alice extended a hand. "I'm Alice Howard."

"Yes, ma'am," the girl mumbled. Alice noticed that her handshake was limp and clammy. "I enjoyed your talk about nursing."

"Thank you," Alice said, "but it's clear your love has a literary bent. Have you thought about a career for yourself when you leave high school?"

Carole raised her head, reluctantly, Alice thought. "I want to do something with words. I'll go to college, of course. Maybe study literature or writing."

"That's wonderful," Alice said. "It's a shame that Carlene Moss could not be here today. She publishes the *Acorn Nutshell*. She would know all about writing."

"Journalism isn't really the kind of writing I have in mind," Carole said. "You have to talk to too many people to get your story. I'm more interested in poetry or short stories."

"Carole is being modest," Nia said, putting an arm around the girl. "Since she's a senior, she's editing the school's literary magazine this year. And doing a wonderful job, too, from what I hear from the sponsoring teacher, Carole."

"Thanks," she said.

"Would you like to tell us about another one of those books?" Viola said, nodding at the stack in Carole's arms. Viola turned to Alice. "Carole helps me identify trends for teens. She lets me know which books she thinks will be popular with the high school students, and I try to stock them. She has an outstanding literary sense."

Carole held up a book with a pair of chopsticks on the cover. "This is about two friends who like Chinese food and compete for the same musical prize. It's part of a series about friends, based on the seasons."

"Sounds like an interesting concept," Alice said.

Viola nodded. "Lots of girls have been asking for it at the store."

"And that's about it," Carole said, seeming to draw back into herself. "I'd better get back to class. Thanks for taking the time to talk to me."

"Thank *you*, Carole," Nia said. "Stop by the library soon."

"And Nine Lives," Viola added.

"It was nice to meet you," Alice said. "I'm always glad to meet a fellow book lover. Good luck with the rest of your school year."

"Thanks, Miss Howard," Carole said, then shuffled off. She opened a book on the top of the stack and started reading while she walked. Instantly, she bumped into a boy.

"Hey, watch where you're going!" he said, then raced down the hall.

"Poor girl," Viola said, adjusting her glasses. "She suffers horribly from shyness."

"She's really quite attractive," Nia said thoughtfully. "She reminds me of myself when I was that age. I thought I was an ugly duckling and hid from people by burying my nose in books."

"She'll grow out of it," Alice said. "Most people do, once they leave high school and begin to find their niche at college."

"I think she's going to find a pretty important niche," Viola said. "What she lacks in social skills, she more than makes up for in literary talent. She could become an editor or a writer, in my opinion."

Nia smiled. "Wouldn't it be wonderful to say that we knew her when she was still young? I hope you're right, Viola. I would love to see one of her own books on the library shelves one day."

Alice watched the girl amble down the hall, ignoring the bustling and jostling of her fellow students. "I would like to see her enjoy the rest of her time in high school," she said. "You're only young once."

Nia squeezed Alice's arm, smiling. "You're not getting senti-mental about your high school years, are you, Alice?"

Alice smiled back. "No, I wouldn't want to go back to that time, but I certainly did enjoy high school while I was there."

"Watermelon, watermelon, watermelon rind. Look on the scoreboard and see who's behind!" Jane and Sylvia could be heard chanting in unison. They were huddled together in one end of the auditorium, practicing their cheers.

"Looks like *some* people would love to go back to their teen years," Viola said. "Do you suppose we can pry those two away from the school so that we can go to lunch in Potterston?"

Alice laughed. "I'm not certain, but we can try."

That afternoon, promptly at three, Louise pulled up in front of Melanie Brubaker's comfortable-looking two-story house. She didn't see Melanie's car in the driveway, but she rang the bell anyway.

Melanie's older child, eleven-year-old Bree, answered the door. "Hi, Mrs. Smith," she said.

"Hello. I'm supposed to meet with your mother."

"She's not here," Bree said.

Alarmed, Louise peered inside the house. "You're not alone, are you?"

"No, Clinton is here too," she said, referring to her younger brother.

Louise drew in her breath. She knew that more and more chil-dren had become what was referred to as latchkey kids—children who stayed at home by themselves—but surely a fifth grader was not old enough to take care of herself *and* a younger brother.

She stepped into the house. "Bree, I—"

"Oh, hello, Mrs. Smith." One of Franklin High's students, Darcy Coldwater, stepped into the hallway. She wiped her hands on a dish towel. "I was just washing up some dishes for Mrs. Brubaker. She should be home pretty soon."

Louise relaxed. "You've been here with the children?"

Darcy nodded. "Sometimes Mrs. Brubaker asks me to pick them up from school when she thinks she's going to be working late. I live next door and get out of school earlier than the elementary school lets out, so it's not a problem. She told me to expect you today. She phoned and said she'll be along as soon as possible. She's running a bit late at the office. I told her I'd be glad to stay as long as she needs me."

"Are you sure she understood you?" Bree asked.

"Of course I'm sure, silly billy," Darcy said, smiling at the girl. "Why do you ask?"

Bree shrugged. "No reason. I'm going to start on my homework now. Mommy said if Clinton and I finished before dinner, she'd take us out for ice cream afterward."

"Sounds like a plan, Bree," Darcy said, smiling as the girl skipped away.

"Now that I'm here, there's no need for you to stay," Louise said. "If you'd like to go home, I'm sure Mrs. Brubaker will be along at any moment."

"Well," Darcy said, considering. "I do have homework, and I know my boyfriend would like to see me tonight. My parents have a strict rule: Homework left undone, Darcy has no fun. And I have a report due tomorrow in social studies."

Louise smiled. "Sounds like you had better go then. We will be fine here."

Darcy gathered her coat and purse. "Thanks, Mrs. Smith," Darcy said. "You're the greatest. Will you tell Mrs. Brubaker that I washed all the dishes and put them away?" Without waiting for an answer, Darcy disappeared out the front door.

Bree joined Louise in the entryway. "Would you like to hear me practice, Mrs. Smith?" the girl asked.

"Why, yes. That would be lovely. Since this is not a lesson, I won't stop to correct you."

"Like a recital then," Bree said, leading the way to the piano in the living room.

"Exactly," Louise said, settling herself on a comfortable cream-colored leather sofa. "I am just here to listen."

Bree smiled, positioned her fingers on the keys, then launched into a short sonata. When she finished, Louise applauded. "That was wonderful, Bree."

"Really? Any mistakes?"

"You didn't hit a single wrong note," Louise said. "You've been working hard, I can tell."

"Thank you," Bree said. "Do you think I'll be able to play it in the Christmas recital?"

"I am quite sure that you will," Louise said.

Bree looked down at her hands, still resting on the keys. "I hope Mom can hear it."

"Surely she can get time off from work," Louise said.

"I don't mean her coming to the recital," Bree said. "Sometimes she doesn't seem to hear all the notes. Or what I'm saying when I talk."

Louise folded her hands. "I am sure she just gets distracted, Bree. Sometimes she has to juggle a lot of things at one time, doesn't she?"

"I guess so. I know she's busy with work and taking care of us. Daddy's busy a lot too. He goes out of town for his job, so it's just Clinton and Mom and me most nights. He's home for the weekends, though."

The front door opened and Melanie entered. "Hi, Mom!" Bree said, hopping down off the piano bench to give her mother a hug.

"Hi, sweetie. How was your day at school?"

"Okay, I guess."

"Hi, Louise," Melanie said. "I'm so sorry I was late." She looked around. "Where's Clinton? Where's Darcy?" She put her hands on Bree's shoulders and looked her full in the face. "Did Darcy show up?"

"Yes, Mom. Then Mrs. Smith got here, and Darcy left."

"I told her there was no need for both of us to stay here," Louise said. "She had some homework to do."

Melanie's expression relaxed. "No doubt she wanted to get it out of the way so that she could spend time with her boyfriend tonight."

"I believe so," Louise said, smiling.

Melanie took off her coat and hung it on the coat tree by the front door. "Well, I appreciate your waiting for me and for letting Darcy go home early. She's good with the kids, and they like her a lot, don't you, Bree?"

"Yep," the girl said happily. "Now that you're home, is it all right if I get back to my homework?"

"Yes, I'm going to talk with Mrs. Smith," Melanie said. "She and I have to talk about the food drive, then you can help me make dinner."

"What are we having?" Bree asked suspiciously.

"Macaroni and cheese."

"Yay! See you later!" Bree rushed out of the room and into the den, presumably to start her schoolwork.

Melanie smiled. "She gets her homework done and isn't a behavior problem. At least not at home. Does she pay attention at her piano lessons?"

Louise nodded. "She's one of my better-behaved students. I am pleased with her musical progress too. Just now she played me a piece that we have been working on for the Christmas recital. She has it memorized already."

"I'm glad to hear that. Sometimes I feel stretched so thin that I worry I'm not giving the kids enough attention. Mac's been traveling a lot for work, so it's just me."

"Bree told me that he was gone a lot," Louise said. "Are you sure that you want to take on this food drive? I can head it up, or someone else will volunteer to do so, I am sure."

"I want to help out. The only thing is—" She broke off, shaking her head. "It's not important," she said, gesturing to the sofa. "Shall we discuss the food drive?"

"Certainly," Louise said, sitting. She opened the notebook that she'd brought along, with her ideas. "Now—"

Melanie sat quite close, as though she was ready to get deeply involved in the discussion. Her proximity unnerved Louise for a moment, but she looked back at her notes. "We can collect canned goods at Grace Chapel and other area churches, but what if we solicit Acorn Hill businesses to donate specific food items or sponsor food coupons for redemption? If you like the idea, you and I can ask around town."

Melanie frowned. "I'm sorry, Louise, I didn't quite catch what you said." She scooted a little closer, smiling. "I'm probably distracted. Could you repeat that?"

Louise complied. Melanie looked at her blankly for a moment, then smiled, as though Louise's words were on a ten-second delay. "Oh, I see! That's a great idea, Louise. Pastor Ken said he'd already set up a box for canned-food donations, but I think you're onto something even better. We can probably get a lot of support."

"I was hoping that the stores and eateries, in particular, would be willing to donate specific food items. I made a list of suggestions here. For example, maybe the Good Apple would donate coupons for pies. Or the Coffee Shop might donate coupons for free meals. Maybe Dairyland will donate some beverages..."

"The General Store might donate coupons for produce," Melanie said, caught up in the excitement.

Louise nodded, adding it to the list. "Gierson's grocery store in Potterston might help out as well." She took out another sheet of paper from her notebook. "I also made a list of businesses that we could probably count on to donate money, if we ask."

Melanie looked at the list, and her eyes lit up. "That is wonderful, Louise. I'm so glad you agreed to help me on this."

"I'll be glad to ask the businesses for help," she said. "I know that you're busy with your family and job."

"But you're busy too," Melanie said. "Can I at least share the list with you? I can contact people on my lunch hour and breaks."

"All right," Louise said. "I'll give you the businesses that are closest to your office. People can bring the money to me, since I'm almost always at home at the inn, or they can take it to Pastor Ken at Grace Chapel."

Melanie's expression sobered. "I hope you don't mind dealing directly with Pastor Ken. I volunteered for this because I heard there was a need, but, well, you probably know I haven't been going to church much lately."

Louise tried to keep her voice light, as she did not like to pry. "Is there any special reason?"

Melanie opened her mouth as though she wanted to say something, then she closed it again. "Just...a series of circumstances. I know I'm a bad person for not going, especially with my kids, but—"

"The Bible says that the Lord made the Sabbath for man, not man for the Sabbath," Louise said. "I don't think God considers you a bad person for not coming to church on a regular basis. I do think, however, that there are people there who love you and want to help you in any way that we can. I've always believed that church is not only for worship, but for support and encouragement. That is what the body is for, isn't it? Each part is important. The body suffers if any one part does...if the foot is lame, or the ear can't hear—"

Melanie's eyes teared up, and she stopped Louise by placing a hand over hers. "Thank you," she whispered. "You're very kind. Maybe I will come back soon. Bree has been asking to see the kids there, but I've been putting her off."

Louise smiled. "There's no need to be afraid. I also know that when my father was the pastor at Grace Chapel, he knew that sometimes members who stopped going to church for a while found it difficult to return. They were afraid of being chastised for their absence. No condemnation will await you there, if you choose to come back."

"Thank you," Melanie whispered again, but she didn't say anything more about returning to church.

Chapter Nine

*A*fter lunching in Potterston, Alice, Jane and Sylvia said good-bye to Viola and Nia and drove back to Acorn Hill. Again, Jane and Sylvia sat in the backseat of Alice's Toyota and discussed cheerleading.

Jane broke off the conversation long enough to talk to Alice. "Mrs. Thrush set up a time for Sylvia and me to meet with the Franklin cheerleaders to give them some pointers."

"When will that be?" Alice asked.

"Because of their busy schedule this week, not to mention the Veterans Day holiday, it will have to be next Monday," Jane said.

"Will that give them enough time to learn the cheers you teach them?"

"Mrs. Thrush says this is the most talented group of girls she's had in years, and they should be able to pick up anything we teach them in time for the game on Thanksgiving," Sylvia said.

"Do you really think they can?" Jane asked. "I know how difficult learning new routines used to be for us."

"I'm sure Mrs. Thrush is a good judge of her girls' skills," Alice said cheerfully. "And you ladies will be excellent teachers, anyway."

"Thanks, Alice," Sylvia said. "That's nice of you to say."

She and Jane huddled in conversation again, excluding Alice for the rest of the trip. Weary of the chatter, Alice was glad to drop off Sylvia at her shop in town. To her surprise, Jane got out too.

"I'll walk home when we're finished talking," Jane said. "Thanks for the ride." She slammed the car door shut.

Alice drove home alone. Feeling a bit left out, she parked the car and hurried up the walk to the house. To her surprise, she saw Trisha Delhomme huddling in her coat on the porch swing. She wiped at her eyes.

"Is anything wrong?" Alice asked as she climbed the stairs to the porch.

Trisha shook her head, silent. But her tears betrayed the truth.

Alice sat beside her on the swing. "I'm a good listener if you need someone to talk to," she said softly.

"I should go inside," Trisha said, rubbing her arms against the chill, "but I needed some time to think."

"I'll leave you alone then," Alice said, rising.

Trisha put a hand on her arm. "I'm sorry, Miss Howard. I didn't mean to drive you away. The truth is, I could probably use someone to talk to, after all. That is, if you have the time."

Alice smiled. "Would you like to come inside where it's warmer? I can make some hot cocoa in the kitchen. Jane will be gone for a while, so we should have privacy and quiet."

"That sounds good," Trisha said, relief in her voice.

In the kitchen, Alice put a pan on the stove, poured in milk and stirred in chocolate and sugar. Trisha sat at the table, and neither spoke until Alice had set steaming mugs of cocoa with marshmallows in front of them. "Where's Libby?" Alice asked.

Trisha sipped her cocoa, then sighed appreciatively. She licked marshmallow from her lips, then said, "She's upstairs taking a nap with Nathan."

Alice drew a deep breath. "Trisha, I don't want to pry, and please tell me if I'm overstepping, but does Nathan suffer from any postwar problems?"

Trisha bit her lip as though she didn't want to speak but felt compelled to do so anyway. "Have your nursing duties ever led you to deal with patients' mental problems?"

"Yes, sometimes. I've also worked with a grief-counseling support group."

Trisha glanced at the doorway as though to verify they had privacy. "Miss Howard, please don't think bad of me for talking about my husband. But I love him, and I want to see him happy again. We married about four years ago, and he didn't seem to have any problems. But in the last year, since his grandfather died and we agreed to come to this Veterans Day celebration, he's been unhappy."

"He seems very happy when he's around Libby," Alice said.

Trisha nodded, taking another sip of cocoa. "He loves that little girl. And I know he loves me too. That's what makes things so difficult."

"What things?" Alice asked.

Trisha drew a deep breath, then faced Alice squarely. "The other night Mort mentioned that Nathan was a hero, remember?"

Alice nodded. "Nathan looked uncomfortable about that."

"He is. He and his buddy were shot down over the desert during the Gulf War. Nathan was eventually rescued and decorated."

"And the friend?"

"He didn't make it," Trisha said softly. "Oh, Alice, do you think that's enough to make him so sad? And if so, why just during this last year?"

Alice sat quietly for a moment so that she wouldn't speak too hastily. "Have you ever heard of post-traumatic stress disorder?"

"I think that's when someone suffers something tragic and relives the memory for a long time, right?" Trisha asked.

Alice nodded. "Does Nathan have any problems like flash-backs or panic attacks or nightmares?"

"Sometimes he has nightmares," Trisha said. "And sometimes he doesn't sleep well. At first I thought it was Libby waking him up, but he'll stay awake even after she finally falls asleep."

"I'm not a doctor," Alice said, "so even if he does have this disorder, I'm not qualified to say. But I'm wondering if this particular Veterans Day has caused him to remember certain events that he's managed not to think about all these years. He probably needs to seek professional help."

Trisha covered Alice's hands with her own. "I've suggested that, but he won't listen to me. Oh, Alice, I feel certain that if you said something, he'd listen to you."

"But, I—" Alice began, alarmed at the notion.

"I know he thinks the world of you and your sisters, and he's enjoying his time here so much. At least until the parade is mentioned. I can tell he's bothered about it. If you could just talk to him and reassure him, I think it would help."

"I suppose I could encourage him to see a professional," Alice said skeptically. "I do want to help, Trisha, but I don't want to just walk up to him and say, 'Hey there, I hear you're having problems. What you need is a good psychiatrist.'"

Trisha giggled. "Maybe that's exactly what he needs to hear— at least from someone else. I do think he would listen to you because you are a nurse. I know he sets great store by the medical profession. He talks about how wonderful the doctors and nurses were to him after he was rescued."

Trisha's eyes shone. "Please, Miss Howard. Won't you speak to him?"

Alice hesitated. Trisha gripped her hands, and Alice could see how much the young wife and mother was hurting for her husband. "I suppose I could try," Alice said. "I don't want him to get angry, though. That might set him back even further."

"How could it? He's already miserable. How about if I set aside some time tomorrow so that you two can talk? I'll make sure that the others are busy, and I'll take care of Libby so that he won't feel obligated to help with her. I'll tell him that you need some help with something, and you can lead into the conversation."

"All right," Alice said, somewhat reluctantly.

"Thank you!" Trisha said, breathing a sigh of relief.

That night Alice lay in bed, having trouble sleeping herself. She couldn't stop thinking about Nathan Delhomme. What could be bothering him? And more importantly, would talking to him really help?

Alice rolled onto her back and spoke softly into the darkness. "Lord, I don't know what's troubling this young father and husband. I don't know what to say to him, either. I promised Trisha that I would try to talk to him, though, so please arrange some time for us to speak. Most importantly, please give me insight into what's bothering him and the wisdom to know what to say."

She poured out her heart further, slipping easily into prayer for her family and friends. The more she spoke, the more she relaxed and felt comforted. Prayer reminded her of talking with her father. He would listen to her problems and only offer advice if she asked for it.

She missed her father. Though Jane and Louise never would have moved back home if not for his death, she missed seeing him every day, missed his wise counsel.

But God was, and always had been, her ultimate Counsel, and He would never leave her or forsake her. "Please tell me what to do about Nathan," she whispered again, coming full circle to the beginning of her prayer.

Alice felt herself drifting toward sleep without an answer to her request about Nathan. But she knew that when the time came she would have the right things to say.

⌒

Once again the veterans returned from dinner and started playing cards. It was quite late, but Jane, who was staying up to work on a new recipe, could hear the muffled sounds of their laughter from the parlor. Long after Louise and Alice had retired for the night, Jane popped her head into the doorway.

"Would anyone like a snack?" she asked. "I've got a tray of goodies here."

"Food!" Mort said, laying down a fresh, unlit cigar. "Jane, you're my hero."

"We'll take whatever you've got," Harvey said.

"All right then," Jane said, entering the parlor. She glanced around the table and saw only Mort, Harvey, Lars and Nathan. "Where are the ladies?"

"Bah!" Mort said. "They said they were tired from the Brandywine Valley sightseeing trip, so they turned in early."

"I told Trisha I'd spell her if Libby woke up and couldn't go back to sleep," Nathan said.

"Got a game of poker going there?" she asked, setting the tray of snacks on the table. She eyed the disarray of cards in front of each person.

"Nah," Lars said. "Hearts."

"Do you want to sit in a hand?" Mort asked.

Jane shook her head. "No thanks, fellas. I'm about ready to head for bed myself." She yawned. "It's getting kinda late."

Harvey laughed. "*Late?* We're just getting started." He eyed the tray suspiciously. "Say, uh, I don't mean to be rude, but what is all this?"

"My special homemade cheese ball, some gourmet crackers and a salmon mousse," she said proudly.

"Salmon!" Mort's eyes lit up. "I knew I liked the looks of you. Thanks."

"Yeah, thanks!" the others chimed in, as everyone started to help himself to some of the food.

"Enjoy," Jane said, then yawned again. "There's some plastic wrap on the kitchen table. Would you guys mind putting the left-overs in the refrigerator?"

The four men looked at each other and laughed. "Leftovers?"

Shaking her head, Jane retreated toward her bedroom. She could still hear their laughter as she started up the stairs.

She relayed the story about the veterans to her sisters the next morning while they were eating breakfast in the kitchen. "Then," she said, finishing the tale, "the men and their wives were up at their normal time this morning, asking me to fix a big breakfast."

"So were there any leftovers?" Louise said, sipping from her coffee cup.

Jane shook her head. "Not unless they stashed them in the guest rooms."

"Yoo-hoo!"

Jane smiled, setting plates of omelets in front of her sisters. "I'd know that voice anywhere."

Ethel entered the kitchen, with Vera Humbert in tow. "Good morning, girls. Look who I found outside your inn."

Vera laughed. "Oh, Ethel, you make it sound as though I were lurking."

"Good morning, Ethel. Good morning, Vera," Alice said. "Won't you join us?"

"I've already eaten breakfast, but thank you anyway," Vera said. "I just stopped by to remind your guests that tomorrow they'll be speaking at the school. I hope you girls will attend as well. Ethel, I know you'll be there, because Lloyd will be speaking."

"Have you had many entries to the Veterans Day essay contest?" Alice asked.

Vera shook her head. "Not many at all. We're extending the deadline to five o'clock tomorrow afternoon. That means that those who've agreed to read the essays may be busy because we've promised to announce the winner tomorrow evening."

"If you'd like to speak to the veterans, they're eating breakfast in the dining room," Jane said.

"Oh, that's all right. I don't want to bother them," Vera said. "They're probably still waking up."

Jane laughed. "I'm not certain that they ever went to sleep last night."

"My goodness," Ethel said. "Do you mean that they all have insomnia?"

"No, Auntie, just that they are such live wires," Jane said. "They are the spryest group of elderly men I've ever seen. They stay up late every night playing cards and talking. Then they sightsee or shop with their wives the next day." She shook her head. "I consider myself in good health, but I couldn't keep up with them."

"Well, please, when the time is right, just remind them about their talk tomorrow at school," Vera said.

"We'll make sure they don't forget," Alice said.

Vera suddenly looked worried. "They don't stay up all night drinking, do they?"

"Not at all," Jane said.

"That's a relief." Vera's face relaxed. "Time to get to school. Thanks, girls. Now, don't get up. I can see myself outside. Good-bye!"

"I suppose I'd better leave too," Ethel said unconvincingly.

"What's your hurry?" Jane asked. "I have some eggs already beaten for another omelet. Are you interested?"

Ethel wavered between heading toward the door and seating herself. Louise smiled and patted the chair beside her. "Sit down, Aunt Ethel. If you don't eat that last omelet, Alice and I will be forced to duke it out to see who gets it."

"I certainly don't want that," Ethel said, seating herself primly. She took up a napkin and placed it daintily in her lap. In no time, Jane set an omelet in front of her.

Alice looked at Louise. "'Duke it out?'" she whispered.

Louise shrugged and sipped her coffee.

Jane left to meet with Sylvia over at her shop, and Louise went into the library to work on some piano teachers' guild business. Alice volunteered to clean up the breakfast dishes. Assuming that the guests had left for another shopping excursion, she went to the dining room to clear the table.

To her surprise, Nathan, alone in the room, was already stacking the dishes on a tray. "You don't have to do that," she said, hurrying to take the tray from him.

"I wanted to do something," he said. "I told Trisha and the others that I didn't feel like going to Gettysburg. I've been there a number of times. But the truth is, I don't want to just laze around, either."

"Did Trisha take Libby?" Alice asked.

Nathan nodded, adding another cup to the tray full of dishes. "I thought I'd bus these dirty things. Maybe help clean up the kitchen, if you'll let me."

Alice smiled. "You know, Nathan, it *would* be nice to have some help, if you're certain there's nothing else you want to do."

"Not a thing," he said. "So here, why don't you give that tray back to me?"

"Why, I can...," she began, then realized that sometimes people just need to feel useful. "That would be wonderful," she finished. "Follow me."

She pushed through the swinging door that separated the dining room from the kitchen and gestured for him to set the tray on the counter. Nathan glanced around the room, taking in the warm-red cabinets, maple butcher counters, stainless-steel appliances and black-and-white checkerboard floor tiles. "This is a nice setup you've got here," he said.

"Jane likes her workspace to be efficient *and* cozy." Alice started running water in the sink. "Would you mind handing me those dishes one at a time? I'd like to rinse them before washing."

Nathan obliged by handing her a saucer. "Why not use the dishwasher?"

"We will for most of the things," Alice said, "but this china has been in the family a long time, and we like to hand wash it to prevent damage."

"I'll help," Nathan said, rolling up his sleeves. "I did my share of KP in the army, though I never washed dishes as fine as these."

"How long were you in the army?" Alice asked, trying to keep her voice casual as she rinsed off each dish and carefully set it aside.

"Too many years, I sometimes think," Nathan said.

When she was finished rinsing, Alice flipped the faucet to his side of the soapstone sink and plugged in the stopper. "If you wash, I'll rinse and dry," she said.

"Be glad to," he said, squirting a little dishwashing liquid into the sink. After adjusting the temperature of the water, he took several pieces of china back from Alice to wash. "Are you sure you trust me with your dishes?" he asked. "I'd hate to break them."

Alice smiled. "I trust you. I'm sure any guest who volunteers to wash dishes is going to be very careful. Though to tell the truth, no guest has ever volunteered to do this before."

"Weeeell," Nathan said, "I have to admit that I did it for self-ish reasons."

"To get out of sightseeing?"

Nathan smiled, carefully sudsing a plate, which he handed to Alice to rinse. "No, I promised Trisha that I'd talk to you today. I figured while I was waiting for the right time, I'd help out. Trisha, ah, she told me she talked to you last night."

"What did she say?" Alice asked.

Nathan paused. "That she thought you might help," he said in a soft voice.

Alice drew a deep breath, saying a quick prayer for guidance. *You've established this time, so please give me the right words.* "If Trisha told you that we talked, then she probably mentioned that I suggested you seek professional guidance."

"Yes, and she's suggested that too," he said. "But..." He trailed off, pretending distraction in a speck of food stuck on a fork.

"But..."

"I just wouldn't feel comfortable stuck in some guy's office filled with leather furniture and a mahogany desk," he said.

"What about a group setting?"

"That sounds even worse. I don't want to talk in front of a lot of strangers."

"You're talking to me," she pointed out.

Nathan sighed. "You're different. You're like talking to my mom. Well, I *would* talk to her if she were still alive."

"If you could talk to her, what would you say?" Alice asked.

Nathan was silent.

"What would you say about being called a hero?" she asked softly.

Nathan set the fork he'd scrubbed into the sink and looked her full in the face. "I'm no hero."

"Why did the army call you one?"

"Because I was shot down during Desert Storm, survived and was rescued. And to be honest, Alice, I think that's the only reason

Grandpa's army buddies invited me to take his place this year. They're buying into the idea that just because I survived, I deserve special recognition."

"I'm sure they invited you not only because they recognize that but also because they miss your grandfather," Alice said.

Nathan looked at her, distressed. "I can't take his place. I'm not their age, I don't share their interests. Sure, they're fun, but I'm not part of 'the greatest generation.' I'm not as good as—"

He clammed up and started washing dishes again.

"So you're not as good as they are?" Alice asked.

Nathan nodded.

"Why?"

He looked straight ahead and smiled. "The only reason I volunteered to march in this Veterans Day parade is to honor someone who *was* as good as Mort, Harvey, Lars and Grandpa."

"Who was that, Nathan?" Alice asked.

Nathan sighed, his shoulders sagging. "His name was Gerald Vickers. He was the pilot and I was the copilot on the plane that was shot down. Gerry was my best friend in the world."

"What happened to him?"

Nathan's eyes filled with tears. "He died," he said, then wiped his eyes with the back of his hand. "Most people know that. It's part of the record, part of history. Our names and photos were splashed all over the national news when I was rescued."

"But Gerry was dead by then?"

Nathan nodded. "We survived the crash, and we managed to find cover in an old building. I had a concussion, and my leg was hurt pretty bad. Gerry, he bandaged it with his own shirt and stopped the bleeding. I was in and out of consciousness, but somehow I knew he was keeping watch for both of us. I knew that he would take care of us."

Alice's heart beat quicker. Nathan had been so much younger than he was now. "What happened next?"

"The next thing I knew, our guys were there helping us. They'd tracked us down and gotten to us before the enemy could. Then they gave me something to knock me out completely, because the pain in my leg was really bad by then. When I came to, they'd operated on my leg and managed to save it. Then they told me that Gerry was gone."

Nathan leaned over the dishwater and let a few tears fall. "He had a chest wound. He needed care more than I did. They told me"—he drew a deep breath—"they told me that he was dead when they got to us."

He turned to face Alice. "Now tell me that I'm a hero, Alice. Tell me that Nathan Delhomme deserves to march in that parade on Veterans Day," he said bitterly.

"You do deserve to march in that parade for precisely the reason that you've given," she said. "You need to honor your friend Gerry."

Nathan nodded, setting his jaw.

Alice put a hand on his shoulder. "But you also need to march for yourself as well because you *are* a hero. You didn't know that your friend was wounded. If you had, I have no doubt that you would have done everything possible to help him as well. That's what friends do. And that's what Gerry, who was aware of both medical situations, did."

"He gave his life for me," Nathan said softly.

Alice nodded. "And the Bible says that man has no greater love than to give his life for a friend. Gerry took care of you until the doctors could. Would you squander the second chance at life that he gave you by not getting the help you still need to fully recover?"

"You mean, like a psychiatrist?"

"Perhaps," Alice said. "Maybe just a grief counselor. It seems to me that you haven't fully recovered from your friend's death. That seems like a good place to start."

Nathan was silent for a moment. "Alice, I've never told anyone, other than the military, what I've just told you."

"The more you tell it, the easier it will become," she said. "I've found that to be true with some of my patients."

"Really?" He didn't sound convinced.

"In fact, I think it might not be a bad idea to start with your wife and your grandpa's friends."

"Trisha deserves to know. But how can I tell Harvey and Lars and Mort that I'm not like them?"

"How do you know you're not?" she asked. "Have you ever heard their more detailed war experiences? I know that there are stories veterans tell, and then there are stories that veterans tell. That's why some of the more recently released World War II movies have been so well received. Veterans who actually partici-pated in the war said that the movies showed things they never mentioned once they got back to America's shores. They're grateful for the chance to talk about them."

"I *have* heard Mort and the others talk of some things that their wives probably don't know about. Stuff about battles and other soldiers and stuff," he said.

"Then tell them," Alice urged. "They, of all people, will understand what you've gone through." She paused. "What you're still going through."

Nathan was silent for a long while, then he soaped the last plate and handed it to her. "I think we're finished," he said.

She rinsed it off and set it in the drainer. "I hope I haven't upset you," she said, worried that his silence meant she had crossed the line.

"Not at all, Alice," he said. "You've given me a lot to think about. I do think you're right about my needing to talk to a professional. But first, I also think I'll take your advice and talk to Trisha and then to Mort, Lars and Harvey. The guys may be angry at me, but I feel like I need to confess. If they don't want me in the Veterans Day parade in place of Grandpa, then I won't participate."

Alice touched his arm. She felt as though Nathan had just achieved some sort of breakthrough. "I have a feeling I know what they'll say, but I'm glad you're taking this step."

Chapter Ten

A lice left for work soon after her talk with Nathan, then came home that evening for a quick supper before going to Grace Chapel for her weekly session with the ANGELs. She heard the veterans laughing and talking as usual when she headed upstairs to bed after the meeting. She wondered if Nathan had spoken to Trisha and to them.

The next morning, the sisters got up and ready in record time. All of them had canceled or refused to schedule any activities for the day so that they could attend the veterans' talk at Vera's primary school.

"Mort and the gang said they'd meet us at the school," Jane said after they had all eaten breakfast.

"Lloyd already stopped by to pick up Aunt Ethel," Louise said. "I heard his car pull up."

Alice's stomach felt full of butterflies. "I hope this goes well," she said, "not only for the veterans, but also for the students. I hope they appreciate what our veterans have done for our country."

Outside the school, more cars than usual were parked at the curb and in the visitors' lot. Inside the school, adults lingered in the hallway to the auditorium. Four students stationed at the doors passed out programs.

"It looks like students were allowed to invite their parents," Jane said.

"I see quite a few of my piano students' parents," Louise said.

Alice noticed that the students had been seated at the front of the auditorium, with parents and other visitors toward the rear. As she scanned the crowd, she saw someone waving and gesturing at Louise. "Melanie Brubaker's waving at you," Alice said, nudging her sister.

Louise turned and waved back. "I hope I get a chance to speak with her after the performance. I need to find out how her solicitations for the food drive are going."

"How is your end of things holding up?" Alice asked.

"I've got some generous pledges from various businesses," she said. "Some are in their busy season, gearing up for the holidays, so they're just donating money. But that's fine. Other businesses are donating nonperishable food or coupons redeemable for free food. It's amazing what you can get if you just ask. Even the electronics firm in Potterston made a nice donation, for example. The owner, Mr. Iberon, is a big supporter of the Community Pantry."

"They're about to start," Jane said, breaking into their conversation.

The stage curtain parted, and the house lights dimmed. "Stars and Stripes Forever" played over the public-address system, and everyone applauded when the curtain had fully opened.

A full row of veterans stood at attention on the stage. Mort and his friends were at stage right. Next to them, standing in the order of the wars in which they served, were Lloyd Tynan, Derek Grollier,

Nathan, then several Iraq war veterans. The applause didn't stop until Vera walked on stage in front of the microphone and held up her hands for quiet.

"Would everyone please rise for the posting of the flags? The color guards are from the school's Boy Scout troop. Color guards, please post the colors."

Everyone in the audience stood, and a boy at the head of each of the two auditorium aisles proceeded toward the stage. One scout held the American flag, and the other held the flag of the Commonwealth of Pennsylvania. The veterans on stage saluted, and the people in the audience put their hands over their hearts.

They posted the flags, and Vera said, "Would you please join me in the Pledge of Allegiance?"

Everyone repeated the words.

"Thank you," Vera said when they finished. "And now, Mrs. Wilma Hutch, our music teacher, will sing our national anthem."

A middle-aged woman with short blond hair took Vera's place at the mike. Without accompaniment, she sang, "O say can you see..."

As Wilma sang "The Star-Spangled Banner," Alice felt chills run down her spine. Seeing the flag and the men and women onstage who had risked their lives to protect it made her feel happy and proud.

When Wilma finished singing, the audience applauded and took their seats, as did the veterans. Vera stepped back to the microphone, beaming. "That was beautiful, Wilma, thank you.

And thank you all for coming today. We're looking forward to hearing from our veterans. We invited you parents and community members because we all want to honor these men and women who have so nobly sacrificed for our country. We're honored to have veterans from several different wars with us today, and each one has a story. It's our wish as a school to honor them, to learn from them and to thank them for their service."

Everyone applauded. Vera smiled. "Our first group comprises veterans from World War II. I understand that they all served together in Europe and have remained friends ever since. We'll start with Mr. Mortimer Fineman, who will tell you more. Mr. Fineman?"

Amid the sound of applause, Mort stepped in front of the microphone and tapped it gently. "Just making sure," he said, smiling. "I could have used one of these during the war. It would have saved a lot of wear and tear on my voice."

The audience laughed. "As Mrs. Humbert said, I'm Mortimer Fineman, and I'm here with two of my best friends in the world. I'll let them tell you more about themselves, but let me just say that when I joined the army, I had no idea that I was going to make such strong friendships. These two guys came from different parts of the country and were nothing like me. I was their sergeant, so I frequently told them what to do. And believe me, they didn't always like it."

Everyone laughed.

Mort smiled. "I'm sure you've all heard about D-Day and the invasion of the beaches of Normandy. We were part of that, though in a smaller way than what you may have heard, or seen in some of the recent films. We were one of the last waves of soldiers to hit the beach, and by the time we got there, the fighting was pretty much over." He paused. "We were a bunch of green kids, but we worked together. Though we weren't with those courageous boys who landed first, we had a job to do after their task was over, and we did it."

He paused again as if organizing his thoughts.

"You know," he continued, "in war movies, you mostly see scenes of fighting and killing, and of course, there was a lot of that. As the Civil War general William Tecumseh Sherman said, 'War is hell.' Even if you're not fighting, you're often cold or boiling hot, hungry and hurting. Yet those awful conditions bring out the best in some men—their bravery, their love of country, their faithfulness to their comrades."

Alice noticed several children whose mouths were hanging open with admiration. Mort evidently noticed, too, for he waved at a few students, barely breaking the pace of his speech.

"My good pals, my faithful comrades, Harvey and Lars will speak next, but before I turn the mike over to them, I want to add that we lost a good friend this past year, one who used to be part of our group."

Harvey and Lars nodded, lowering their heads for a moment.

Mort continued. "His name was Jackson Delhomme, and he is greatly missed. You'll hear from his grandson later." Mort pointed to Nathan and smiled. "That's Nathan Delhomme over here, and like us old guys and all of us here on stage, he did what all us veterans have done—answered the call of our country. Thank you."

The audience applauded wildly, then applauded even more after Harvey and Lars spoke. They, too, spoke of the friendships forged during the war and how it was a good thing to come out of a bad situation. Lars looked directly at the students and told them that no one wanted war, but that sometimes it was necessary to keep peace. He tried to explain it on a level that they could understand. Alice appreciated his efforts, because it was a difficult subject for even adults to comprehend.

Lloyd spoke about his time in Korea and how North Korea was still a politically unstable area. "But like Mr. Fineman said, American veterans and soldiers all have answered our country's call to protect and defend. Theodore Roosevelt said that 'the things that will destroy America are prosperity-at-any-price, peace-at-any-price, safety-first instead of duty-first, the love of soft living, and the get-rich-quick theory of life.' We must always be ready to take action when action is needed and be prepared for sacrifice."

Everyone clapped. "Go, Mayor Tynan!" someone yelled.

Lloyd waved his hand in a dismissive gesture, and the audience laughed.

"Thank you, Mayor," Vera said. "Students, one thing I want you all to keep in mind while you listen to our speakers is what these fine men and women have done after they served in the military. Mayor Tynan is an example, and the next person we'll hear from is another important figure in our town. A veteran of the Vietnam War, our next speaker is also one of Acorn Hill's longest active firefighters. Please welcome Derek Grollier."

Amid the applause, Derek walked to the podium. A sixty-ish man with a full head of thick gray hair and a mustache to match, he smiled warmly at the audience. "Thank you for having me here today," he said. "I didn't fight in a popular war, but I didn't know that until I came back to the States. I was greeted at the airport in California by protesters who said some horrible things. I never understood how they could react that way when I was only doing what my country asked. I was pretty low when I took the flight from California to Philadelphia, then the bus from Philadelphia to Potterston. But when I got to Potterston, I saw a whole flock of folks from Acorn Hill, hometown people, who'd turned out to cheer my return. I made up my mind then that I would always live here and protect everybody by becoming a firefighter. Thank you."

Applause rang out. Vera stepped to the microphone. "I understand, Derek, that you've served thirty years and are about to retire, is that correct?"

He nodded.

"Acorn Hill thanks you for your service both in the military and in the fire department, don't we students and parents?" she asked.

Everyone clapped, and Derek nodded in acknowledgment.

Vera turned back to the microphone. "And now we'll hear from a veteran of the Gulf War, Nathan Delhomme."

Alice applauded along with the others, her stomach fluttering with nervousness for Nathan. She saw Trisha and Libby down front. Trisha was all smiles, and she held up Libby so that Nathan could see.

Nathan smiled at his daughter and wife, sending them a little wave before he spoke. "Thank you all. I'm honored to be here. And Mort, Harvey, Lars...Grandpa Delhomme was honored to serve alongside such fine men. You truly are part of the greatest generation."

Everyone applauded. Mort, Lars and Harvey looked bashful but nodded in acknowledgment of the tribute.

Nathan continued speaking to the audience. "Mayor Tynan spoke about sacrifice. Serving your country does mean a sacrifice for everyone, not only the soldiers who leave their homes but those who are left behind."

He shifted his weight. "But really great sacrifice is sometimes made by one soldier for another on the battlefield. I am a living testimony to that."

His gaze focused on Trisha and Libby, and he smiled. "I owe my life to a dear friend and combat buddy who gave his life to save mine."

Nathan's voice cracked slightly, and he coughed to cover his emotion, then he continued. "Our plane was shot down and we were both injured. After we crawled to shelter to wait for rescue, I blacked out from a concussion. Gerry, who I later learned had a mortal chest wound, tended my injuries and made sure that I'd make it even though he didn't."

Nathan paused and scanned the audience. "It's for him that I'm marching in the Veterans Day parade tomorrow, and I hope that you'll remember a brave soldier, Gerry Vickers, when you wave your flags and applaud those of us who are blessed to be here marching. Thank you."

As Nathan took his seat, he was met with thunderous applause. Mort, Harvey and Lars stood, applauding in Nathan's direction. Everyone in the audience rose as well. Alice wiped tears from her eyes. Louise and Jane applauded enthusiastically.

Seated again, Nathan searched for Alice in the audience. When he caught her gaze, he smiled, then gave her a small salute. She saluted him back and knew then that he would seek the help he needed.

Several more veterans spoke, including a young woman who had served a tour of duty in Iraq and another woman who had just joined the military. "I look forward to one day being a veteran myself," she said to a wave of applause.

Vera took the microphone one last time. "Don't forget, students, that we've extended the Veterans Day essay deadline until five o'clock this evening. We hope we'll receive some more entries by then. In the meantime, thank you, soldiers, for taking the time to speak with us today. And thank you, parents and members of our community, for your attendance. If you'll make your way to the cafeteria, we have some refreshments."

Vera joined the sisters, who reassured her that she had done a wonderful job of emceeing the event. They all watched as the soldiers left the stage and were soon surrounded by several students who wanted to ask questions. Mort Fineman seemed particularly touched by one youngster who asked for his autograph.

"That's Michael Wister," Vera said to Alice as they walked to the cafeteria. "He's one of the shyest kids in my class, but look at the light in his eyes. He's hanging on Mortimer Fineman's every word."

Alice and Vera walked into the cafeteria with Jane and Louise trailing close behind. Alice saw that Michael Wister now had the attention of Mort, Harvey and Lars, asking them questions and listening attentively to their answers.

Nathan Delhomme, she noticed, was sequestered in a corner with Trisha, and both of them were smiling. Nathan lifted Libby from Trisha's lap and held the baby high in the air. When he laughed out loud, Alice smiled.

"There you are," Melanie said, rushing to catch up with Louise in the cafeteria. "I was hoping to get a chance to speak with you."

"Hello, Melanie. I was hoping to speak with you too."

"I'll leave you two to chat about the food drive," Jane said. "I'm going to go congratulate Lloyd on his speech."

Left alone, Melanie and Louise drifted to the quiet end of a long cafeteria table. "The speeches were wonderful, didn't you think?" Louise asked.

"The what?" Melanie looked at her for a moment, as if processing what she'd said, then nodded. "Yes! The speeches. I thought they were great."

"How are your solicitations for the food drive going?" Louise asked.

"The food drive? Yes, the food drive. Wonderful, Louise. I was at Grace Chapel today, and there were a lot of donated canned goods already there. I also set up bins in the General Store and in the Potterston grocery store. It's easy to buy an extra can or two and drop it in the bin on the way out, don't you think?"

"That was a good idea," Louise said.

Melanie leaned forward as though hanging on every word. Suddenly it dawned on Louise what the young woman's problem might be.

"Melanie," Louise said, "do you have a hearing problem? I notice you sometimes have difficulty understanding other people when they speak."

"A what? A hearing problem?" Melanie laughed. "Why would you say that?"

"Because you sometimes misunderstand what people say. And because you sit so close whenever we talk. I don't mean to offend you. I just wondered if hearing had become difficult for you."

"Of course not." Melanie's face flushed. "I'm not that old, Louise Smith."

"I know that, dear. But I know from working with musicians all my life that sometimes people have hearing loss earlier in life than is normal. For instance, if they've worked around loud equipment or frequently worn headphones to listen to music, it might cause their hearing to diminish."

Melanie laughed. "If that's the case, then everyone in my generation will be in hearing aids before long. We *all* listened to rock and roll at earsplitting decibels."

"That may be," Louise said, "but whatever the cause, I'm wondering if you have a problem with your hearing. Have you thought about having it checked?"

Melanie folded her arms across her chest. "I'll admit that I don't hear things as well as I used to, but I don't have time to get my hearing checked."

"Hi, girls. I'm back." Jane put her hand on Louise's back, ending the conversation.

Melanie looked relieved as she turned to Jane. "How are the plans for the Thanksgiving Day feast going?"

Louise's heart sank. Apparently Melanie was going to fall further into denial.

"You know, I haven't spent much time planning the feast," Jane said, frowning. "I really need to get with Craig Tracy about that. Seems like all I've done lately is work with Sylvia on our cheers."

"Your *fears*?" Melanie asked, surprised.

"No, our *cheers*," Jane said, raising her voice a little. "Sylvia and I are going to help the Franklin High cheerleaders come up with a new routine for the play-off game with Billings High."

Melanie smiled but didn't say anything. She nodded as though in agreement with something.

Jane frowned, confused by Melanie's response.

To cover the awkward moment until she could explain the situation to her sister, Louise said, "I'm sure you and Craig will work things out splendidly, Jane. Since the feast has become an annual event, everyone knows what jobs have to be done and are volunteering to do them. And you know that you can count on my or Melanie's help with any Thanksgiving Day needs."

"I certainly don't want to dip into your food drive," Jane said.

"Of course not," Melanie said. "Louise and I wouldn't mind driving anything on Thanksgiving Day."

Jane looked even more puzzled. "No, I said I don't want to interfere with your food drive. I don't want to take any of your canned goods for the feast."

"Oh." Melanie looked hurt, as though she'd been scolded. "I'm sorry. I thought you said that you didn't want to ask Louise or me to drive anything for you. My mistake."

"That's all right." Jane glanced sideways at Louise, who shook her head slightly. "Well, listen, I see Craig Tracy over there, so I'll go have a word with him about that feast. Good luck with your plans, you two."

"Thanks, Jane. See you later," Melanie said brightly.

After Jane left, Louise said quietly, "You didn't hear her very well, did you?"

"Of course I did," Melanie said. "She was only right across the table from me. How could I not hear her?"

"There's no shame in having hearing difficulties," Louise said. "It's not a problem just for old people, and even if it were, that doesn't mean ignoring it is going to make things better for you."

"I just need to pay better attention," Melanie said. "That must be the problem. I need to concentrate more."

"Melanie," Louise said, covering the young woman's hand, "please see a doctor. At least get a hearing test. I understand they don't take long, and I don't even believe there is a sizable cost involved. At least you'll know what you're dealing with."

Tears filled Melanie's eyes. "I know what I'm dealing with," she said softly. "Do you want to know why I haven't been to church lately?"

Louise patted her hand. "If you wish to tell me."

Melanie wiped her eyes. "It's because I can't hear Pastor Ken well enough to know what's going on. Do you know how embarrassing it is not to be able to hear prayers? Not to know when the amen has sounded?"

"Melanie, I am so sorry," Louise said. "It must be awful."

"And I know my singing during hymn time has gotten bad, because I never seem to hear the right pitches anymore. I'm afraid to sing loud enough to be heard. I don't want people turning around and looking at me."

Louise squeezed her hand. "Please go get your hearing checked. At least then you will know."

Melanie shook her head vehemently. "I can't, Louise. I appreciate your concern, but I'm just too young for hearing aids. I'll just have to try harder at listening."

"Hey, there's Louise!" Mort said, approaching the table.

Lars and Zoë followed close behind. "Hello, Louise," Zoë said. "Weren't the boys wonderful?"

Louise smiled at Zoë's referral to the eighty-plus-year-old men as boys. "They were wonderful indeed. Let me introduce you to my friend Melanie Brubaker. Melanie has two children in this school. Melanie, this is Zoë and Lars Olsdotter, and their friend is Mort Fineman."

"It's a pleasure to meet you," Melanie said, shaking hands with Mort. "Thank you for speaking today. The students learned a lot, I'm certain. I know I did."

"The pleasure is all ours," Mort said, bowing.

Lars nodded. "We're always happy to pass the torch, so to speak."

"Hey, guys," Nathan said, joining them beside Louise and Melanie. He held Libby in his arms, and she was looking around with interest. Trisha stood close at hand, smiling, her hand on Nathan's arm.

"Nathan!" Mort said, clapping him on the back. "I'm proud of you, boy, mighty proud."

"Thanks, Mort."

Melanie smiled at Nathan. "Is that your daughter, Mr. Oldham?"

"Delhomme, ma'am. No offense to the school, but you know how microphones can be. It got slurred in the introduction, I'm sure."

"That must be it," Melanie said, laughing nervously.

"But yes, she is my daughter," Nathan said. "And this is my wife, Trisha. And you are...?"

"I'm sorry," Louise said. "Nathan and Trisha, this is my friend Melanie Brubaker. I was just telling the others here that she has two children at the school."

"Nice to meet you," Nathan said, trying to extend a hand to shake, but unable to do so because of Libby in his arms. He laughed and handed the baby off to Trisha, then shook Melanie's hand.

"I'm sure my kids won't forget this day," Melanie said. "We try to teach them about Veterans Day, but it means so much more when they have personal stories to put with the holiday. It's important."

"Are you coming to the parade tomorrow?" Mort asked.

"The parade?" Melanie asked, and Louise knew she was verifying that she had heard correctly. She nodded her head vigorously to compensate. "Of course we'll be there. We wouldn't miss it."

Mort pulled a cigar stub from his pocket and set it between his teeth. "As the senior veterans in attendance, we old guys get to ride in an automobile."

Lars leaned forward. "A *convertible*," he said, as though divulging a confidence.

"Oh dear," Zoë said, gasping.

"What's the matter?" Louise asked, taking her hand. The elderly woman seemed agitated.

Zoë smiled. "I'm going to need a scarf for my hair if we're riding with the top down."

Everyone laughed. Louise breathed a silent sigh of relief.

"She's such a kidder," Mort said to Melanie.

"Oh, really, Mort!" Zoë said, giving him a dismissive wave. "It's not the kind of thing that you and Lars and Harvey would notice, because you hardly have any hair left. But we women, well, that's a different story. Isn't it, honey?" Zoë said, looking straight at Melanie.

"Well..." Melanie looked like she had lost track of the conversation.

Louise leaned in to help. "She said—"

"Nathan, does Libby feel warm to you?" Trisha asked suddenly.

"I didn't notice." He touched the baby's forehead. "Now that you mention it, she does seem a bit warm."

Trisha frowned. "Maybe we'd better get her to a doctor."

"There's Alice," Louise said, spying her sister a few tables over. "Alice!" she called. Normally, she would not resort to raising her voice in a public place, but she was hemmed in by the veterans, and expediency seemed to be the order of the moment.

Alice glanced up from her conversation. Louise gestured for her to join them, and when she arrived at the table, she bypassed all formality. "Feel Libby's forehead. She feels a bit warm to Trisha and Nathan."

"She does feel as if she might have a temperature," Alice said to Trisha. "How long has she been like this?"

"Not long," Trisha said, her lip quivering. "She's never been sick before."

"I think she's fine," Alice said, smiling her reassurance. "But if you want to be on the safe side, I'd be glad to drive you to see Dr. Bentley here in Acorn Hill."

Trisha looked at Nathan. "What do you think?"

Nathan ran a hand through his hair. "Gosh, I've never been a dad before, but it seems to me like we should have this checked out."

Trisha looked relieved. "I think so too. Oh, Alice, I hope you don't think we're a couple of overreacting new parents. Of course we are, but I can't help it." She looked like she was ready to burst into tears.

"There's nothing wrong with erring on the side of caution," Alice said. "Do you have a car seat for Libby?"

Nathan held up a carrier. "Right here."

"I hope the kid's okay," Mort said, his expression concerned.

"The poor dear," Zoë said, then put an arm around Trisha's shoulder. "If there's anything we can do, sweetie, you let us know, all right? We'll be at the inn."

"Thank you," Trisha said, returning Zoë's hug. "Everyone's been so friendly and loving. You feel like family."

"We *are* family," Lars said quietly.

Chapter Eleven

Alice drove Nathan, Trisha and Libby to Dr. Bentley's office. He was in for patient hours and Alice felt certain that the doctor would be able to make time to see the little girl.

"Howdy, Alice," Dr. Bentley's receptionist, Kris Ferrell, greeted them with the drawl that betrayed her Southern upbringing. A petite brunette, she had only been out of high school two years. After graduation, she'd decided to work for Dr. Bentley full-time rather than attend college. While Alice would have liked to see the girl pursue a higher education, Kris was extremely proficient at single-handedly running the doctor's office.

"Kris, these are guests at the inn, Nathan and Trisha Delhomme. Their two-month-old daughter feels warm to the touch, and we'd like Dr. Bentley to check her out."

"Y'all are in luck," she said. "He just finished up with a patient and doesn't have another for thirty minutes. I'll tell him you're here. Have a seat."

She headed through a door to the back of the office where the exam rooms were located. Alice knew that Nathan and Trisha probably didn't feel like sitting, but she gestured at the leatherette sofas. "I'm sure it won't take long."

Holding Libby, Trisha perched on the edge of the sofa and felt the little girl's forehead. "She still feels warm," she said.

"The doctor will take good care of her," Nathan said. "I'm sure he'll give her some medicine, and we'll see that she gets lots of rest. I certainly don't have to march in the parade tomorrow."

"Yes, you do," Trisha said. "We came all this way for you to do just that."

Kris entered the waiting room. "Unfortunately, I've got some forms for y'all to fill out while I get the exam room ready."

"I'll take them," Nathan said, glancing at Trisha, who still had her hands full with Libby. "Don't worry. We have insurance."

"That's fine," Kris said. "If you have your card, I'll take that for a photocopy. I'm sure we'll get an approval, even though you're from out of town, but I've found that it's always best to talk to the insurance company before treatment so that there's no problem later."

Libby started to cry, and Trisha rooted around in her diaper bag. "I'll see if I can find a pacifier for her. It isn't time for her to eat yet."

Kris looked at Libby and must have read the frustration on Trisha's face. "Come on back, Mr. and Mrs. Delhomme. Y'all can fill out those forms later. If you'll give me your insurance card, I'll go ahead and call while the doctor is seeing you. We can always fudge the time of the visit."

"Thank you," Trisha said, sounding relieved.

"I'll wait right here," Alice said.

"Actually, you can come on back too, Alice," Kris said. "Dr. Bentley knows you're here and suggested you do so. His nurse had to step out for a minute, and he said that he could probably use your help. If you don't mind, that is."

"Not at all," Alice said.

They went back to one of Dr. Bentley's exam rooms, which was decorated with soothing prints of Victorian women at the beach and in gardens. Trisha had just laid Libby on the exam table, when the doctor entered.

"Mr. and Mrs. Delhomme, I'm Dr. Hart Bentley. I understand you're staying at Grace Chapel Inn."

"Hello, Doctor," Nathan said, shaking his hand. "Yes, we are. We were at the primary school for a Veterans Day program when we noticed that Libby here felt warm to the touch."

"Alice, do you mind helping me?" Dr. Bentley asked.

"Not at all."

"Would you please take Libby's temperature?"

Alice proceeded to do so while Dr. Bentley asked about Libby's medical history. "And she's never had any trouble or been sick before," Trisha finished.

"Her temperature's 99.8 degrees," Alice said.

"Has she been coughing or seemed congested?" Dr. Bentley asked.

Trisha shook her head.

"Let's have a look-see." Dr. Bentley listened to her heart with his stethoscope, then checked her throat and ears. "*Hmm*."

"What is it?" Alice asked.

"It looks like she might be starting an ear infection," Dr. Bentley said. "It looks a little bit pink around her left eardrum, and there's a little bit of fluid. Most likely you would have noticed tonight because she probably wouldn't sleep too well. But I think we caught it early enough. We'll start her on antibiotics, and if we're lucky, she won't lose any sleep tonight. And neither will you," he said, winking.

"So it's not serious?" Nathan asked.

"I don't think so. I think a course of antibiotics will clear things right up. Are you staying at the inn much longer?"

Nathan shook his head. "We're leaving in two days, on Saturday."

"So you'll be home by Monday? Let's start her on the antibiotics. Meanwhile, call your pediatrician back home and set up an appointment for Monday or Tuesday so that you can take her in for a recheck. I'll make a copy of today's paperwork so that your doctor can see it and keep it in her chart."

He reached into his drawer and pulled out a prescription pad. "She's not allergic to any medicines that you know of?"

"No," Trisha said.

Dr. Bentley scribbled for a moment. "This is for amoxicillin. You'll probably become familiar with it. My young parents call it 'the pink stuff.' It smells a bit like bubble gum."

"How are we supposed to give it to her?" Nathan asked. "She can't eat from a spoon."

"The pharmacist will give you a special syringe you can use to squirt the medicine in her mouth a little at a time," Alice said.

Dr. Bentley handed them a bottle. "These ear drops should help ease the pain, especially if she's fussy at night. Ear infections often hurt more at night when children are lying down. You're in luck that the pharmaceutical rep stopped by recently, so I've got all these new samples."

"Thanks, Doctor," Nathan said, taking the bottle.

"You've got a cutie here," Dr. Bentley said, patting the little girl's tummy. "I know the first illness is scary, especially when you're away from home, but you're in good hands with Alice around to help."

"We know, and we're grateful for all that she's already done," Trisha murmured.

"Call me if you need anything, day or night," Dr. Bentley said.

"I'm supposed to march in the parade tomorrow, Doctor, but with Libby being sick, maybe we should all stay back at the inn," Nathan said.

"It'd be a shame for you to come all this way and not march with the others," Dr. Bentley said. "As for Libby, if she's not any worse tomorrow, cover her ears and dress her warmly. She should be fine," Dr. Bentley said.

"Chances are that Trisha and Libby can find a spot along the parade route where there's a heated building they can duck into so that they're not standing out in the cold the entire time too," Alice said.

Dr. Bentley smiled. "Capital idea."

"Thanks again for seeing us, Doctor," Trisha said. "Especially on such short notice."

"Any time."

On the way out, they stopped by Kris's desk. She had contacted the insurance company, which had authorized payment for the visit. Nathan filled out the necessary paperwork, made the copayment, then accepted the receipt.

"Don't hesitate to call Dr. Bentley if y'all need anything," Kris said. "In a small town like Acorn Hill, he's pretty much on call all day, every day."

"What do you do when he's on vacation or out of town?" Nathan asked.

"Nobody's allowed to get sick," Alice said, smiling.

"That's right," Kris said, giving them a wink.

"Miss, ah..." Trisha said.

"It's Kris. Kris Ferrell," she said.

"If you don't mind my asking," Trisha said, "I noticed your accent. Where are you from?"

"Jackson, Mississippi," Kris said proudly. "I moved up here two years ago with my mama and haven't been back since. Acorn Hill is home now, but I can't seem to get rid of this accent," she added, laughing.

"It's a fine accent," Trisha said. "It sounds a bit like home. Nathan and I are from Louisiana."

"Well, listen, y'all take care during the rest of your trip, okay?" Kris said. "You got a cute little girl there, and that medicine should fix her right up."

Back in the car, Trisha sighed with relief as she buckled Libby into her car seat. "I'm so glad Dr. Bentley doesn't think it's serious."

"Me too," Nathan said, rubbing his hand against his face.

Alice smiled. "As Dr. Bentley said, it's always frightening when it's your child's first illness."

"How are we going to make it through eighteen more years?" Trisha asked, laughing.

They stopped by the pharmacy, where Chuck Parker filled the prescription. Back at the inn, they found that the others hadn't returned from the school yet. Or perhaps they were off on another quick sightseeing trip. Alice invited Nathan and Trisha into the kitchen for something warm to drink, and they readily accepted.

While she brewed tea, the Delhommes sat at the table. Nathan balanced Libby on his lap while he gave her the medicine. She took it without a fuss, then promptly fell asleep.

"I think she'll be just fine," Alice said, setting a cup of tea in front of each guest.

"I still don't think I'll march tomorrow," Nathan said. "It wouldn't be fair to leave Trisha and Libby here."

"But the doctor said we could go," Trisha said. "You heard him."

Nathan sighed, splashing tea into the saucer as he set the cup down. "It just doesn't seem important anymore, Trisha. I know I have to work through some issues, but I've been thinking about it, and I've lost sight of the whole reason we came here."

"But...!" Trisha started to protest, then turned her head away as though she was about to cry.

Alice felt it was time to step in. "If you don't mind my interrupting, I think it's important for you to march, Nathan," she said.

"I appreciate all you've done for me, Alice," he said, "but Gerry won't even know that I'm marching for him," he said.

Alice put a hand on his shoulder. "There's a bigger reason for your coming to town. You need to march for yourself."

Nathan blinked. "I don't understand."

Trisha turned back around and nodded. "Tell him," she said softly.

Alice looked at the young man who still had so many good years ahead, with a wife, daughter and who knew how many more children to love and raise. "You need to march for yourself as much as for your friend," she said. "Yes, you can honor him, but you need to march to let people honor you. You *are* a veteran. You *were* injured while serving your country. It seems to me that Memorial Day is to honor the dead, but Veterans Day is to honor the living."

"She's right," Trisha said, her eyes shining. "I know you don't like the term *hero*, but from what you've told me, you are one. All the years we've been married, you never talked about what happened to you. I'm glad you've opened up to me about it now, and I'm eager to hear more when you're willing to talk about it."

She drew a deep breath. "You also need to march for me and our daughter. I'm proud of you, and even if she can't say so yet, Libby is too. Remember why we named her what we did?"

Nathan nodded, reaching out for his wife's hand. "Liberty," he said softly.

"If you fought for it, shouldn't you now march for it, as well?" she asked.

Nathan's jaw tightened for a moment, then he nodded.

Alice gently cleared her throat. "Would you like me to take the baby so that you two can enjoy your tea?"

"Sure," Nathan said, handing her over. He smiled at his daughter, sleeping peacefully in Alice's arms, then he smiled at his wife. He took her hand. "If it means that much to you, I'll march tomorrow."

Trisha smiled and nodded.

Libby continued to do well the rest of the day. By dinnertime she seemed comfortable, and her temperature was normal when Alice checked. After they returned from dinner, the veterans had hunkered down for a night of charades. The sisters had settled in the library for needlework when they heard the doorbell.

Jane answered the door to find Vera Humbert and a young boy standing on the porch. "I'm sorry to bother you when you're relaxing," Vera said, "but we have something to tell you."

Alice and Louise joined Jane at the doorway. "Come in," Alice said.

Vera moved the young boy in front of her. He seemed bashful, but she was all smiles. "This is the winner of our Veterans Day essay contest, Michael Wister. He was so excited when I told him that he had won that he wanted to come right over and tell the veterans himself."

Jane smiled at Michael. "Congratulations! You met them this morning, didn't you? I saw you talking to them."

Michael nodded. "They were really nice. I had written an essay before listening to their talks, but I wasn't going to hand it in because it just didn't seem right. Then I listened to the veterans about how they cared for each other and were brave and how they still cared for each other. That's what I added to my essay to make it have real meaning."

"Would it be all right if we spoke with them?" Vera asked. "We won't bother them for long."

"They're in the parlor," Louise said, "and I'm sure they'd be delighted to see you, Michael. Come right this way."

Alice and Jane took up the rear of the group, and they could all hear the shouting through the doorway.

"Beach!"

"No, shore...shoreline! Is it shoreline?"

Vera looked confused.

"Charades," Louise said. She knocked on the door.

Lars let them in, his face red with the exertion of trying to act out whatever book or film he'd been charged with miming to his team. "You have good timing," he said, panting slightly. "I've been doing my level best, but I don't think they're going to get it."

"*Sands of Iwo Jima!*" Penelope cried, leaping to her feet.

"Thank goodness," Lars mumbled, sinking into a nearby chair.

Mort walked to the door. "Come on in, Louise," he said. "Hey, it's Mrs. Humbert the teacher and our favorite pupil, Michael Wister."

Michael's face lit up. "You remember me?"

"Of course we do, kid," Mort said. "What? You think we're so old that we can't remember you more than a few hours?"

Michael looked panic-stricken. "Gosh, I didn't mean that."

Mort laughed. "Of course you didn't. I was just joshin' with you."

"We came to share the good news. Michael won the essay contest," Vera said proudly, putting a hand on the boy's shoulder.

"Hey!" Mort said, "That's great!"

"Yes, congratulations, Michael," Harvey said, patting the boy on the back.

The others clustered around, offering congratulations. His smile stretched from one side of his face to the other.

"Do you have this masterpiece with you?" Mort asked. "I'd like to read it."

Vera held up a piece of paper. "I have it here, but it's up to Michael. Do you mind if they read it?"

"No," Michael said, but he ducked his head, embarrassed.

"Don't worry, kid. We won't read it out loud, if that makes you feel better," Mort said.

Michael nodded, then let out a little sigh of relief.

Mort took the paper from Vera. Harvey and Lars looked over his shoulder, each removing a pair of reading glasses from a shirt pocket. Mort laughed at them. "Old timers," he said, then held the paper out at arm's length.

They read silently and at last Mort lowered the paper. He looked like he was about to cry. "That was a winning essay all right," he said in a quiet voice.

"You captured perfectly how we feel about being veterans," Lars said.

Harvey tried to speak but cleared his throat.

"Hey," Mort said, shaking himself. "What are we getting so maudlin about? The kid did a good job, but let's not get all *far-klempt*. Say, Michael, have you ever ridden in a convertible?"

Michael shook his head. "No, sir."

"Why don't you ride with us tomorrow?" He held his hands out wide. "Whaddya say?"

"He's getting an award, right?" Zoë asked. "If he rides in the convertible, it won't interfere, will it?"

"He just has to be at the stage by noon," Vera said. "I think it would be wonderful if he rode with you...that is, if you want to, Michael, and if your parents say it's okay."

"Of course I do, and they've gotta say it's okay. Oh boy! Thanks!" The young boy's eyes shone.

Mort put his hand on Michael's shoulder. "You did a good job. Your teacher is proud of you, the judges are proud of you, and we're proud of you. You've captured what this day means to us. We'll be honored to have you with us."

Michael was speechless.

"I'd better get you home, Michael," Vera said. "It's been an exciting day for all of us."

"We'll see you out," Jane said, ushering Vera and Michael toward the hall with Louise and Alice following.

"See you tomorrow, kid," Mort yelled after them.

After Jane had given Michael some celebratory cookies in the kitchen, and the sisters had seen him and Vera out the kitchen door, Alice went down the hall and peeked into the parlor but didn't see Nathan, Trisha or the baby. "Did the Delhommes go to bed?" she asked.

"Little Libby sacked right out," Penelope said, "and poor Trisha and Nathan didn't look like they were going to be able to stay awake much longer either."

"They've had a hard day," Alice agreed. "I was hoping to get a chance to check on Libby before bedtime."

"She was cool as a cucumber," Zoë said. "I told Trisha to wake me up if Libby got fussy. I may be an old lady, but I've walked my share of babies late at night."

"I told her I could help take care of Libby too," Penelope said, sounding slightly miffed.

Alice tried to keep a straight face. "I'm sure Trisha would be glad for help from both of you, if she needs it. Maybe Libby will sleep well tonight. In the meantime, if either of you ladies *do* see Trisha tonight, let her know that I'm available as well."

"Hey, Alice," Mort said, "how about joining us for another round of charades?"

The others groaned. "I don't think I can handle another one," Lars said.

"Me either," Zoë said.

"How about some cards?" Harvey said. "Or some dominoes? We haven't played any Chicken Foot yet, and our trip is almost up."

Revived, the others cheered.

"Good idea," Lars said, clapping his friend on the back. "I'll get the dominoes from upstairs."

"I'll leave you to your game," Alice said. "Good night then."

A chorus of voices said, "Good night!"

She suppressed a smile as she left the parlor and headed back for the library, where Louise and Jane had once again taken up their needlework.

"Are all the veterans heading for bed soon?" Louise asked.

Alice sank into a leather chair, studied her needlework, then rose again. "No, but I am. I'm too tired to cross another stitch. It's been a long day and tomorrow is *the* day."

Jane yawned. "I know what you mean."

Louise yawned. "Now you're making *me* tired," she said, laying aside her needlework. "I think I'll go to bed."

"Yes," Alice said. "Let's leave all the fun and games to the old live wires. We young fogies need our rest."

Chapter Twelve

*V*eterans Day dawned clear, bright and chilly. "I am always grateful on a morning like this that we do not have a dog that must be walked," Louise said, sipping her breakfast coffee in the kitchen with Jane and Alice.

"I've already been off for a jog myself," Jane said cheerfully.

"I'm proud of you for getting some exercise," Alice said. "Vera and I have been lax about walking together lately. It's so much easier to do when the weather is warmer. But like Louise, I'm afraid cold mornings don't do much for me."

"It's bound to warm up as the sun gets higher in the sky," Jane said.

"I hope so," Alice said. "Even though all the schools and most businesses are closed, people may just stay home if they think they will get cold standing along the street."

"Thank goodness it's not raining," Louise said. She sipped coffee from her cup, then set it down in the saucer. "This tastes wonderful, Jane. Is it a new blend?"

Jane nodded. "Wilhelm Wood brought it back from a trip he took recently to Seattle. Since you like it, I'll get some more."

"These scrambled eggs are good too," Louise said, dipping her fork for another bite. "What are our guests having for breakfast?"

Jane grinned. "They asked for what they called a good old-fashioned American breakfast—scrambled eggs, bacon, pancakes with lots of maple syrup, and a stack of buttered toast with strawberry jam on the side. Oh, and lots of strong, hot 'joe,' as Mort called it."

"I am guessing they are not drinking this blend then," Louise said.

"Nope. Those guys want nothing but straight old-fashioned java, and lots of it. I've been refilling that coffee pot all morning."

"I've read recently that a cup of coffee a day is actually good for you," Alice said. "It helps your liver."

"Are you going to turn into a coffee drinker?" Jane said, her eyes twinkling. Although Jane and Louise drank coffee, Alice drank only tea.

Alice sipped green tea from her cup, smiling over the rim. "Old tastes, like habits, die hard," she said.

"Yoo-hoo!" Ethel said, entering the kitchen from the back door.

Jane slipped into a chair and sipped from her own coffee cup. "You could set your watch by her," she murmured.

"Come in, Aunt Ethel," Louise said. "Would you like some breakfast?"

Ethel took a seat at the table. "No thank you, dears, I'm far too nervous."

"About the parade?" Jane asked.

Ethel nodded. "I'm so nervous for Lloyd. He's going to be the grand marshal." She patted her hair. "And he's invited me to ride with him in the convertible."

"Oh, Auntie, how fun!" Jane said. "Have you practiced your wave?"

"Well..." Ethel looked sheepish. "I must admit that I have posed in front of the mirror, practicing different styles. Which style do you think I should choose?"

"Style?" Alice asked, bewildered.

"I know what she means," Jane said. "Show them, Aunt Ethel."

"There's this style," she said, waving her arm from the elbow to her fingers, side to side.

"The 'window washer,'" Jane said.

"Then there's this." Ethel shook her hand back and forth, fingers straight, from the wrist.

"The 'howdy,'" Jane explained.

"But what about this?" Ethel held her hand still, but wiggled her fingers quickly, one at a time.

"Ooh, the 'flirt,'" Jane said, smiling at her sisters.

"That doesn't seem quite appropriate for a parade," Alice said, frowning.

"What about this?" Louise asked. She held her fingers close together, curving them at the tips so that her hand made a slight cup, then waved. The gesture was small and dignified.

"The 'queen's wave,'" Jane said. "That's what you want, Aunt Ethel."

"Like this?" Ethel practiced, waving first at one side of the table, then the other, as though she were riding down a street to an adoring crowd.

"Yes," Alice said. "That looks very elegant, Aunt Ethel. It makes you look like royalty."

"Or at least somebody important," Jane said. "All the home-coming queens use that."

"As well as the queen of England, I believe," Louise said.

Ethel put down her hand. "Oh, fine. Now all I need is one of those silly-looking little dogs and a big hat and I'll be in busi-ness." Ethel laughed at her own joke. "Anyway, I know Lloyd will get all the attention, and that's as it should be, but a girl should know how to look nice when she's invited to ride with the grand marshal, don't you think?"

Jane gave her a hug. "Of course, Auntie. And you'll be fabulous."

Ethel went back to her house to change clothes, and the sisters cleaned up the breakfast dishes. Alice and Louise waited in the foyer for Jane, who decided to change shoes at the last minute. Out of the corner of her eye, Alice thought she saw Jane descend-ing the stairs. When she turned, she saw that it was Trisha hold-ing Libby. They were both dressed in navy-blue coats with red piping.

"You look very nice," Alice said. "How's the baby?"

Trisha smiled. "She slept pretty well last night."

"Did you get Zoë or Penelope to relieve you when she woke up?"

"I didn't have to. When Libby did wake up, she nursed for a little bit, then went right back to sleep."

Louise glanced up the stairs. "Where's Nathan?"

"He's not dressed yet, but he said he'd be down in a minute."

They chatted for a few minutes, then Alice heard movement at the top of the stairs and turned. She signaled Trisha and Louise, who turned in the same direction.

Trisha sucked in her breath. "Oh, Nathan," she whispered.

Wearing his dress uniform, Nathan descended the stairs with dignity, eyes straight ahead. Only when he reached the bottom of the stairs did he break his concentration by smiling at his wife and daughter.

"You look wonderful," Trisha said, her eyes misting. "I wish I had known you when you served in the army. I would have been just as proud then as I am today."

"I'm proud of you too," he said, kissing her on the cheek. Libby cooed, and he bent to kiss the tip of her nose.

He turned to Alice and smiled. "I didn't think I would go through with this today. Thank you for your encouragement."

"Gerry would be proud of you," she said. "He would know that his life was not given in vain."

Nathan reached into his pocket and held out a small gold cross. "He used to keep this in his pocket with his coins. Whenever he needed change, he would see this cross, and it would be a reminder of the faith he needed. We always joked about how it kept us safe in battle, even though we knew our protection really came from above."

His face clouded, but he drew a deep breath and continued. "After he died, the hospital staff gave it to me. I had it put away until now, but I'll carry it all the time from now on, starting with this parade."

Trisha leaned against him, squeezing his arm with wordless pride.

A car horn honked outside. "That's our ride," Nathan said. "The Veterans' Association in Potterston sent someone over to pick us up. Will we see you ladies at the parade?"

They nodded, and the Delhommes promised to look for them.

Just as they walked out the front door, the sisters again heard footfalls. Mort came down the staircase, followed by Harvey and Penelope, followed by Lars and Zoë. All the men were wearing crisp-looking suits, and the women were wearing 1940s full skirt–style dresses, and hats with netted veils.

"Unlike Nathan, we haven't fit into our uniforms for a long time," Mort said, smiling broadly.

"You look wonderful just the same," Alice said to each of them.

Jane came down the stairs behind them. "I *love* those hats, ladies."

"Thank you," Zoë said, giggling, putting a hand to the brim. "It makes me feel like a girl again."

"I've always been a bit mad for this style," Penelope said.

"If you dames are finished primping, we'd better get a move on," Mort said.

"When is your driver supposed to pick you up?" Louise asked.

"What driver?" Mort said, dangling a key chain. "They brought the convertible around this morning, and guess who's driving?"

"Something tells me it must be you," Jane said.

"You got it, sweetheart." Mort winked. "A 1946 Buick convertible. Cherry red."

Jane whistled. "What a sweet ride."

"Are you picking up Michael?" Alice asked.

"No, he'll meet us at the parade, which starts on Main Street and ends at the courthouse in Potterston. Speaking of which"—he turned to Harvey and Lars—"are you boys ready to shove off?"

"Yes, sir!" they both said, snapping to a salute.

"If you guys don't have any better plans after the parade, come back here. I've made some refreshments to celebrate." Jane glanced at her sisters. "We'd better head out ourselves," she said. "I want to get a good spot on the route so that we can check out Aunt Ethel's wave."

"Don't forget to wave to us," Zoë said. "We'll see you when we get back. Bye now." With a flounce of her full skirt, she and the others were out the door.

Louise sighed. "I hope I'm that spry when I'm in my eighties."

"I hope I'm that spry tomorrow," Alice said.

During the drive to Potterston, Jane acted as though at any minute the parade would start without them. "Can't you drive any faster, Louise?" she asked, leaning over the front seat to exhort her sister.

"I'm driving the legal speed limit," Louise said calmly. "I don't want anything to happen to this car."

Alice smiled. Louise took excellent care of her twenty-year-old Cadillac, which accounted for its spotless condition. "Someday this car will be used in parades," Alice said, "just like the sixty-year-old Buick Mort will be driving."

Louise laughed. "I won't live to see the day, but it is certainly a nice thought."

When the sisters arrived at Potterston, they were amazed. Cars with patriotic magnets lined the side streets, along with pickup trucks decorated with red, white and blue crepe paper. American-flag buntings hung from nearly every building in sight. "This is an even bigger crowd than I expected," Jane said. "Do you think we'll be able to find a place to park?"

"Look, there's Lloyd and Aunt Ethel in that first spot off Main Street," Alice said.

"Why are they getting into Lloyd's SUV?" Jane asked. "Doesn't he get to ride in a classic car? He is the grand marshal, after all."

"Can you pull up alongside them?" Alice asked Louise. She obliged, and Alice rolled down her window. "Hi. Why aren't you in the parade?"

"We thought we could walk from here down to where it begins, but it's a little too far. We're going to drive down there," Lloyd explained. "Would you girls like this parking space?"

"Thanks," Louise said, leaning across the front seat to talk through Alice's window. "I'll pull back and let you out."

"See you girls after the parade," Ethel said. Lloyd pulled out and headed up the street.

Louise carefully moved forward into the crosswalk so that she could back into the now-empty parking space. "Parallel parking has never been one of my favorite driving endeavors—or one of my better skills. I'm glad that I only have to be concerned about the car behind us."

"You can do it, Louise," Alice encouraged her. "Jane, since you're in the backseat, tell us how close we are to the curb."

Jane craned her neck. "Cut your wheel in a little more. Yes, that's it. Now cut it the other way. You've got it. Good job, Louise."

Sighing with relief, Louise put the gear shift into park and turned off the ignition. "Thank goodness that's over."

The sisters buttoned up their coats and got out of the car. "Hey, it's not too cold out here," Jane said. She had brought a knitted cap to wear, but she stuffed it into her pocket.

"The sun is quite bright," Louise said, blinking against the rays.

"Where should we stand?" Alice asked. "Near the beginning of the parade or the end?"

Jane stepped forward and looked up and down the street. "We're about halfway along the route. Why don't we stay here?"

Alice scanned the street, which was rapidly filling with people along the curb. "This seems to be as good a spot as any."

"Great," Jane said, perching on the hood of the Cadillac.

Louise looked horrified. "Jane Howard! Get off my car!"

"Why, Louie? I'm not hurting anything." She faced the street. "This is a wonderful view, and I don't have to stand."

"She doesn't seem to be hurting anything," Alice said.

"Yes, but..." Louise clamped her mouth shut, then broke into a smile. "Is there room for Alice and me? I do hate the thought of standing for the entire parade, and no telling when they'll get started."

"Sure," Jane said."

"Er, how did you get up there?" Louise asked.

Jane grinned. "I hopped. Here, I'll give you a hand."

Jane got off the front of the car and helped Louise up first. Then she helped Alice. With the two of them sitting on the hood on either side of the insignia, there was little room left for Jane.

"I'll sit on the roof," Jane said.

"Jane Howard!" Louise grabbed for her sister, but Jane was already perched on top of the car.

"The view's really great from here." Jane shaded her eyes with her hand, scanning the street.

"The car seems fine," Alice said to Louise, then lowered her voice. "We do have more room this way."

Louise sighed. "How that woman continually manages to surprise me is beyond my understanding."

Alice just smiled.

It *was* a good view of the route, and from where they sat, Alice could see up and down Main Street. The sidewalks were wide and the stores set back, so the view from the car was not blocked. The people in the car across the street had the same idea and were perched on the top and the trunk of their car. On the sidewalk were men, women and children, families, friends, inhabitants of Potterston, and inhabitants of Acorn Hill and other, even smaller local communities.

The street was lined with two- and sometimes three-story buildings dating back to the early twentieth century. The businesses that filled the buildings were varied: law offices, antiques stores, small eateries. Madeleine Berry Howard, the sisters' mother, had taken Alice and Louise as young girls to a nearby mom-and-pop shoe store twice a year: once for new school shoes in the fall, and once for Easter shoes in the spring.

Some of the shops were open for business, particularly those selling hot beverages and takeaway treats like bagels or sandwiches. Besides the expectant onlookers lining the street, scampering children and several elderly women who were passing out American flags filled the busy sidewalks.

One sprightly woman handed each of the sisters a flag. "I'm affiliated with the Veterans of Foreign Wars," she said. "We want all our parade participants to feel welcomed."

"What a lovely idea," Alice said, giving her flag an experimental wave as the woman moved to the next car.

"Alice! Louise! Jane!"

"It's Melanie Brubaker," Louise said, pointing across the street. Alice saw the young woman waving, along with her two children, Bree and Clinton.

"Hi!" they called back.

"Yay!" Jane said from above Alice and Louise, waving her flag. "Two bits, four bits, six bits, a dollar. All for the veterans, stand up and holler!"

Louise closed her eyes as though trying to compose herself. "Please tell me that she is not standing on my car," she murmured. "Jane is slender, but I don't know what kind of weight the car can take without the top caving in."

"Don't worry," Alice said. "She's still sitting. Practicing her cheers, but she's still sitting."

Jane waved her flag. "We are the Patriots, and no one could be prouder. And if you don't believe us, we'll yell a little louder!"

"Jane!" Louise hissed. "Please do not cause a fuss."

Jane shrugged. "Somebody needs to get this crowd pepped up. The parade's supposed to start any moment." She cupped her hands around her mouth and yelled, "We are the Patriots, and no one could be prouder. And if you don't believe us, we'll yell a little louder!" She waved her flag and cheered.

This time, some young girls on the sidewalk near them cheered and waved their flags along with her. "Yay!" The youngest, a girl of around ten, yelled out, "We are the Patriots and no one could be prouder..."

Across the street, a group of young moms with toddlers took up the cheer. "And if you don't believe us, we'll yell a little louder!"

All around the Cadillac, people started to take up the cheer. Jane clapped her hands in time with the words, leading them on, but the enthusiasm took on a life of its own. Louise shrugged and started clapping, as did Alice.

"Ladies and gentlemen," a voice boomed over the speakers lining the street. "Welcome to the annual Potterston Veterans Day Parade!"

The crowd roared.

Louise strained to look up the street. "I can't see the parade starting."

"I can from up here," Jane said. "Can you hear the music? That's the Franklin High band."

Alice cocked her head. "I hear it." She felt like a girl again, and she squeezed Louise's hand. "This is exciting!"

Two Korean War veterans were first, carrying a large banner between them that read THE ANNUAL POTTERSTON VETERANS DAY PARADE. Below that, it read GRAND MARSHAL, then, ACORN HILL MAYOR LLOYD TYNAN.

A 1955 white Packard convertible was next. Lloyd and Ethel sat in the back seat, waving to the crowd on both sides of the street.

"Yay, Lloyd!" Jane cheered. "Over here, Aunt Ethel!"

Ethel turned, saw the sisters, and waved like royalty.

They laughed and waved back with exaggerated "howdy" and "window-washer" gestures.

Next came two drill-team members holding a banner that said THE FIGHTING PATRIOT BAND OF FRANKLIN HIGH. The band followed, marching to a drummer's cadence. Then, instruments raised in precision, they launched into the theme from the film *Patton*. The crowd cheered.

Jane leaned down toward Louise and Alice. "Mort and the others are coming," she shouted as the band passed by. "They're next!"

Alice felt the low notes from the tubas, in the band's last row, reverberate against her heart. Then she saw two VFW men carrying a banner that read OUR OLDEST VETERANS and under that WORLD WAR II.

Following was Mort Fineman behind the wheel of the cherry-red convertible. He nodded and waved to the crowd, clearly in his element. Michael rode in the front seat beside him, waving hard enough to dislocate his shoulder.

"He seems to have lost his shyness," Louise said to Alice.

The speakers along the street boomed with the announcer's voice. "Riding in the car with our World War II veterans is Michael Wister. Michael was the winner of Acorn Hill's primary-school essay contest on Veterans Day. Way to go, vets, and way to go, Michael!"

Together in the back seat of the Buick were Lars and Zoë, with Harvey and Penelope. The women looked lovely in their 1940s attire, and the men smiled and waved in sincere appreciation.

"Hey, ladies!" Mort took one hand off the wheel to wave at the sisters. "Look at us!"

"Hi!" Michael yelled.

Lars and Harvey waved from the back seat, along with Zoë and Penelope. "Woo-hoo!" Jane called. "Looking sharp, ladies and gentlemen!"

The convertible drove past, and Alice turned to see what was next. Another drill team marched past, then the voice on the loudspeaker returned. "Our next group of veterans served during the Vietnam War."

"There's Derek Grollier," Louise said, pointing him out to Alice. He was in the last row, smiling broadly, as were his fellow veterans. Alice swallowed hard and waved enthusiastically. Remembering his story from yesterday at Vera's school, Alice was proud to be part of a town that had given him such a warm reception all those years ago when he returned from the war. He had more than repaid them in his work as a firefighter for all the ensuing years. She hoped that he enjoyed his retirement and especially hoped that he chose to remain in Acorn Hill. He was a good man and a good example to the town's young people.

Next came a men's fraternal organization wearing red fezzes and whizzing in circles on minimotorbikes. They tossed candy into the crowd, and Alice nearly fell off of Louise's Cadillac trying to grab some.

"Careful," Louise said, steadying her sister.

"Didn't you get any?" Alice asked.

Louise arched an eyebrow. "Do you think I would jeopardize myself just to catch some candy?" She laughed. "Of course I got some."

Alice glanced up at Jane to see if she'd gotten any candy, but Jane was laughing and pointing up the street. "What is it?" Alice asked.

"It's...it's..." Jane was laughing so hard she couldn't speak.

"What is that sound?" Louise asked.

Several men wearing sunglasses and fedoras marched in single file, each one carrying a sign that had a few words printed on it, like the old Burma-Shave road signs. Alice read the first one out loud, then Louise, then Alice, then Louise again.

"We don't play real instruments"

"We haven't the nerve"

"But we honor our veterans"

"Because they served"

Then came twenty men dressed in black tuxedos and tennis shoes marching in perfect formation, each one tooting a kazoo to the tune of "Colonel Bogey March" from the movie *Bridge on the River Kwai.*

"It's Craig Tracy!" Jane said.

"Is that Fred Humbert?" Alice asked, nudging Louise.

"Yes!"

Alice laughed out loud. "That was a nice touch."

"Here come the Franklin High cheerleaders," Jane said. "Yay, girls. Go, Candace! Go, Sophie!"

The girls marched with precision, then stopped long enough to perform a cheer routine for the crowd. Alice noticed that Jane seemed to be moving in sync with them, trying to keep up. At the end of the routine, she cheered back with the crowd.

The announcer came over the loudspeakers again. "Though they did not serve together, our youngest group of veterans are next—soldiers who served in the Middle East."

Alice gripped Louise's arm. "There he is," she said quietly.

Marching determinedly, eyes straight ahead, oblivious to the cheering crowd, was Nathan Delhomme. "Go, Nathan!" Jane yelled.

"Yay!" Louise cheered.

Scarcely thinking, Alice yelled, "Go, Gerry!"

Nathan heard her yell, for though he never broke stride or concentration, he looked at her, nodded his head slightly and smiled.

Alice knew that Nathan had a long way to go to overcome the trauma of his past. She knew it was not unusual for post-traumatic stress disorder to manifest itself for many years. But he had taken the first step, and she was confident that with good counseling and the love of his family, he would let go of his unfounded guilt. The friend who had died to save his life would no doubt be pleased.

"Good for Gerry," Alice whispered. "Good for you, Nathan."

Chapter Thirteen

everal more marching bands, an ROTC unit and the Daughters of the American Revolution float filled out the rest of the parade. When it was over, Jane came down from her perch and helped Louise and Alice down from the hood. They chatted about the people they had seen, the music they had heard and the pride they felt in seeing the veterans march.

"I can't wait to get back to the inn to give each one of those old guys and their wives a big hug," Jane said. "And then I'm going to hug Nathan, Trisha and Libby."

"I hope Trisha and Libby found a good place to stand in the sun," Alice said.

"I thought I could see them up the road," Jane said. "They looked fine."

"I hope that we can get out of this parking space," Louise said. "It was tough getting in, but it will be even tougher getting out now that everyone's heading for home at the same time."

The sisters got into the car. With help from Jane, who kept an eye out the back window for oncoming traffic, Louise pulled out of the spot and turned right onto Main Street to make her way home.

"There are Melanie and her kids," she said, nodding at the car just in front of them. Melanie had pulled her late-model Volkswagen into a right-hand turning lane, preparing to head back to Acorn Hill. Louise pulled behind her while they waited at a red light.

The light turned green just as Louise heard a siren coming from their left. She looked just in time to see a fire truck whizzing through the intersection. Melanie had started to make a right turn at the light, however, and the fire truck blasted his horn.

"Oh no!" Louise said, gripping the steering wheel.

Too late, Melanie saw the fire truck and swerved her Volkswagen to the right. Horn still blaring, the fire truck steered wide and barreled down the street. Melanie's car jumped the curb, banged over a newspaper stand, then crashed into the side of a red-brick building. Steam rose from under the hood, which had crumpled.

"Melanie!" Louise pulled the Cadillac around the corner and into a parking spot and shut off the engine. She and Jane jumped out of the car. Alice was ahead of them. A crowd quickly gathered. Louise's heart pounded.

The Volkswagen had come to rest with its right side against the building, so it was impossible to open either door on that side. Alice and Louise opened the doors on the driver's side, asking simultaneously, "Are you all right?"

Bree and Clinton sobbed, tears running down their cheeks. "Mom!"

Leaning over the steering wheel, Melanie clutched her forehead, which was bleeding and already showing signs of bruising. "I'm all right, kids. I'm okay."

Alice helped her out of the car while Bree and Clinton scrambled to safety. Louise gathered the children to her. Both seemed all right, though it was hard to tell because of their tears. "Are either of you hurt?" she asked, checking arms and legs for injury.

Sobbing, Clinton held out his elbow and pointed. "I... hit...this."

Louise checked. It looked like a lump was forming, but it didn't seem to be anything major. "Bree, are you all right?"

"I'm...scared," she wailed, but couldn't say anything else.

Melanie tried to gather them to her. "It's okay, kids. It's okay." She brushed off Alice, who was trying to check her out. "I'm fine, Alice, really. It was just a little accident. Just..."

She broke into sobs, turning into Alice's arms for comfort.

Louise held Clinton and Bree close but didn't try to hold them back when they went to their mother. They clung to her waist and sobbed along with her.

A man approached Louise. "I called for an ambulance," he said. "Even if these folks don't need to go to the hospital, they should be checked out."

Louise nodded.

"It's all right," Alice was saying, holding Melanie close. "It's okay. Here, sit down a minute."

"Is there anything I can do to help?" Jane whispered to Louise.

She shook her head. "I don't think so." They stepped back, letting Alice do what she did best. While she and Jane waited for the ambulance, they surveyed the Volkswagen. Twisted metal and chrome, along with thousands of shards and bits of glass, littered the sidewalk.

The ambulance arrived, and the paramedics leaped out to check Melanie and the kids. It took all their best efforts just to get her to sit on a gurney long enough to be examined. "I have to get home," she kept saying. "My husband is out of town, and he might phone."

Alice joined Louise and Jane. "Melanie's in shock," she whispered.

"What about the kids?" Louise asked. "Clinton said his elbow hurt."

"He probably banged it against the door on impact. I looked him and Bree over, and though I don't know about any internal injuries, they seem all right."

One of the paramedics, a young man in his midtwenties with a name tag that said Rafael, approached Alice. "Are you the nurse that helped Mrs. Brubaker?"

"Yes, I work in Potterston," she said, squinting at his name tag. "I think I recognize you from a few times when I've worked in the emergency room, Rafael."

"You're Alice. I remember you too," he said. "We're going to take Mrs. Brubaker and her kids to the hospital for observation. We think they're all right, but we want to get them checked out as quickly as possible."

"Good," Alice said. "May we follow you?"

"Actually, that's what I was hoping. We want the kids to ride in the ambulance so that they won't be separated from their mother. Once we get to the hospital, they'll probably be released fairly quickly. It'd be good for them to have someone there that they know."

"We'll meet you at the emergency room," she said.

Louise nodded, and the sisters piled into the Cadillac.

"Now is one of those times I wish I had a cell phone," Alice said. "I'd call Aunt Ethel and ask her to check in on our guests. They'll be wondering where we are."

"I'll pull over at this gas station so that you can use the pay phone," Louise said. "Lloyd usually keeps his cell phone on, doesn't he? Aunt Ethel is bound to still be with him on the trip back from Potterston."

She pulled into the station, and Alice placed the call. "I spoke to Aunt Ethel," she said, "and she and Lloyd are going to head right over to the inn. It seems that Lloyd wants to visit with the veterans anyway, so that worked out well. She'll explain our situation, and she also said that she would contact one of Melanie's neighbors. Maybe they have Mac Brubaker's cell phone number so that they can contact him. He'll probably want to come home as soon as possible." Alice paused. "Thank goodness Aunt Ethel is so quick thinking."

At last they pulled into the Potterston Hospital parking lot near the emergency room. In the waiting area, they asked about Melanie and her children "They're back in an examination room," the receptionist said, "but you can't go back there if you're not family."

Alice flashed the security card that she used when working at the hospital. "I just want to check on her. If the doctors are finished examining her children, my sisters and I are here to take care of them while Mrs. Brubaker is being examined."

The receptionist studied Alice's ID, then relented. "You and one of your sisters can go back."

"I'll wait here," Jane said.

Louise nodded. The receptionist let Alice and her through the security door, then said, "They're in room 2A." Louise followed Alice back into the maze of examination cubicles, where she led the way to Melanie.

They found her lying down on a bed, a child lying on either side of her, huddled close. They had stopped crying and were fast asleep. Melanie appeared to be sleeping too, but as the sisters stepped closer she opened her eyes. "Hi, Alice. Hi, Louise," she whispered, trying to smile. Her face was bruised, with a good-sized lump on her forehead and a swath of gauze covering her cut.

Alice took her hand, careful not to disturb the children. "How are you, Melanie? Has a doctor seen you yet?"

Melanie shook her head. "The admitting nurse examined me briefly, but I'm still waiting for a doctor. She said the children were all right, though shaken up, of course."

"I'll be glad to take care of them when the doctor comes to see you," Louise said. "Jane is also in the waiting room."

"Thank you," Melanie said, looking embarrassed. "I'm sorry to cause you such trouble. It was just a little accident. We'll be fine."

"We're all part of the body of Christ," Alice said in a quiet voice. "And when one part of the body hurts, we all do." She squeezed Melanie's hand. "We are all thankful that you are safe.' Cars can be repaired or replaced."

Tears pooled in Melanie's eyes. The children woke up, rubbing their eyes. "Mom," Bree said, clutching at her.

"It's all right, sweetie," Melanie said, wiping her eyes with the back of her hand. "The doctor will be here soon to examine me. I want you to go with Alice now, will you? Alice, you don't mind, do you? I want to speak with Louise alone for a minute."

Alice nodded. "Would you like to get something to drink out of the vending machine while we wait for your mother?"

They nodded, then sat up. Though obviously reluctant, they obediently climbed out of the bed and followed Alice. Louise pulled up a chair beside Melanie and took her hand. "What is it, Melanie?"

"I didn't even know how the accident happened until the paramedics told me," she said. "Louise, I never heard that fire truck until it was right on us. The kids told me they did, but I didn't." She blinked back tears. "I could have gotten us all killed."

"But you didn't, Melanie."

Melanie wiped away her tears. "You were right, though. I do need to get my hearing checked. And if I need hearing aids, so be it. I can't risk my life or especially my children's lives anymore."

"I think that is a wise idea. If you need any help at all—someone to watch the children or whatever—please let me know."

"Louise, I feel silly admitting this, but I'm afraid of doctors," she said. "I have been since I was a little girl. Fortunately, I don't get sick very often, but I panic sometimes. Would you go with me when I make an appointment to have my hearing checked?"

"Of course," Louise said. "And I will stay with you now until the doctor arrives to check you out. Alice and Jane will take good care of the children."

Melanie breathed a sigh of relief. "I'm so glad you were riding behind me when I had the accident and that you're here now. What would I do without you three? You're good friends."

Louise squeezed her hand again and smiled. "We're more than friends. As Alice said, we are all part of the body of Christ."

Alice returned to the examination room and reported that Jane was entertaining the children, who were ready to go home now that they were over the initial shock of the accident.

The doctor arrived and, after examining Melanie, said that he would release her. "I'll give you a prescription for a painkiller, if you need it. Otherwise, just take aspirin and put an ice pack on that bump."

"What about this?" Melanie said, gingerly touching the gauze covering the cut on her face.

"It doesn't need to be stitched," he said. "Change the dressing before bedtime and once a day after that. Of course, you can call us if you have any concerns."

"Thank you, Doctor," Melanie said.

After he left, Alice and Louise helped her gather her things. "Aunt Ethel arranged, through Pastor Ken, for someone from church to take you home. They'll also stay with you for the rest of the day to help with the kids and get your dinner."

Melanie looked like she was going to cry.

The sisters waited until the Grace Chapel family arrived to help Melanie and the children. When Louise, Alice and Jane returned to the inn, it was late afternoon, and they assumed the postparade festivities would be long over.

To their surprise, they heard music blaring through the front door. "What in the world?" Louise asked, looking at her sisters.

They opened the front door and found Lars and Zoë jitterbugging to "In the Mood" in the foyer. The others lined the wall, clapping their hands or snapping their fingers to the beat. A boom box sat on the staircase.

"Come on, Ethel, let's have a go at it," Lloyd said, taking Ethel's hand, then spinning her around.

She giggled like a schoolgirl and waved at the sisters. "Hi, girls!"

The sisters were speechless. Jane grinned. "I'd forgotten that they took dance lessons."

Mort sidled up to Jane and held out his hand. "May I have this dance?"

"Sure!" Jane said and joined him on the makeshift dance floor.

"My goodness," Louise murmured to Alice. "I never dreamed they would turn our inn into a dance hall."

"I think it's fun," Alice said.

"Hello, Alice," Trisha said over the noise. She held Libby up for inspection. "She's feeling so much better. She did very well at the parade. Didn't cry at all."

Nathan came over to Alice. "I saw you all wave at me when we marched past." He smiled. "I heard what you said too. Thanks."

Alice nodded, then smiled. "Why don't you let me hold Libby so that you two can dance?"

Nathan looked at Trisha questioningly. She smiled and handed the baby to Alice. "I'd love to, thanks."

The music on the boom box changed to a slow tune, "Sentimental Journey." Lars and Zoë seemed lost in their own world. Harvey and Penelope joined the others, and Mort and Jane continued dancing.

"I am not surprised that he is a good dancer," Louise whispered to Alice. "He's a smooth operator, isn't he?"

Alice grinned. "Indeed. But he didn't sway Aunt Ethel. Look at her over there with Lloyd." The two of them were holding each other close, dancing smoothly and comfortably.

Trisha smiled at Nathan and put her head on his shoulder as he held her close, and they danced, oblivious to the others. Alice held Libby close and whispered, "Look at your parents. They're something, aren't they?"

Libby looked back at her with thoughtful eyes, and Alice could swear that the little girl smiled.

The veterans, the sisters, and Lloyd and Ethel danced till suppertime, when Jane served chicken salad with toasted almonds on croissants with tomato bisque in the dining room. They all sat around the table, laughing and chatting about the day. "It was a ball having that kid Michael in the car with us," Mort said. "He made the day fun. He even got a certificate from the parade organizers. He said he was going to hang it on the wall of his room and that he'd never forget us."

"We'll never forget him either," Zoë said.

"I'm so glad to see that young people haven't forgotten us old folks," Penelope said as she passed the fruit platter. "So many of them don't have much use for us or for the stories from our generation."

"We'll make certain that Libby never forgets," Trisha said, smiling at the baby in Nathan's arms. "We'll not only tell her about her great-grandpa Delhomme, but about all his wonderful friends."

"Your grandpa was a great man," Mort said, turning to Nathan. "Out of all these mugs here, he was my closest buddy. He alone knew what I shouldered as a sergeant, and he understood. He knew that I had to motivate them into action, and I knew that he encouraged the others. I know he certainly encouraged me."

Mort wiped his eyes, then, as if embarrassed, smiled. "We miss him this year. We're glad you joined us, though. You're a great man too." He rose and held up his glass. "Here's to the memory of your grandpa, but here's also to you, Nathan. May you have a long, prosperous life with your loved ones by your side as you carry on the family name and bravery."

"Hear hear," everyone said, rising.

Nathan flushed, but he held up his water glass in return. "And here's to all of you—Harvey, Zoë, Lars, Penelope...Mort." His gaze lingered longest on his grandpa's friend. "You truly are the greatest generation."

Jane applauded, and Louise and Alice followed suit.

The next morning, the veterans packed up to leave. The breakfast sounds from the dining room seemed muted to the sisters as they ate in the kitchen.

"I'm sure they're sad because they won't see each other for another year," Alice said.

Jane sighed as she spread strawberry jam over her toasted English muffin. "I'd be sad too. In fact, I *am* sad, because they'll go to another city, a different parade, next year and we'll probably never see them again."

"Maybe they'll come visit sometime," Alice said.

"But they probably won't be all together," Louise said. "I am quite happy to bid farewell to some Grace Chapel Inn guests, and there are others that I would like to invite to live with us."

"Maybe we could open a veterans' retirement home," Jane said brightly. "Do you think they would move in with us?"

Alice knew that Jane was only teasing and laughed. "I don't know that we could keep up with them for more than ten days."

Later, when they met in the lobby to say good-bye, each one of the group hugged each one of the sisters. More than a few tears were shed. "This has been our best reunion ever," Zoë said. "I'm certainly going to thank my friend who recommended your inn."

"We hope you'll consider coming back to see us," Alice said. "We've enjoyed having you here."

"We've enjoyed it as well," Lars said. "Do you ladies like to get postcards? Penelope and I travel when we're able, and we enjoy sending cards to our friends."

"We would be delighted to receive them," Louise said.

Mort took the unlit cigar stub from between his teeth. "Ladies, it's been a pleasure."

Trisha hugged Alice, then took Libby from Nathan's arms. "Thank you so much for everything, particularly with Libby. Not only was it nice to have a nurse around, you were so kind as well."

Nathan nodded, his eyes meeting Alice's to show his appreciation.

"You're welcome," she said. "Don't forget to get Libby checked by your pediatrician on Monday."

Trisha smiled. "We've already got an appointment."

"Good-bye, ladies," Zoë said, waving.

"Please take care," Penelope added, tearing up. She dabbed at her eyes with a handkerchief. "I do hate farewells. We'll have to do it here and then again at the airport when we go our separate ways."

"I think we'd better sing our happy song now," Zoë said.

The men groaned.

"What happy song?" Jane asked.

Penelope and Zoë linked arms. "We always sing 'Happy Trails.'"

"The Dale Evans song?" Jane asked.

Penelope nodded. "We usually sing it at the airport."

"I suppose if you've got to sing it, it might as well be here," Mort said.

"We'll have to sing it again before our planes depart, of course," Zoë said with a mock-indignant expression.

Mort threw up his hands with a sigh. "Dames."

"All right, everyone," Penelope said. "Let's begin."

The men sighed, then, from long practice, linked arms with the women. Penelope gestured for Jane, Alice and Louise to join them at one end of the chain. At the other, Nathan and Trisha joined. At the end of the chain, Trisha held Libby, and Nathan put his arm around her. Penelope started the song with her clear British soprano, and the others joined in.

"...until we meet again," they all sang, finishing the song.

"Good luck, dears," Penelope said, giving the sisters a final hug. "I wish we could stay to see you whip those young cheerleaders into shape," she said to Jane.

"Or to see how the food drive works out," Zoë said to Louise.

"Come on, ladies," Lars said, rounding them up, "or we'll miss our plane."

"Good-bye, good-bye," they said, hustling out the door, blowing kisses as they got into their cars and left.

The sisters watched them drive off, then linked arms. Each one felt a certain sadness at seeing their guests leave. They looked at one another, and each one had tears in her eyes. Jane smiled and started singing, "Happy trails to you..." She was slightly off-key, as usual.

Chapter Fourteen

The next round of guests was not due until Wednesday, but they would be staying through Thanksgiving. The sisters were somewhat relieved to have the break, because it gave them a chance to recuperate and clean the rooms now that their long-term guests had checked out.

They agreed to rest on Sunday, leaving the room cleaning for the following day. Other than visiting the Brubakers, they took things easy.

On Monday they began housecleaning in earnest. For many months the Sunset and Garden rooms had been reserved by two women. The other two rooms would be occupied by two sisters and their two cousins, all of whom used to attend Franklin High. They no longer had family living in the area but wanted to spend Thanksgiving together and decided to return for the play-off game with Billings High School.

"I can't recall us ever having only women for such a long stay," Alice said as she and Jane polished the staircase banister.

Jane paused to wipe her forehead with the back of her hand, her fingers covered with polish. "We'd better get some fashion magazines and romance novels and have plenty of chocolate truffles on hand."

"Some people would say you're being sexist," Alice said with a smile.

"Actually, I was just being hopeful, but I'm afraid I won't have much time for fun," Jane said. "This afternoon Sylvia and I are meeting with Candace, Sophie and the other cheerleaders to show them a few of our old routines. Between helping them before the big game and arranging the Thanksgiving feast with Craig Tracy, I'll be busy."

"As always," Alice said, smiling at her talented sister. She gave another swipe at the railing. "How are your holiday meal plans going? Is there anything I can help with?"

Jane shook her head. "We already have volunteers for all of the committees. Craig and I haven't actually gotten together to finalize things, but we've done this enough times now for it all to run like clockwork."

"How many people are coming?"

"Hmm." Jane paused in her work. "You know what, Alice? I have no idea. I know how many usually come, but it would probably be best to get a head count. We always assume more people will come than tell us in advance, but it's still wise to have an estimate."

"And people are volunteering to bring food?"

"You bet," Jane said. "Say, I thought of something you can do to help."

"What's that?'

"Remember that sweet-potato casserole you made last year, the one with the secret ingredient that you won't share?"

"Yes." Alice smiled, avoiding Jane's face while she studiously worked on a staircase spindle.

"You still won't tell me, will you?"

"Nope," Alice said.

Jane sighed. "Will you at least consider making a big batch of your mystery sweet potatoes for the Thanksgiving dinner?"

"I'd be delighted," Alice said. "But I still won't give you the recipe. The person who gave it to me asked me not to."

"And just who was that?" Jane narrowed her eyes.

"That, too, is a secret."

Jane sighed, tossing her rag aside with mock exasperation. She thought for a moment, then said, "I bet you that if you make up a batch of the casserole I can figure out all the ingredients. Even the secret one."

Alice smiled. "Really? That would be quite a challenge. I'd like to see if you can do it. I'll be impressed if you can, though not surprised."

"If you make me a batch, I'll get right on it," Jane said cheerfully.

"I've got some time this afternoon. I'll make it while you and Sylvia are helping the cheerleaders."

"And I'll have all the ingredients figured out before Thanksgiving," Jane said.

"You're on."

Jane glanced suspiciously at Alice. "No cheating. That is, no substituting ingredients now that you know I'll be studying them closely."

"Not me," Alice said. "I'm actually rooting for you. If you succeed, you might have a whole new career started. Jane Howard, recipe investigator."

"Maybe the networks can make it into a new entertainment program called Forensic Chef," Jane said, smiling. "I play the chef who goes to different restaurants and tries to figure out the ingredients of all the recipes."

"Would this be with or without the aid of laboratory equipment?" Alice smiled.

"For the TV program, with. For your sweet-potato casserole, without. I'll rely entirely on my sensitive palate."

Alice nodded. "Then the game is afoot."

"Or, should we say, a-mouth."

That afternoon, Sylvia Songer picked up Jane so that they could meet with the cheerleaders at Franklin High. After much consultation, they had each decided to wear navy-blue stretch pants and white long-sleeved T-shirts.

"I think we look pretty good," Sylvia said as they drove to Franklin.

"Too bad we don't still have our cheerleading uniforms," Jane said.

Sylvia looked sideways at Jane. "I don't know about you, but even if I had that uniform, I wouldn't be able to fit into it."

Jane laughed. "Good point."

When they got to Franklin, they parked the car and gathered up the red-and-white pom-poms they'd ordered online. After checking in at the front office for visitors' passes, they walked down the hall toward the gym.

It was between periods, and students dashed past them on their way to their next classes. Jane's face warmed with pleasure as memories of her high school days came back in a rush. Game day had always been exciting, because it meant flouncing around the halls in a ponytail and a short skirt. Now that she could look at the past with the honesty of an adult, she recognized that she had loved the attention then and didn't mind it so much now either.

"It's fun to be here again," Sylvia whispered.

In the gym, the boys' basketball team was practicing on half the court. The cheerleaders were talking in a corner. Candace and Sophie broke away from the other two girls and walked up to Sylvia and Jane. "Hi, Ms. Songer, Ms. Howard."

The girls were wearing short, flouncy navy-blue skirts with red-and-white long-sleeved shirts.

"Why don't you just call us Jane and Sylvia?" Jane said.

"Well, okay," Candace said, but she looked doubtful. "Let me introduce you to the other girls on the squad. Hey, girls!"

They bounded over to Sylvia and Jane. "Oh, you're the old cheerleaders we've been hearing about," one said. "Hi, I'm Lashaunda Derito."

"Hi, Lashaunda," Jane said, feeling a little miffed that she'd been referred to as old.

"And I'm Mai Holtmeier," the other said, her short black hair swaying as she talked. "Let's get started. We're really psyched to learn some new routines."

"And we've been working on them," Jane said. "Right, Sylvia?"

"Right!" Sylvia stood beside Jane. The high school girls sat against the wall, expectant looks on their faces.

Jane looked at Sylvia. "Ready? Okay!" They moved their pom-poms in sync with their words. "Lean to the left, lean to the right, stand up, sit down, fight fight fight!" Jane and Sylvia returned to their starting position, smiles on their faces.

The girls looked at one another and shifted uncomfortably. "Do you know another one?" Sophie asked.

"Oh sure," Jane said. "We know a lot." She and Sylvia lined up again, then started running in place, clapping their pom-poms together. "We've got spirit, how about you? We've got spirit—"

Candace rose. "Um, I hate to interrupt, but we kinda know that one, Ms. Howard."

"Call me Jane," she said, her stomach beginning a slow descent.

"Yeah," Sophie said, rising to her feet. "We need something with some movement to it, you know?"

"Let's try choo choo," Sylvia whispered to Jane.

"Okay," Jane said to the girls. "We've got another one."

Candace and Sophie sat back down, looking hopeful.

Jane and Sylvia went into their routine.

Choo choo, bang bang
gotta get my boomerang
Uhh. Ungowa. Patriots are the best
Hit 'em in the chest
What cha gonna do?
Dance the boogaloo!
C stands for can
And D stands for do
Us a-mighty Patriots gonna sock it to you
Hey hey hey sock it to YOU

They finished with a flourish on their knees, pom-poms out-thrust. Jane felt her heart beating against her chest.

Candace's expression said it all. "Um—"

"Never mind," Jane said, rising to her feet. Sylvia groaned and Jane helped her up. Sylvia immediately bent over to catch her breath.

The girls looked at one another as if agreeing on something. "We really need to get to class," Sophie said, her expression showing that she was trying to be nice. "Do you have anything else to show us?"

Jane had known there might be a moment like this, and she and Sylvia nodded at one another. Time for the ace in the hole. "This is a really old cheer, from the 1930s, I think, that we learned from some former Franklin High cheerleaders when we were in school. We'd love to pass it on to you."

"Let's see it," Sophie said, settling in again.

Jane got that sinking feeling in her stomach again. "It doesn't have much movement. Nothing flashy, anyway."

"That's okay," Sophie said.

Jane and Sylvia lined up and moved their pom-poms in time with the cheer.

> *Down by the river*
> *Skit! Skat!*
> *Beat that team and send them back.*
> *With a hidy-hi and a hody-ho.*
> *Truckin'! Truckin'!*
> *Truck some mo!*
> *Our team is red hot!*

Breathing hard but exultant, Sylvia and Jane looked at one another. When they saw the expressions on the girls' faces, they knew their cheerleading days were truly over.

Sophie and Candace looked at each other, then they looked at Mai and Lashaunda, who were staring at the floor as if in embarrassment. They stood up and approached Jane and Sylvia.

"You don't have to say anything," Jane said.

"We appreciate your efforts," Candace said, "but we need something a little more..."

"Yeah, um, Mrs. Thrush mentioned that she had a DVD recording of the national cheerleading finals from last year. We'll look at that and see if we can get some ideas."

"You two are really good," Mai said, "for older women, but—"

"What she means is that we know you've worked hard to prepare those cheers for us," Lashaunda said hastily, "but..."

"Cheerleading is more athletic now than in your day," Sophie said.

"We did jumps and cartwheels back then," Sylvia said, sounding slightly irritated.

"We do a lot more than that now," Sophie said. "We do choreographed routines. More gymnastic and dance stuff."

"Come to the game and you'll see," Candace said. "We don't have enough room here on this portion of the basketball court or we'd show you. Meanwhile, we're really glad you worked so hard and came all the way out here to show us what it was like when you were cheerleading at Franklin."

"You're welcome," Jane said, trying not to let her disappointment show. "I guess we're ready then, Sylvia."

She nodded, scooping up her pom-poms. "I'll get back with you girls about the Patriot costume."

Mai giggled. "We don't know who it will be for."

"What?" Jane asked.

"Apparently only two people asked to audition," Mai said. "So Mrs. Thrush decided that each of them should work on a routine. Then during the game, they'll each get to perform."

Sylvia smiled. "And since it has a head-to-neck covering, no one will know who it is when he comes out onto the field."

"I didn't think of that," Candace said. "It'll be a real surprise to the school."

Sylvia sighed. "I'd better get home and get to work. There's only a week left until the game."

Candace put a hand on Jane's and Sylvia's arms. "No hard feelings?"

Sylvia and Jane looked at each other, then smiled at Candace. The girl smiled back and put her hand out, palm down. Jane put hers on top, then Sophie, Sylvia, Mai and Lashaunda followed suit. "Yay, go!" they yelled as one, breaking the huddle by throwing their hands upward.

On the ride back to town, Jane and Sylvia were silent. Finally, in exasperation, Sylvia whacked the steering wheel and laughed. "What were we thinking, Jane?"

Shocked, Jane was speechless, then she began to chuckle. "I'm not sure."

"Those poor girls looked so hopeful. I'm sure *we* looked so hopeful."

"I guess it has been a few years," Jane said. "And I'm sure cheerleading styles have changed."

"I hope they find the help they want. It's a big game for them, and their job is to keep the crowd motivated. Plus, they want to look good in front of the other team."

"The mascot for the other team is a goat, Sylvia. How good do they have to be?"

They fell silent a moment, then Sylvia said, under her breath, "Choo choo bang bang."

Jane smiled. She took up the cheer, just as softly, "Gotta get my boomerang..."

Louise finished her last piano lesson for that Monday afternoon. She was heading upstairs when the phone rang. "Grace Chapel Inn," she answered.

"Louise? It's Melanie Brubaker."

"How are you?" Louise asked. "And Bree and Clinton?"

"They're fine," she said. "Mac went back on the road this morning. That's how well we're doing. I have the day off, but I'll be back at work tomorrow."

"I am glad to hear it. Do not go back before you are ready, though."

"I'm ready." Melanie paused. "There's something I'm not ready for, and that's why I've called. I made an appointment with an ear, nose and throat specialist in Potterston. Are you still willing to go with me?"

"I..."

"I know it's silly, but I'm so nervous. I'd feel better if someone...if you...were with me."

"When is your appointment?"

"Wednesday afternoon at three o'clock. I know it's short notice, and you probably have a piano lesson or something."

"No, actually, I don't," Louise said. "I would be happy to go with you, if you think my presence will help."

"I know it would. A lot."

"Shall I pick you up?" Louise asked.

Melanie laughed softly. "That would be great, Louise. I still don't have a car."

They arranged a time for Louise to pick her up, then they ended the call.

Alice walked down the stairs. "I heard the phone ring. Was it someone making a reservation?"

Louise shook her head. "It was Melanie. She's worked up the courage to see a doctor about her hearing, and she asked me to go with her."

"Is she going to an ear, nose and throat specialist?"

"Yes, someone in Potterston."

Alice smiled. "I think there's only one in town, and he's a wonderful doctor. If she truly does have a phobia, he'll be sensitive to her needs. Some doctors aren't so patient and just make matters worse."

"What makes a person afraid of doctors?" Louise asked. "I know I never cared for shots as a child, but I was afraid of the needle, not the man on the other side."

"People are usually afraid of doctors because of a traumatic event as a child. Maybe a doctor had her held down for a shot or an exam. I'm sure that having you there will help her immensely," Alice said. "Sometimes all it takes is having a friend by your side to get you through the rough moments."

Louise opened the calendar book that recorded the reservations of guests. "I cannot believe that no one is coming until Wednesday."

"When are our guests due to arrive?"

Louise consulted the book. "The high school reunion group is coming in the morning. Oh, so are the two other women."

"It's been so quiet," Alice said. "It always feels strange for a day or two, having the house to ourselves, and then it feels strange when we have company again."

"Especially when we're completely booked, as we were with our last guests and will be with the next group."

Alice smiled. "Sometimes I wonder that Father and I weren't more lonely, living here by ourselves. Even now when we don't have guests, the house seems so warm and full of life."

"Could it be my piano students?" Louise grinned. "Some days it seems as if they're always in and out."

"I meant you and Jane," Alice said. "It's nice to know you're here to stay and not just passing through."

The front door slammed. "Hi, girls!" Jane said.

"How did it go with the cheerleaders?" Alice asked.

Jane smiled. "Let's just say we gave them two bits, four bits, six bits, a dollar, but they didn't stand up and holler."

"They don't need your help?" Alice asked.

"Nope," Jane said cheerfully.

"I'm so sorry," Louise said. "I know that you and Sylvia worked hard."

Jane waved her hand. "It's all right. Sylvia and I apparently have rusty cheerleading routines. And, I've just discovered, my muscles are a little rusty too." She held her hand at the small of her back in mock emphasis. "Anyway, Sylvia's involved with making the new Patriot costume, so she'll feel like she's contributing. And I"—Jane shrugged —"well, I'll go to the game and cheer from the bleachers."

"That's the spirit," Alice said. "And we'll be right there with you."

"Speaking of spirit," Jane said. "Did you make your sweet-potato casserole while I was gone, Alice?"

"It's warming in the oven."

Jane smiled. "As soon as I shower and change clothes, I'll be ready to tackle a new challenge. I'll have more time to figure out your secret ingredient."

"Good luck," Alice said, smiling.

Chapter Fifteen

*B*y the next day, Jane had nearly forgotten the cheerleading incident. Except when she twisted a certain way and felt certain muscles pull, such as when she tried to mix chocolate cake batter too quickly by hand.

"Ouch," she said, dropping her wooden spoon into the batter. "I may have to use the electric mixer for a while."

The phone rang, and Jane answered the extension in the kitchen. "Grace Chapel Inn."

"Ms. Jane Howard?"

"Yes?"

"I've heard that you and Sylvia Songer are pretty good at cheerleading."

Jane laughed. "Is this a joke?"

"Oh no," the voice said. "I'm someone in need of some cheerleading help."

"Why not go to the current cheerleaders?" she asked, intrigued.

"Well, I'm auditioning for the Franklin High mascot role, and I need some routines. The other person auditioning is already working with the Franklin cheerleaders."

"You must not have heard that our cheers were rejected by the spirit squad," Jane said. "I don't think Sylvia and I would have any good advice for you."

"I really need help, and you are the only ones I know who can give it to me," the voice said, "if you have the time, that is."

"Who is this?" The voice was low and Jane could not even tell if the caller was male or female. It sounded somewhat distorted, as though the caller was speaking on a cell phone.

"I'm sorry, but I'd rather remain anonymous at this point. Will you help me?"

"You won't remain anonymous while Sylvia and I are showing you our routine, will you?" Jane asked.

The voice laughed. "No. But if you agree to help, I hope you'll keep my identity a secret."

Alice walked into the kitchen.

Jane waved at her sister, then went back to the conversation. "Why do you want to keep your identity a secret?"

Alice's eyes widened.

"I promise I'll explain later," the caller said. "Please, Ms. Howard, will you help?"

Jane sighed. It seemed those cheerleading muscles would be getting in shape after all. "I'll give it a go. Have you contacted Sylvia yet?"

"No. I wanted to start with you. Can you meet this afternoon?"

"That's pretty short notice."

"I know, but I just worked up the courage to try out. I can meet wherever you and Ms. Songer agree."

"I can make it," Jane said. "Why don't we meet at Sylvia's shop? She has some space in the back where we've been working on our routines. That way we can continue to practice in secrecy."

"All right, I'll give her a call. If she agrees, I'll meet you both there at three o'clock."

Jane said good-bye, hung up the phone and shook her head. "That was the strangest phone call I think I've ever received."

"Someone wants to remain anonymous...about what?" Alice asked.

"Whoever it is, he or she wants to try out for the mascot position at Franklin, and wants Sylvia and me to help work up a new routine."

"But the cheerleaders didn't like what you two did."

"I know. That's the crazy thing," Jane said. "But apparently this person heard about what we did and is interested just the same." She shook her head, laughing softly. "Must be pretty desperate."

Alice laughed too, then glanced over at the counter. "What are you making?"

Jane rubbed her arm. "Chocolate cake. I got interrupted by the mystery mascot."

"No chance to taste my sweet-potato casserole?" Alice affected innocent interest.

"I gave it my first taste test last night," Jane said.

"And, Inspector Holmes?"

"Nothing conclusive yet, but I'll figure it out. It's sure to be 'alimentary,' my dear Watson."

Jane got back from Sylvia's shop so late that she barely had time to put dinner on the table. Alice and Louise helped her, and Alice hoped Jane would talk about how the meeting with the mysterious mascot-wannabe had gone. Jane didn't say a word about the matter, however, smiling secretly and humming marching-band music.

Once they all sat down, said grace and started eating, Alice said, "All right, Jane, curiosity has gotten the better of this cat. Are you going to tell us about your cheerleading lessons?"

"Sylvia and I have agreed to help...this person," she said. "And since we've been sworn to secrecy about the person's identity, I'm afraid I can't divulge that information even to my dear sisters."

"Can you tell us *why* you can't tell us?" Alice asked.

Jane shook her head. "Not even if you offered to reveal your casserole's secret ingredient."

"Looks like both of you are in the secret-keeping business lately," Louise said.

"Here's your chance to join the club," Jane said. "Any mysteries up your sleeve, Louise?"

She shook her head. "Not a one. I've told you about agreeing to accompany Melanie tomorrow to the doctor. That's about the only big item in my life lately."

"Is Melanie going to be able to work on the food drive?" Alice asked.

"She hasn't said anything about quitting. I can't imagine that a hearing problem would affect that."

"Hearing aids might even boost her enthusiasm," Jane said.

"Is there anything I can do to help with the food drive in the meantime?" Alice asked.

"Could you put out a donation box at the Potterston Hospital?" Louise asked. "Maybe we could get some canned goods from the staff."

"That's a wonderful idea," Alice said. "I'd be glad to help."

"Great. Melanie and I have some cardboard boxes already assembled, with an explanatory sign attached. If you can find a prominent place for the box and bring everything you collect to us early next week, that would help immensely." Louise passed the spinach salad to Alice. "Now back to you, Jane. Why did the mystery mascot choose you and Sylvia?"

"He...or she...heard about our performance for the cheerleaders and realized that he needed someone to help him learn some basic spirit routines. The other candidate has already begun work with the cheerleaders, so the mystery mascot thought we might be able to help him."

"So both people auditioning will actually get to perform as mascot on the day of the game?" Alice asked.

Jane nodded. "That's right. Then Mrs. Thrush will decide which one gets to continue for the rest of the season—if there is any season left after the play-off game. Sylvia and I think that our mascot has a good chance of winning."

"Any special reason?" Louise asked.

"He has what it takes here," Jane said, pointing to her heart. "He cares about Franklin High and wants to help the fans get enthusiastic about the game."

"Speaking of fans," Alice said, "our Franklin alumnae are checking in tomorrow."

"As are our other two guests," Louise said. "Although I must confess I don't know anything about them other than that they are friends. Many times guests making a reservation will tell me why they are coming to Acorn Hill, but the woman who made the reservations didn't specify. In fact, she didn't say much at all. I don't know if she was just busy or extremely shy."

"I'm sure we will find some way to engage them in conversation," Alice said.

The next morning, all three sisters were home when the Franklin alumnae arrived. The house had been thoroughly cleaned, and the Sunrise and Symphony rooms were ready for their first guests, two sets of sisters who were cousins. All looked to be in their forties.

"Hi, I'm India Coppersmith," said the first, a woman with stylish frosted hair, a trim figure and kitten heels. "This is my sister, Lois Swantek."

"Hi," Lois said with a little wave. Unlike her sister, she was shorter, plumper and dressed in a blue-denim jumper with school buses embroidered around the hem.

"And these are our cousins, Christal Ocana and Misty Locascio, who are also sisters," India said.

Christal and Misty were identical twins with short dark hair and engaging smiles. Even though they were middle-aged, they were dressed identically in red suede jackets, designer jeans and black boots. They looked at each other and laughed in unison.

"As you may have guessed," Christal said, "our parents call me Christy, but I insist on Christal with everyone else."

Christy and Misty, Jane thought. *Hmmm.*

"We're here for a girls' week off," India said. "We'll rejoin our husbands and kids late on Thanksgiving Day, but we wanted to have a girls-only party before the holidays begin."

"We've all been working hard, and we needed a break," Lois added. "And our hardest work starts at Thanksgiving and isn't over until after New Year's Day."

"The holidays are hard on moms and wives," Christal said.

"And since our old high school is in the play-offs, we thought this would be a good time to get away," the other twin said.

"You're originally from this area?" Louise asked.

India nodded. "Yes, we all grew up outside Riverton, but it's been years since we've been back. We don't have any family here now, but we thought we'd take a trip down memory lane."

Louise wore a bemused expression. "I hate to be rude, but I should warn you in advance that I do not think I will be able to tell you two women apart. Is there a distinguishing feature, or should I just guess when I need to address you?"

The twins looked at each other and giggled. "Can't you tell?"

Jane looked at each one closely. "I'm afraid I can't see a difference."

"It's the eyes. We each have one green and one brown eye. I'm Christal, and I have the green left eye."

"And I'm Misty, with the green right eye."

"So it's Christal, green left, and Misty, green right," Jane said. "Correct?"

"You've got it," Christal said.

"I'm afraid I don't," Louise said. "So just forgive me if I call you by the wrong name."

"That's all right," Misty said. "Everyone does at one time or another."

Jane showed the four women to their rooms, where they oohed and ahhed over the décor. They were also delighted to be sharing a bath, although several jokes were made about setting up a morning schedule.

"Do you have any plans while you're here?" Jane asked.

"I brought a portable TV and DVD player, and we're going to spend a lot of time watching romantic movies," Lois said.

"Yeah, stuff that our husbands and kids laugh at us for watching at home," Misty said.

"And I have a small suitcase full of books," Christal said.

"And I have some board games," India added. "And if we get really bored, we each brought new makeup and hairstyling magazines, and we're going to give each other makeovers."

"Wow," Jane said. "You really *are* planning to have a slumber party."

Christal studied her hair. "I'm a stylist, Ms. Howard. You have great hair. I'd love to experiment with some styles if you have the time while we're here."

"I never do anything special with my hair," Jane said, flipping the ponytail she'd chosen for the day. "I lead a pretty active life and don't have time to fuss with it."

"How about if I fix it for you on Thanksgiving Day?" she offered. "That's a day to look special."

"I'll think about it, thanks, but I may not have time," Jane said. "I'm in charge of a big Thanksgiving dinner at Grace Chapel, which is right next door. Speaking of Thanksgiving dinner, don't tell me that you ladies are going to have a fun week, then leave on Thanksgiving Day and rush right home to cook a big meal."

"Not us," India said. "Our husbands said they would take care of everything. So on Thanksgiving, right after the game, we'll fly back to Kansas City, where we live, and they'll pick us up at the airport and take us straight home for a late celebration."

"I'm not sure how they'll manage to talk the kids into helping—you know teenagers—but that's their worry," Lois said.

"I'll let you girls get started on your partying then," Jane said. "If there's anything you need, please let us know."

She headed back downstairs to the foyer and there found Alice, Louise and two women, each of the latter with a suitcase at her side. One woman wore a loose brown polyester pantsuit, and the other wore a shapeless gray knit dress. They wore no makeup and had their hair pulled back in severe ponytails.

Jane offered her right hand. "Hi there. I'm Jane Howard."

Louise placed a card in her outstretched hand. "They don't talk," she whispered.

"*What?*"

"Read the card," Louise said.

We are on a retreat of silence until Thanksgiving Day. Please excuse us for not speaking and please do not ask us to write out anything.

Jane handed the card back to the woman in gray. "Have you taken a vow of silence?"

She shook her head.

"Just temporarily?"

She nodded.

"Well," Jane said, "I can't ask you your names then."

"This is Avis Goodwyn," Alice said, gesturing to the woman in gray. "And that is Hillary Perrino."

"Nice to meet you," Jane said.

Each woman nodded slowly, closing her eyes.

"Shall I show you to your rooms?" Jane asked, slightly unnerved. She felt like she was in a silent movie.

Avis nodded and lifted her suitcase. Hillary did the same.

"Right this way then," Jane said, ascending the staircase once again.

When she showed the women the Sunset and the Garden rooms, they, of course, said nothing. Jane thought she saw one of them blink, which she took as a sign of approval. After she'd gone through her routine speech about the room, bathroom and breakfast time, she asked them if they had any questions.

They looked at her, blinking like two orphaned owls.

"*Oops*, I guess not. Well, holler if you do...I mean, let us know... somehow...if you do."

She retreated back down the stairs, grateful to find Alice and Louise. "How did you ever get their names out of them?" she asked.

"I held out the reservation book and they pointed to their individual names," Alice said.

"I do not think they will be much trouble while they are here," Louise said dryly.

"At least we know they won't have any yelling matches or loud parties," Jane said.

Alice smiled. "Speaking of parties, I wonder how they will fare with our reunion women sharing the same floor."

Jane got an impish look on her face. "This could be an interesting week."

That afternoon, Louise drove to Melanie's house to take her to her doctor's appointment. Melanie's hands were shaking as she got into Louise's Cadillac, and she dropped her purse on the floorboard.

"Are you all right?" Louise asked.

"I'm just nervous, but I am also excited about getting my hearing checked out," Melanie said. "The thought of being able to hear clearly what's going on around me, being able to hear my kids..." She broke off, tearing up a bit. "I should have done this a long time ago."

Louise smiled at her. "Well, you're doing it now."

Melanie sniffled, then smiled back. "Yes, I am."

When they arrived at the parking lot of the doctor's office, Melanie squared her shoulders and walked with a look of resolve into the building. A pleasant-looking receptionist handed her insurance and medical papers to fill out, and soon Melanie was being called back to the examination room.

Melanie shot Louise a nervous glance as though her confidence had taken a nosedive. "Would you like me to go with you?" Louise asked.

Melanie released a pent-up breath. "That'd be great, Louise. Thanks."

The nurse led them back to the room. Melanie slowly seated herself in the examination chair and gripped the arms.

"The doctor will be with you shortly," the nurse said, smiling.

A minute ticked by, and Melanie didn't move. "Would you like a magazine?" Louise asked, gesturing to a full end table.

Melanie shook her head. "What do you think he'll do, Louise?"

"Why, I imagine he'll look at your ears and then—" A man in a white lab coat strode through the door and went directly to Melanie. "Hi, I'm Dr. Hal Paulis. You must be Melanie Brubaker."

"I am," she said, unclenching her grip on the chair long enough to shake his proffered hand. "This is my friend Louise Howard Smith. She came with me for support."

"Hello, Louise," Dr. Paulis said, shaking her hand as well. "Melanie, I think it's wonderful that you brought someone with you. Facing the unknown can be frightening, but it's always easier to bear when someone you trust is with you."

Melanie seemed to relax a little at his words, for she didn't cling to the chair again but dropped her hands in her lap.

"What brings you here today?" he asked.

Melanie took a deep breath. "I've noticed lately that my hearing's not as good as it used to be," she said. "To be honest, it hasn't been good for a long time."

"Let me tell you what I'm going to do, and maybe that will put you at ease," he said, smiling in a warm manner as if they'd been friends for a long time. He held up an instrument with a black cone-shaped piece attached at the end. "This is an otoscope, which will let me look inside your ears a bit."

"What do you expect to see?" Melanie asked, flinching as he brought the instrument to her ear.

"Nothing, I hope. But we want to rule out any blockage or physical damage that could be the cause of your hearing loss."

"Blockage?" Melanie's hands gripped the arm of the chair again.

Dr. Paulis smiled. "Well, there could be something unusual, but most likely something like a buildup of ear wax."

"Oh," Melanie said, relaxing.

Dr. Paulis examined her ears. When he was finished, Melanie said, "That's it? That's all that's involved?"

He smiled and nodded. "I don't find anything wrong, Mrs. Brubaker. No blockage or infection or anything abnormal that might cause your hearing loss. What I recommend at this point is that you see the audiologist who works with my office. Her name is Susannah Howell, and she'll guide you through a series of hearing tests so that we can get a better idea of what's going on."

"I have to see someone else?" Melanie asked in a small voice.

"Susannah is wonderful, and she'll put you right at ease," Dr. Paulis said. "If she finds anything of a physical nature, she'll report it to me. But if hearing aids are your best option and you choose to take that path, she can help you." He reached over to a counter and plucked a business card from a stand. "Here's her information. You can call her directly and make an appointment."

"Thank you so much, Doctor," Melanie said.

"If I don't see you again, good luck to you," he said. "It was nice to meet you, and you too, Mrs. Smith."

Louise nodded, and Dr. Paulis left. Melanie smiled wistfully at Louise. "I was hoping we could take care of everything today."

"You have one hurdle down," Louise said. "Just one or two more, and you'll be at the finish line."

"Will you go with me to the next appointment?" Melanie asked. "I know it's asking a lot."

"Not at all." Louise smiled. "I was never much of a runner, but I can definitely go the distance alongside you."

Chapter Sixteen

While Louise was out with Melanie and Alice was working, Jane took out the sweet-potato casserole, spooning
out a small portion for a taste test. While she waited for it to heat
in the microwave, she got out a piece of paper and a pen so she
could write down the ingredients she already recognized.

"*Hmm.* Sweet potatoes, of course," she mumbled to herself,
scribbling on the paper. "And coconut, pecans and probably a
little salt."

The microwave chimed, and she took out the dish. She
spooned out a small portion and tasted. "Butter. It has some kind
of sweetener, but what? White sugar? Brown sugar? No, those
wouldn't exactly be secret ingredients. It's not molasses or corn
syrup either."

Defeated for the moment, she finished eating the rest of the
portion she'd heated. Whatever was in the recipe, it made the
potatoes tasty.

Jane sighed. *That's enough recipe guessing for today. I'd do well to talk
to Craig Tracy about Thanksgiving, though. I've got Alice on board for her casserole, but I must get a list of the other donations.*

She put on her coat, gloves and scarf and walked toward town.
The trees were stripped of their leaves, the mighty oaks looking

like shivering hat racks against a somber sky as she trudged down Chapel Road. There was something dignified and sacred about the coming of winter, she mused. Just like the dignity and sacredness of old age. Of course, age was a matter of perspective. To the high school cheerleaders, she was older than winter, but she was still considered young by the World War II group.

A breeze scuttled leaves at her feet, and she hunched her shoulders against the chill. Mortimer Fineman and his group were still so energetic, even after having been through so much: a major depression, a world war, the social revolution of the 1960s. There was a time when she would have dismissed anyone over the age of thirty, but now that she was well past the three decades' mark herself, she thought differently.

"Let me be receptive to all people, of all ages," she murmured in prayer.

At Hill Street, she took a left and headed past several stores. Hope Collins, the waitress at the Coffee Shop, waved at her through the window. Jane thought about stopping in for a hot beverage but decided to press on to Craig's floral shop, Wild Things. The wonderful scents wafting from the Good Apple Bakery on the corner of Hill and Acorn Avenue almost caused her to abandon her resolve and pop in for a snack. As she hesitated near the bakery's door, she saw Lorrie Zell, who sometimes filled in as sales clerk at Nellie's dress shop for the eponymous Nellie Carter. The store was across the street from the Good Apple on Acorn Avenue. Lorrie was a tall, willowy woman in her late twenties who had a penchant for eclectic looks, although she worked in a store that sold mid- to high-priced classic clothing.

"Hi, Jane," Lorrie said, brushing back a dark lock of long wavy hair. "I'm taking a break to get a cup of tea at the Coffee Shop. Want to join me? There's something I'd like to talk to you about."

"Well, I..." Jane glanced at Craig's shop across the street. He would no doubt be there the rest of the day, so their discussion could wait. "Sure, Lorrie."

They headed back up the street to the Coffee Shop. Out of the corner of her eye, Jane studied Lorrie's ensemble. Her clothing was a marvel to most of Acorn Hill, because one never knew whether she would be dressed in the latest couture design or a peasant skirt and a T-shirt. Today she wore a stunning pale lime-green wool suit that she had adorned with chunky Mexican silver jewelry. Lorrie looked fabulous.

"That's a great outfit," Jane said. "That green is a good shade for you."

"Thanks," Lorrie said. "I was feeling a little down this morning, what with winter coming on soon, and green never fails to pick me up."

They entered the Coffee Shop and settled into a red vinyl booth. "Did you ever model?" Jane asked. "You've got great features, and I don't think there's anybody in town who can make an outfit look as good as you do."

Lorrie laughed. "Nia Komonos makes suits look pretty great. Nellie has been selling a lot more of them since Nia's been living in Acorn Hill."

"Hi, ladies," Hope said, approaching them with her order pad at the ready. "What'll it be today?"

"A cup of decaf for me," Jane said.

"Do you have any white tea?" Lorrie asked. "I'm trying to cut back on coffee."

Hope nodded. "I think June ordered a box of the stuff. She read that it was even healthier than green tea, so she figured others would have read the same thing and want to get in on the health craze."

"June's smart," Lorrie said.

"Coming right up," Hope said, heading for the kitchen.

"Is the shop busy?" Jane asked. "I haven't had much of a chance to pop in lately."

"I'm just working a few hours this week to help Nellie with her shipment of winter styles. She got in some interesting jackets, a little less mainstream than what she usually carries. You might want to check them out."

"Thanks," Jane said, hoping that she had been given a compliment.

Lorrie cleared her throat. "I wanted to talk to you about Thanksgiving. I heard you and Craig were heading up the feast at Grace Chapel."

"Yes, and I hope you know that you are invited if you'd like to join us."

"I'm not a member of your church," Lorrie said, "or any other church, for that matter."

Jane shrugged. "Yes, I know, but that doesn't matter. You're still welcome. You can bring a dish if you want to, or not. I'm sure we'll have plenty of food."

Lorrie looked uncomfortable. "That's just it. I'm concerned about the menu."

"That's a coincidence," Jane said, smiling. "I was just on my way to talk to Craig Tracy when I ran into you. He and I are working on the dinner together, and I'm afraid we're behind in getting things done. Would you like to help us?"

"No," Lorrie said. She folded her hands together on top of the table. "Jane, I'm not pleased that you're serving turkey for the dinner."

Jane sat up straight. "What? But it's Thanksgiving. Thanksgiving means turkey."

"Exactly," Lorrie said. "Do you know how many turkeys are executed for the holiday?"

"I haven't taken an exact count, no," Jane said. She leaned forward. "Are you a vegetarian, Lorrie?"

She nodded. "I recently decided to make a lifestyle change, and now I'm concerned about holidays like Thanksgiving being a time of slaughter."

Hope brought their mugs and set them down. "White tea for you, Lorrie, and decaf for you, Jane. Anything else?"

Jane shook her head, wordless, still trying to absorb what Lorrie had said. Hope retreated and Lorrie sipped her tea. "Good stuff," she said.

Jane took a sip as well, then set down her mug. "What do you want me to do, Lorrie?" she asked.

"I want you not to serve turkey for the dinner."

Jane drew a deep breath. "I can't do that, Lorrie. Most people like turkey and think of it as the central part of the Thanksgiving meal." She paused. "I like turkey. It's tradition to have it."

"Then I'm afraid I can't attend," she said, draining her cup. She put a few dollar bills on the table. "I'm sorry you won't change your mind, Jane. I'd better get back to work."

"But—" Jane turned, but Lorrie was already heading for the door. Jane sighed and finished sipping her coffee. She had known many vegetarians, particularly when she lived in San Francisco, but she couldn't remember any who had been quite so militant.

"Everything okay?" Hope said, picking up Lorrie's empty cup.

"I'm not sure," Jane said, still bewildered.

⌒

After finishing her coffee, she didn't have the heart to talk to Craig just yet, so she headed for Sylvia's Buttons. She needed to talk to Sylvia anyway about their mascot friend.

Sylvia had gotten into the spirit of the season, for her window was decorated with smiling male and female pilgrim and Native American mannequins, a papier-mâché blunderbuss and a large ceramic turkey. Jane winced at the sight of the last item.

When Jane entered the shop, it appeared to be empty; Sylvia soon entered from the back room. Seeing it was Jane, her face relaxed. "Oh, I'm glad it's you."

"I'm always glad it's me too," Jane said, smiling. "What's up?"

"Our mascot is here," Sylvia said, nodding toward the back. "We were just going over some ideas. Do you have time to join us?"

"Absolutely," Jane said.

She followed Sylvia to the back of the store. Standing in the corner was the Patriot costume, not yet completed. "How's that going?" Jane asked.

"Very well," Sylvia said.

In the back of the store was the mystery mascot who had phoned Jane.

"Hi, Carole," Jane said, greeting Franklin High's biggest bookworm.

"Hello, Ms. Howard," Carole said.

"How's the Franklin High literary magazine going?"

"Really well." The magazine was one subject that made Carole's eyes sparkle. "I think we're going to have an outstanding one this year. We're getting lots of excellent contributions."

Jane sat down on one of the stools around Sylvia's cutting table. "Tell me again why you don't want anybody to know that you're auditioning as the mascot."

Carole looked at the ground and worked the toe of her shoe against the carpet. "I'm not very popular at school."

"And so...?" Jane prompted.

"And so I don't want anybody to laugh at me. If they don't know who I am, and I bomb, then they won't have a chance."

"But what if you do well?" Sylvia asked, putting an arm around the girl. "I think you've got potential, kiddo."

"I'm not really a cheerleader type," Carole said. "To be honest, I don't know why I'm doing this. I just wanted to try something new, to break out of my usual routine and see what it's like to be extroverted for a change."

"There's nothing wrong with being introverted," Jane said. "You do have friends, don't you?"

Carole nodded. "They're like me, though. Brainy." The way she said the word, it sounded like an affliction rather than a gift.

Jane glanced at Sylvia. Since they'd been playing at cheerleading again these past weeks, they had reminisced about high school and what a difficult time of life it was. It would be easy to tell Carole that her intelligence would be more highly valued later in life than all the social action of the more popular kids, but she would learn that soon enough when she went to college.

"There's no reason you can't be brainy *and* have fun doing something new and exciting," Sylvia said.

"Yes," Jane said. "And as long you'd like, we'll keep your secret."

Carole smiled. "Thank you. You two have been so helpful already."

"I wish I could let you practice with the Patriot costume," Sylvia said, "but it wouldn't be fair to the other kid who is auditioning."

"I understand," Carole said.

"Since the costume involves a large foam and latex head, though," Sylvia said, "you might want to try rehearsing with a box. I don't think that's unfair. So I took this cardboard box and cut out some eye holes so that you can see what you're doing."

She handed Carole a large box, and the girl smiled. "This is great. Thanks. Do you two have time to show me a cheer or two?"

"Sure," Jane said. "You know, I was thinking...remember that 1930s cheer, Sylvia, the one that the cheerleaders looked at us like we were crazy for using?"

Sylvia nodded. "Down by the river, skit skat?"

"That's the one," Jane said. "How about if Carole wore some 1930s clothes over the Patriot costume so that she would look like an authentic 1930s cheerleader?"

Sylvia smiled. "Something really old school?"

"That's what I'm thinking," Jane said.

"I've got some old clothes that I've used in window displays over the years. They might work for that."

"They'd have to be big to fit over the costume, wouldn't they?" Carole said.

"Somewhat big," Sylvia said. "But remember that from the neck down, the Patriot costume is just regular clothes—a blue vest with a white lace cravat at the neck, a navy blue cutaway coat, red breeches and white stockings."

"It's going to be great," Carole said, "even if I don't win."

Jane glanced at her watch. "If we're going to practice, we'd better get started. I still need to talk to Craig about Thanksgiving dinner."

"All right, Carole," Sylvia said. "Pretend that you're the Franklin High Patriot. People are looking for you to lead them, but mostly they're looking for you to have fun. Because if you have fun at what you're doing, they'll have fun."

Carole nodded, then put the box over her head. She put her hands on her hips and struck an authoritative pose. "Now what's this skit-skat cheer you two were talking about?"

Jane and Sylvia grinned, lining up beside her. "Watch how we move and follow along," Sylvia said. "We'll go slowly. Ready? Okay!"

After they finished practicing, Jane drank a bottle of spring water that Sylvia gave her. Carole snuck out the back door and headed home, and after she cooled down, Jane left for Craig Tracy's. Since it was near the end of the day, she was glad to find him still in Wild Things.

"Hi, Jane, I'm glad you caught me," he said. "I was about to close up shop."

"Slow day?" she asked.

He nodded. "I think it's going to pick up tomorrow, though, and stay busy until Thanksgiving. Then after that it will be really busy. Business is pretty steady until Christmas, what with people buying poinsettias, wreaths and holiday arrangements."

"I'm sorry I haven't contacted you about the Thanksgiving feast," she said. "It's not like me to put things off."

"I hear you've been busy."

Jane leaned her elbows on the counter, grinning. "And just what have you heard?"

He smiled back. "That you were first practicing to help the cheerleaders, and now you're helping someone practice for the Patriot mascot auditions."

"My, my, word travels fast, doesn't it?"

Craig spread his hands wide. "This is Acorn Hill, Jane."

Jane looked at him sideways. "You don't know *who* I'm helping for the mascot job, do you?"

He shook his head. "Apparently it's still possible to keep some secrets in this small town."

Jane let out a sigh of relief. "Thank goodness. Okay, let's get down to business. Do you have any idea how many people we should expect?"

Craig gave her a figure, based on people he'd talked to.

Jane whistled, like the sound of a bomb being dropped. "That many?"

"'Fraid so."

She sighed. "I really want this dinner to be special. I want to include people that normally don't come to church events. I already lost one person today."

"Who was that?"

"Lorrie Zell." Jane told him about her request that they not serve turkey.

"We could have an all-vegetarian dinner," he said jokingly.

Jane smiled. "I don't know of any other vegetarians in Acorn Hill. Lorrie would be our only guest. Anyway, how are we on turkeys? Do we have enough volunteers cooking them?"

"I think there are enough, but I'll cook one just to have extra."

"I'll do one as well," Jane said. "Alice is going to make several sweet-potato casseroles, and we have lots of people bringing mashed potatoes, stuffing and cranberry sauce."

Craig agreed to check with friends and parishioners about filling the slots for other side dishes and desserts, and Jane said that she'd do the same.

Heading back toward Grace Chapel Inn, she saw Lorrie locking the front door of Nellie's, preparing to leave for the day. Jane crossed over to her side of the street. "Lorrie?"

She jumped. "Oh! You startled me, Jane."

"I just wanted to say that I'm sorry we left on such a bad note. I hope we can still be friends. I wouldn't want a little turkey to divide us," she said, trying to make a small joke.

Lorrie frowned. "It's not a laughing matter, Jane. Turkeys are animals, just like dogs and cats. They may not be as cute and cuddly, but they have a right to exist."

"I understand your position, but not everyone feels that way. Are you going to shun the rest of us because of your beliefs?"

"Are you going to shun *me*?" Lorrie shot back.

"No," Jane said patiently. "You are welcome to attend the dinner. You don't have to eat the turkey. There will be lots of other food."

Lorrie shook her head. "I can't sit there and pretend it's all right."

"I'm sorry, then," Jane said. "But I do hope we can still be friends."

"I'm not sure. See you later, Jane," Lorrie said, then turned and walked toward her home.

With a slightly heavy heart, Jane did the same.

Alice returned from work that afternoon tired but not bone weary. Nursing demanded more some days than others, and today had been fairly slow, just routine work with no emergencies and no surprises.

She went upstairs to change out of her uniform. After putting on her jeans and a blue plaid shirt, she sat in her easy chair for a few moments to read some of the mystery she had started,

Deadly Silent. Written by her favorite mystery author, the novel centered on a villain who never said a word as he methodically plotted and executed his crimes.

The book became a little too unnerving, especially with the coming of dusk. She set the book aside and decided to head for the kitchen. No doubt Jane would appreciate some help with dinner preparations.

When she reached the second floor, where the guest rooms were located, Alice ran into Christal and Misty. The twins were chasing their cousins, India and Lois, down the stairs. India wore three-inch spiked heels, and Lois wore navy-blue Keds. Both were giggling like school girls.

"What's the hurry?" she asked, hoping the women didn't collide with one another or fall down the stairs.

"We're playing tag," Christal said, pausing long enough to answer Alice. Her dark eyes were shining.

Her sister Misty yelled, "Come on, Christal. They're getting away!"

"Oops, gotta run!" Christal said. Before Alice could say another word, or warn them to slow down, the four women were through the front door and outside on the porch.

Two doors opened on the guest room floor. Avis Goodwyn and Hillary Perrino, the silent retreaters, peered out like disapproving bookends.

How did they time that to the exact moment? Remembering the mystery she'd been reading, Alice felt a chill. There was something unnerving about people who refused to speak.

"Did the noise bother you?" she asked.

They nodded slowly, two pairs of unblinking eyes staring back at her.

"I'm sorry," she said. "I'll speak to them about it." Inspiration struck, and she smiled. "Actually, my sisters and I were going to have a little after-dinner coffee and dessert in the dining room for our guests. Would you like to join us?"

Without mutual consultation, the women shook their heads in rhythm, two slow measured shakes indicating no.

Alice cleared her throat, edging toward the staircase. "If you change your mind, feel free to join us around seven thirty."

The doors shut resolutely and Alice fled down the stairs.

I'm just being ridiculous. I probably shouldn't read books that frighten me so much.

Nevertheless, she hurried into the kitchen, delighted to find both Jane and Louise. Jane chopped vegetables on a cutting board, and Louise sat at the table, sipping a cup of tea and reading the weekly edition of the *Acorn Nutshell*. Wendell, the tabby cat who had been Daniel Howard's before his death, was playing with a catnip mouse under the table. He gave it a swat, and it skittered under the refrigerator.

"You'll have to wait until later to get that back, I'm afraid," Alice said, lifting the tabby. She pulled a chair away from the table and put Wendell in her lap. Forgetting the errant toy for a moment, he curled up for a quick snooze.

"I ran into our guests, almost literally," Alice said, describing her encounter with the women's group and the two silent retreaters.

Louise laid the newspaper aside. "I saw Hillary and Avis earlier too. They had wandered down to Father's library and were studying the books."

"I saw them walking outside when I came back from Craig's," Jane said. "They seemed to be in their own world."

"Maybe they are," Alice said. "Maybe they're from another planet."

Louise laughed. "That doesn't sound like you, Alice. Jane, maybe."

"Hey!" Jane said. "I think I should be offended at that."

"I just meant that you had a mind more given to speculation, dear," Louise said soothingly.

"Yes, and one much more creative than mine," Alice said. "Although I have to admit that I've let my imagination get away with me once today already."

"It's this time of year," Jane said, sighing. "It's getting dark much earlier. Winter is on its way."

"Winter has its charms," Louise said. "It allows for solitude and reflection."

Jane sighed again, and Alice turned to her. "What's wrong?"

Jane explained about the situation with Lorrie Zell.

Louise smiled at the thought of Lorrie being so insistent that they not serve turkey, but Alice frowned. "I understand how she feels, but I can't say that I've felt the urge to become vegetarian over my beliefs. As much as I love animals, God did put them on earth to serve man."

"I don't think I could give up turkey for the holidays," Louise said. "Nor give up meat altogether. I can understand not wanting to be cruel to animals, but it's not as if turkeys are killed merely for sport."

"I know, but I hate that she feels alienated," Jane said. "I don't want anybody to feel like she's not welcome at the Thanksgiving dinner, for whatever reason."

"I wish there was something we could do," Alice said. "I feel the same way you do, Jane." Alice rose and put her arm around her sister. "Thanksgiving is about more than turkeys or food, for that matter. It's about thanking God for what He has given us. And it's about fellowship."

"Yes, and the Grace Chapel feast combines both of those elements," Louise said.

Jane smiled at her sisters. "You are right. I just wish there was some way for us to show Lorrie that she is part of this fellowship no matter what she prefers on her plate." Jane's eyes lit up and she snapped her fingers. "I got it!"

"What?" Alice asked.

Jane shook her head. "I don't want to say anything yet. I want to talk to Craig first, since he's my cochair."

Alice and Louise looked at each other. They knew that when Jane got that light in her eyes, something creative was certain to follow.

Chapter Seventeen

The next morning, which was Thursday, Louise picked up Melanie to take her to the audiologist's office. She had been fortunate to get an appointment for the day after she called to schedule one. Susannah Howell met them at the door to her office, offering a big smile along with her hand. "It's nice to meet you, Melanie."

"This is my friend Louise Howard Smith," she replied. "I brought her for moral support, if that's all right."

"It certainly is," Susannah said. "Come in and let's get started."

She led the way into a large room dominated by an audiometer, a large tabletop panel filled with knobs, buttons and switches. In one corner was a floor-to-ceiling booth with a door. "We'll get started right away, Melanie. Is it all right if I call you Melanie?"

"Certainly."

"Have a seat in the booth here. Mrs. Smith, you can sit on that chair against the wall, behind where I'll be sitting."

Melanie sat on a stool in the booth, and Susannah stood in the doorway where she could be heard by both women. "What I'm going to have you do is put on these headphones, and I'll be speaking to you from the audiometer. You'll be able to see me through the side window. We'll run through a series of tests that will tell me more about your hearing loss. Okay?"

"I guess that's what I'm here for," Melanie said.

"The booth eliminates environmental sounds that might interfere with the tests," Susannah explained. "If you're all right, I'll close the door and we can get started."

Louise could see Melanie through the window directly in front of the audiometer. Susannah sat and tweaked a few of the controls. "All right, Melanie," she said. "I'm going to test your speech-reception threshold first. I'll say a few words, and I'd like you to repeat them after me. If there's something you don't understand, just guess, if you can. Do you understand?"

Melanie nodded.

"Say baseball."

"Baseball," Melanie responded.

"Fire truck."

"Fire truck."

Susannah ran through a list of words, working the controls of the machine as she did so. Several times she said a word, and Melanie didn't respond or looked through the window quizzically at Susannah.

When she was finished, Susannah made some marks on a chart. "All right, Melanie, now I'm going to give you a pure-tone test, which checks your ability to hear sounds under good conditions. I'll give you a series of tones, and you raise your hand when you hear one. All right?"

Melanie nodded. Again Susannah adjusted the controls, and Louise could see Melanie raise and lower her hand. A few times she started to raise her hand, then lowered it quickly or looked at Susannah as though she wasn't certain she'd heard anything.

When she was finished, Susannah made some more marks on the chart. "I'm coming into the booth now, so you can remove the headphones."

Melanie did, and Susannah opened the door, another head-phone-looking device in her hands. "This is a bone-conduction test. In laymen's terms, we're testing your hearing nerve. I'm going to put this end, a vibrator, on your mastoid bone, which is behind your ear. This can tell me more about your hearing loss—whether surgery or medicine will help, or whether hearing aids would be the best answer."

"It won't hurt, will it?" Melanie asked.

"Not at all," Susannah said.

In no time, she was finished and smiling. "One more test, then we're finished, Melanie. Step on out of the booth to my tym-panometer. This will tell me how well your eardrum is moving and whether your middle ear is normal."

"I think my kids have had this test before," Melanie said.

"I'm sure they have. It's something doctors often check for in young children when they suspect an ear infection, to make sure they don't have fluid in their ear. When they do, or if there is some other problem in the middle ear, it can keep your eardrum from vibrating..."

"...and cause hearing problems," Melanie finished.

"Exactly," Susannah said.

She performed the test, then wrote some notes for several minutes. At last she looked up. "Based on your results, I'd say that hearing aids would be your best answer. You have a relatively flat forty- to fifty-decibel hearing loss, bilaterally."

Melanie blinked. "What does that mean?"

Susannah held out a piece of paper. "Mrs. Smith, you might want to move closer to see this too."

Louise did so, and she saw a graph on the paper.

"This is how we measure hearing," Susannah explained. "The lines at the top measure frequency levels in hertz, and the lines along the side measure hearing levels in decibels. Normal hearing is anywhere from around the zero to twenty-five decibel level. Your normal level is around forty to fifty decibels, and it stays pretty constant, even when the frequency is higher. That's why we call it flat."

Louise could see a series of dots connected by lines ranging from the forty to fifty level on the chart.

"Normally, as people lose their hearing with age, the graphed line drops off. In other words, people generally lose the ability to hear higher pitches as they get older. Since yours remains flat, I suspect that unless you've worked around loud noise a lot, your hearing loss is most likely hereditary."

"Is that bad?" Melanie asked.

"No hearing loss is good, but fortunately, I think you'll find life much improved if you get hearing aids. Are you interested in learning more about those?"

Melanie looked at Louise. Louise could see the look of unhappiness on her friend's face. Then, as if she remembered the car accident, Melanie turned toward Susannah again. "I'm interested. Tell me all about them."

The audiologist retrieved a clear plastic box with several items inside. "Based on your particular hearing loss, I have several brands to recommend, but what is best for you mainly depends on the style you'd like and, like purchasing any major item, on how much money you want to spend. Most hearing aids today are digital. They've come such a long way since I first became an audiologist. Think of each one as a computer in your ear, and the different models are different types of computers, ranging from an ATM to a sleek laptop."

She opened the lid to the box, which was filled with hearing aids. Louise could see that they were of different shapes and sizes. Susannah held up one for Melanie's inspection. "Let's start with the low end first. This is known as a behind-the-ear model and is the type that people normally think of when you say *hearing aids*. This plastic piece fits over the ear, and this smaller attached piece fits in your ear. It's the most visible of all the hearing aids, with the microphone on the outside."

"My grandfather had something like that," Melanie said.

Susannah laughed. "I don't know many people who actually prefer that model anymore, but sometimes it's just the right hearing aid for someone with, say, severe hearing loss. It's also the least expensive model." She held up a small version, without the over-the-ear piece. "This fits in the ear canal and fills the bowl of your ear."

"That's still a little big," Melanie said.

"I figured you might say that." Susannah smiled. She went on to show Melanie one that half filled the bowl of an ear, and then one that was hardly visible at all.

Melanie examined them all, one at a time. Then Susannah handed her a tiny hearing aid and said proudly, "And this is known as a CIC—completely in the canal. It's the smallest hearing aid made."

"Wow," Melanie said, taking it. "That *is* small. Is it possible to lose it inside your ear?"

"No, because it's custom made to fit. It can't go in the canal too deep. See that little plastic string? It's what you use to take the aid out of your ear."

Melanie giggled. "I thought that it was an antenna."

Susannah smiled. "The next thing we should talk about is cost." She held up each hearing aid and gave an average price. By the time she got to the smallest hearing aid, Louise noticed that Melanie's eyes had widened considerably.

"What do you recommend?" she asked.

"I tell my patients to think about their lifestyle. If you're very active and around a lot of people, you would probably need a top-of-the-line model. If you're more solitary and don't get out much, then you would do fine with an entry-level or midrange model. The cost is linked to performance."

Melanie thought for a moment, then she smiled. "I already know what I want," she said.

"That was fast." Susannah glanced at Louise, and they both laughed.

"I don't want the tiny one. I'm still afraid I would lose it. I want the next size up."

"The one that's still in the ear?"

Melanie nodded. "I don't think it would show very much, and it seems like it would be a good model."

"For your level of hearing loss, I think it is a wonderful choice." Susannah set the box of samples on the counter. "If you're sure that's what you want, let's do a few more hearing measures to test your hearing comfort level. Then I'll make molds of your ears to send to the manufacturer."

Susannah directed Melanie back into the booth, then determined where speech was more and less comfortable for Melanie's hearing level. Then Susannah had Melanie sit on a chair, and she used what looked like a caulking gun on first one of Melanie's ear canals and then the other. When the impressions were finished, she said, "I'll send these off, and you should have your hearing aids next week."

"That fast?"

Susannah smiled. "I'll give you a call, but with luck they'll arrive before the holiday."

Melanie signed a contract for the hearing aids, and after they thanked the audiologist, she and Louise headed for the parking lot. "Won't it be great if I *do* get the hearing aids by Thanksgiving? It will be so wonderful to be able to hear while we're all gathered together to eat."

For some reason, Louise thought of Lorrie Zell alone on Thanksgiving, and a wave of sympathy flooded her.

That afternoon, Jane met with Sylvia and Carole Keith in the back of Sylvia's shop. Try as they might, she and Sylvia were not able to get Carole enthusiastic about practicing that day.

"What's wrong?" Sylvia asked the girl.

"Everything," she said, slumping to the floor. "I just don't think I can do this."

Sylvia and Jane took a breather and sat cross-legged beside

her. "Sure you can," Jane said. "You've come too far to back out now. Besides, you've already said that you're committed to this."

"Even with that giant Patriot's head hiding my face, I feel people will know who I am. And besides, the mascot isn't supposed to talk. How can I do any cheers?"

Sylvia looked at Jane. "I hadn't thought of that."

"Me either," Jane admitted. "Sylvia and I have been so focused on learning the cheers ourselves, we didn't stop to think about what you actually needed."

"Yes, and we're so sorry, Carole," Sylvia said. Jane nodded in agreement.

Carole sighed. "At least the cheerleaders have each other to help out. The mascot is pretty much by himself."

"Who says?" Jane demanded. "It seems to me that I remember the cheerleaders doing routines with the mascot at the last game."

"Yes, but they'd rehearsed those in advance. The other person auditioning for the mascot position is working with the cheerleaders already."

"You still have a week. Why don't you do that too?" Sylvia asked.

"I don't want anyone to know I'm doing this, remember?"

Jane looked at Sylvia and grinned a lopsided smile. "Well, what do you think?"

Sylvia blinked. "What do I think about what?"

"Why can't we help Carole out?"

"What, and cheerlead?" Sylvia got to her feet.

Jane stood up as well. "Why not? If Carole's going for a humorous routine, what could be funnier than two women our age trying to do some cheers?"

Sylvia thought for a moment. "We *could* cobble together some funny, old-timey cheerleader costumes before next week."

"Sure!" Jane said. "You and I can yell all the cheers, and Carole, you can do funny moves."

"You can lead us!" Sylvia said. "You sign to us which cheers to do and—"

"Signs!" Jane said. "That's brilliant. We can hold up signs to get the crowd to cheer back, and—"

She broke off, glancing down at Carole, who was still seated on the floor. "I'm sorry. I'm rambling and running away with ideas when you should be the one to come up with them." She looked guiltily at Sylvia, who lowered her head.

"I'm sorry," Sylvia said. "We shouldn't have overstepped."

Carole looked at each of them in turn, then broke into a wide smile. "I think you two have wonderful ideas. And it would be fun to do them with you. If you helped me, I wouldn't be as scared, and I think the three of us could really pump up the crowd."

"Great!" Jane said. She flopped back down onto the floor, and Sylvia joined her. "Let's do some more creative planning."

Late that afternoon, Alice sat in the living room in the overstuffed burgundy chair, a fire burning in the fireplace. She had decided to give *Deadly Silent* another chance, promising herself that she would keep one foot in reality, so to speak, while she read. Instead she became so engrossed in the book that she lost track of time. When she glanced up, she saw that the sky had grown dark. It was just after five o'clock, and the weather had taken a turn for the worse.

"It's dark in here," she whispered to herself, wishing she had turned on more lamps than just the one she had been reading by.

Wind whipped through the trees, and rain pelted the window.

Alice heard a creak. She turned her head in the direction of Madeleine Howard's antique rocking chair. Was it her imagination, or was the chair in motion?

She forced herself to relax. "This is ridiculous," she muttered, rising from her chair to head for the door. "There's nothing frightening about—" A branch smacked against the window, and she automatically looked toward it. When she turned back, Hillary and Avis stood in the doorway, watching her. Alice dropped the book, and her hand went to her throat. "I'm sorry. You startled me."

They stepped forward, and Hillary put a hand on Alice's arm. Alice could feel the goose bumps rise under the woman's hand. "It's chilly in here," she said by way of explanation, not wanting to hurt the woman's feelings.

Hillary smiled. Avis moved behind Alice, out of her peripheral vision.

"What are you—?" Alice tried to turn so that she could keep an eye on both of them, but Hillary's hand seemed to clamp tighter. Alice sucked in her breath, just as the rain began to come down even harder. Sensing someone behind her, Alice let out a small squeal. "Ah!" She jumped, half expecting to feel the cold blade of the silent murderer's knife in her back.

Instead, she felt Avis arranging the sofa throw around her shoulders.

"Thank you," she said, feeling slightly more than ridiculous. Hillary patted Alice's hand, then dropped her hold. Avis stood beside Hillary, and they both smiled, silent as always. "Were you two looking for me?" Alice asked.

Hillary nodded, pantomiming drinking from a cup.

"You want something to drink," Alice said.

Hillary and Avis nodded.

"Something hot?"

They nodded faster.

"Coffee?"

They looked at each other, then shook their heads.

"Tea?"

They nodded.

Alice let out a quiet sigh. How was she ever going to find out if they wanted black, green or white tea, not to mention caffeinated or decaf? She supposed they could always point to what they wanted.

"Why don't you two follow me to the kitchen? We'll see what Jane has in the pantry there."

They stood back, allowing Alice to lead the way through the door. Feeling a bit like Sacagawea, still warmed in the throw, Alice led the way.

Rain was still falling steadily when Alice recounted the story to Louise and Jane over dinner. The corner of Louise's mouth turned up slightly in amusement, but Jane let out a spirited laugh.

"It was an honest mistake," Alice said. "Between the book and the weather—"

"—and the way those two creep around. Honestly, I don't blame you, Alice, but it's still funny," Jane said.

"Perhaps you should not bother finishing that book," Louise said gently. "If it is only going to upset you and make you suspicious of our guests, you might do well to set it aside and move on to something more uplifting."

"I suppose you're right," Alice said with a sigh, "but it's so well written. And it's by one of my favorite authors."

Louise took a bite of the jambalaya Jane had made for dinner. "This is delicious, Jane. Thank you for going easy on the spices."

"You're welcome." Jane grinned. "I made a spicier portion for myself because I like a little more *zing* to my food than you and Alice prefer."

"How is the mascot rehearsal coming?" Alice asked.

Jane smiled broadly. "I think our mascot has a good chance at winning. If he doesn't, it's certainly not for lack of practice or brainstorming."

"Speaking of storm," Louise said, "if you think the weather tonight is bad, Melanie and I heard a weather report on the way back from Potterston. It's still a week away, but things don't look good for the holiday."

"Not more rain," Jane said, groaning.

"I heard the same report," Alice said. "It could mean rain or even snow."

"But not only is Thanksgiving next Thursday, that's also the day of the football game!" Jane said. "What if they have to postpone it? Everyone would be so disappointed. Is there an anti-rain dance we can perform?"

"I don't think so," Louise said, "but I am sure that if there is, you will find out the steps for the routine."

Chapter Eighteen

*S*unday afternoon, Louise played the piano alone in the parlor. It was something that she loved to do, but between giving lessons and seeing to the needs of Grace Chapel Inn's guests, musical time for herself was rare. Today, she spent the time with Chopin, as the mood of his nocturnes seemed to fit the weather. The rain had stopped, but an ominous gray lingered outside.

When she finished, Louise stacked the sheet music neatly and exited the parlor. She decided to go upstairs to her room for a brief nap. On the second floor all was quiet from the Garden and Sunset rooms where Avis and Hillary were staying, but laughter emanated from the Symphony Room.

Louise paused on her way to the third floor. She sniffed the air. Something was burning! The odor was coming from the Symphony Room, so she tapped on the door. "Is everything all right in there?"

Christal opened the door. A multitude of tiny rollers loaded down her hair, and a cucumber-green cosmetic masque covered her face. "Oh hi, Louise," she said. "Are we making too much noise?"

Louise glanced into the room. Behind Christal, Misty, India and Lois were styling each other's hair and were surrounded by an assortment of cosmetics. "I thought I smelled something burning," she said.

"Yikes!" Christal made a dash for a travel iron on a book on the floor in the corner. "Girls, the sandwich!"

Christal lifted the iron, which had been facedown. Misty picked up a bundled square of foil. She managed to open it, revealing burned slices of bread with equally burned oozing cheese.

Christal sighed. "So much for the grilled cheese sandwich."

Louise didn't know what to say. As far as she could remember, no one had ever before tried to cook in their rooms. "It's not a good idea to do that," she said, as gently as she could under the circumstances. "Please don't do so again."

"Sorry 'bout that," India said, bounding over. She deftly unplugged the iron, taking care not to smudge her obviously fresh nail polish. Proceeding to wave her hands in the air to hasten the drying process, she smiled at Louise. "You probably think we're a little crazy."

Louise resisted the urge to raise an eyebrow and chose to say nothing.

India kept smiling. "You see, the four of us used to be suite mates in our college dorm. We used to make grilled cheese sandwiches with our iron all the time. We thought we'd try it again, but obviously we got involved in our beauty session."

"I'm glad it was only the sandwich and that nothing else burned," Louise said.

"I'm sorry," India said. "We won't try to make any more."

"What about the cheese dip in the coffee pot?" Misty asked.

"*What?*" Louise tried to keep calm, but that was becoming difficult.

Misty held up a small plastic electric coffee pot. "In college we always used one to heat up soup..."

"...and cheese dip," Lois said, smacking her lips. "*Mmm.* Velveeta and tomatoes."

Louise grimaced. Jane had obviously spoiled her, for she had no taste for such culinary adventures. "If you'd like a snack—of nearly any sort," she was careful to add, "ask Jane. She can usually whip something up in the kitchen and you can, ah...you can pretend she's the head of the cafeteria or something."

"Thanks, Louise," India said, putting a manicured hand on Louise's arm. "I'm sorry about the grilled cheese and the dip. We promise not to cook anything in our rooms again."

"Just let Jane know whatever you want." She closed the door. In the hallway, she saw Hillary and Avis peeking out their doors, their unadorned hair and faces a stark contrast to the four beauty queens in the other rooms.

Louise nodded to the women. "I'm sorry to disturb you. If our other guests are too loud, please let me know, and I'll speak to them."

How Avis and Hillary would signal this was beyond Louise's comprehension, but she had to mention it anyway. The two women shrugged, however, and ducked inside their rooms, shutting their doors softly.

The next day, Jane and Sylvia met with Carole Keith. Only three days remained until the Thanksgiving Day game. Sylvia had started sewing cheerleading costumes for herself and Jane, which she proudly showed off in the back of her store.

"They're adorable," Carole said. "I'm so glad you two will be there to help me."

"We won't be able to perform Herkies very well," Jane warned, referring to the well-known cheerleading jump.

"But that's the fun of it," Carole said. "I've done some research into the history of cheerleading, and they didn't jump a lot way back when, and they certainly didn't choreograph their routines the way I'm sure the Franklin High cheerleaders will."

"She's right," Sylvia said. "These costumes will play up our weakness."

"What? Bad joints? Varicose veins?" Jane asked, laughing.

"Hey, we can still yell with the best of them," Sylvia said. "Rachel Holtzmann at the antique store is lending us these old cheerleading megaphones."

Jane grinned. "This really *is* going to be fun. Carole, thanks for letting Sylvia and me have one more go at cheerleading."

"Thank *you* for letting me have my first try at it," she said, smiling shyly.

"You did check this out with Mrs. Thrush, the cheerleading sponsor, right?" Sylvia asked. "I don't want to get you in trouble if we appear on the football field with you."

"Other than my parents and you guys, she's the only one who

knows that I'm auditioning. When I told her what we wanted to do, she was behind us all the way."

Jane grinned. "Then on Thursday, let's go go, get 'em get 'em!"

～

On the way home, Jane stopped by Nellie Carter's clothing store. Fortunately, Lorrie didn't have any customers, so Jane sat with her for a while, discussing the plans for the Thanksgiving dinner that she and Craig had come up with.

"You would do that...for me?" Lorrie finally said in a quiet voice.

"I count you as a friend," Jane said, "and I would hate for you not to attend the dinner because you were uncomfortable. I can't *not* have turkey, but I can try to make it easier for you."

"By having tofu turkey?"

"Yep." Jane grinned. "I've eaten tofu turkey, and other tofu dishes, and they're good."

Lorrie nodded. "I don't understand why more people don't at least try it before they pass judgment."

"So you'll come?"

Lorrie shifted uncomfortably. "I don't know, Jane. It still bothers me to be there when other people are eating meat."

"I understand how you feel," Jane said, "but until someone opens a vegan restaurant, you'll have this dilemma whenever you eat outside your home."

"That's true." Lorrie thought for a moment. "I don't have anyone to spend Thanksgiving with, and I would like to be with friends."

"Then you'll come?" Jane asked.

Lorrie smiled. "What dish can I bring?"

"Any kind of casserole or dessert would be good," Jane said, then smiled. "I'm so glad you'll be with us, Lorrie."

ॐ

When she got back to Grace Chapel Inn, Jane went straight upstairs to Alice's bedroom and knocked on her door. When Alice invited her in, Jane found her sister reading *Deadly Silent*. "You really should give up that book," she said. "At least wait until summer when the weather's nicer."

"How's it looking outside?" Alice asked, marking her place with a piece of paper.

"Not good." Jane shook her head. "I think we're going to be in for a storm. We should have a contingency plan for our guests, in case they aren't able to leave to go home because of the weather."

"That's a good idea. We should speak to Louise," Alice said, rising.

Jane blocked the door. "Not so fast. I have a few questions for you first."

"This must be about the sweet potatoes."

"The secret ingredient must involve something with sugar, am I right?"

"Guess the ingredient, and I'll tell you," Alice said, smiling.

Jane thought for a moment. "Maple syrup?"

Alice shook her head.

"Corn syrup?"

"No."

"Molasses? Honey?"

"No and no," Alice said.

Jane sighed, frustrated. "It's something more than sugar, but something with sugar in it. Okay, Alice, you win this round. I'll keep investigating."

Alice grinned. "Let's go talk to Louise."

By Tuesday, the gray weather had still not lifted. By that evening, the weather forecast predicted a snowstorm. By Wednesday morning, the snow was a reality.

The sisters called all the guests to the dining room before breakfast, but it was obvious that they already realized what was at stake, as they could see the rapidly growing layer of snow that blanketed the ground.

"Isn't it beautiful?" India asked. "I don't know about you girls, but let me at that white stuff. I want to make snow angels!"

The others agreed with noisy enthusiasm, except for Hillary and Avis, who sat silently, waiting for the next word from one of the Howard sisters. Louise held up her hands to silence the giggling and planning among the reunion group. "I'm afraid that the weather forecast is more of the same. It's supposed to snow all day and into tomorrow. There's a good chance the airport will be closed."

She turned to Hillary and Avis. "Did you fly, then drive to Acorn Hill, or did you drive all the way here?"

Avis made a flapping motion with her arms, and Louise smiled in spite of herself. "You flew. Is your flight scheduled to leave tomorrow?"

Avis nodded.

Louise turned to India. "I know that you ladies are scheduled to fly out tomorrow too."

"We're concerned that they will close the airport and you all won't be able to get to your homes on Thanksgiving," Jane said. "You're welcome, of course, to head for the airport tomorrow, but if you need to wait an extra day, my sisters and I invite you to stay here as our guests. There will be no charge, of course. We just want you to have a safe place to stay if the airport is closed. I know it would be a disappointment to miss Thanksgiving dinner with your loved ones, but if you have to stay here, we're having a dinner at Grace Chapel. No matter how bad the weather is, I think enough people can make it to the church for dinner."

"I hope they don't cancel the Franklin and Billings game," India said. "That was the big reason for our girls' week."

"I'm sure they'll wait to see how the weather is tomorrow, but we hope they don't cancel the game either," Jane said.

"We'll keep you updated on the weather," Alice said. "But we thought you might want to know now, so that you can notify your families that you might be a day late."

Hillary and Avis nodded, their eyes clearly showing their thanks. India and her relatives looked at one another. "I guess we'd better get on our cell phones and make a few calls," India said.

"Then can we play in the snow?" Christal asked.

India smiled. "I plan to."

India and her friends spent much of the day outside. Avis and Hillary stood at the window, watching silently, smiling occasionally at the women's childlike antics. Early in the afternoon, however, India and the rest of her group were forced inside, as the once gently falling snow turned into a good old-fashioned blizzard. Thankful that the furnace was going full blast and that they had a good supply of wood, the Howard sisters invited their guests to dine with them that evening on spaghetti and meatballs served with Jane's homemade sauce. Afterward, they all popped corn in the fireplace with an antique popper.

During the night, the blizzard tapered off, and by Thanksgiving morning, the sun shone bravely, giving everyone hope that the football game and airline itineraries might proceed as scheduled. Alice hung up the phone after listening to a recorded message at the airport's switchboard, then headed for the dining room, where her sisters and all the guests sat waiting.

"All flights are canceled until tomorrow," she said. "They want to make certain the runways are clear and that there's no problem with deicing the planes."

"Looks like we'll be your guests for at least another day," Christal said.

Hillary and Avis nodded in unison.

"We are happy to have you," Louise said.

"We want to make sure that you're safe," Jane added. "Avis and Hillary, the rest of us will be going to the high school play-off game. That is, if they're going to hold it."

"The kickoff was scheduled for one o'clock," Alice said. "I'll call Vera Humbert and see if she knows anything."

After Alice left, Jane continued to talk to the guests. "All of you are welcome to join us tonight at Grace Chapel for Thanksgiving dinner. With any luck, we'll get started around six o'clock this evening. We're getting a late start because of the football game. Most people in town are going, so there was no point in holding the dinner earlier in the day."

"It's going to be cold at the stadium," India said, involuntarily shivering. "I'm glad I brought my heavy coat."

"I've been gathering blankets to take. And I'll make a lot of hot chocolate," Jane said.

Alice entered the room. "I talked to Vera. She checked with the school district, and the game is going on as scheduled. There are too many people visiting the area because of the game for them to postpone it. They've also talked to the transportation department, and the roads will be plowed for people to get to the stadium. The forecast is clear, too, so there shouldn't be any problem with more bad weather."

Everyone cheered. "Wonderful!" Jane said. In her excitement, she hugged Louise, while India, Lois, Christal and Misty danced in a circle. Even Avis and Hillary looked pleased.

Jane noticed that Alice was smiling, but she didn't seem as excited as the others. "Is something wrong?"

"I can't go to the game," Alice said. "Right after I spoke to Vera, the hospital called. They want me to come to work. They need extra people on hand because of the bad weather."

"Oh, Alice," Louise said. "I am so sorry."

"I'm concerned that the roads might not be plowed yet," Alice said. "I'm sure they will be by the time you all leave for the game, but I need to go now."

The phone rang again, and Alice excused herself to answer it. When she came back, she was smiling. "My dilemma has been solved. Another person on staff at the hospital is going to pick me up. She has four-wheel drive."

"I'm glad for that," Jane said. "I would worry about you if I knew you were driving alone."

"I'm sorry I won't be able to see you perform as a cheerleader again," Alice said, giving Jane a hug. "Promise me you'll stay warm, all right?"

"I think the temperature is supposed to go up as the day wears on," Louise said. "And I'm sure Jane will be warmer than the rest of us, since she'll be jumping and cheering." She thought for a moment, then smiled. "That sounds like a good idea. Perhaps she and Sylvia would like some help."

Chapter Nineteen

*A*lice's ride arrived, and she left for the hospital. The others dressed warmly for the game. As they stood in the foyer, rounding up coats, hats and scarves, Christal reminded Jane that she had offered to fix her hair. "If there's time after the game, I'll be glad to do it before the dinner."

"Thanks, but I'm not sure I'll have time," Jane said. "As soon as we get back, I have to start taking food over to Grace Chapel." She had stayed up late the previous night, baking. That morning she had also put the turkey into the oven for its lengthy cooking process. The tofu turkey was ready to bake as well, once they got home. Just in case she was flustered from the cheerleading, she left a to-do list on the kitchen table.

Louise had called the transportation department and learned the roads to the stadium were already plowed, so she volunteered to drive Jane and Sylvia to the game. Lois was driving her sister and cousins in a rental car. All four women were reminiscing fast and furiously about their high school days, especially football games they had attended.

"Were any of you cheerleaders?" Jane asked.

Christal laughed. "Not us. We were in the home ec club..."

"...and the chess club," Misty added.

"I was in the choir," Lois said.

India raised her hand. "Drama club for me, could you guess?"

They all laughed. "We'll watch for you today, Jane," India said. Jane had told them about cheering with the mascot.

As Jane drew a heavy coat over the cheerleading outfit Sylvia had made, she saw Hillary and Avis standing in the foyer. "Did you ladies decide to go with us?"

"Actually, no," Avis said.

Everyone turned and stared. "You spoke!" India said.

Hillary smiled. "Our temporary vow of silence was only until Thanksgiving."

"And that's today," Avis said.

Jane had many questions, but Louise was tugging on her arm to signal that they needed to leave.

"We'll be glad to explain it all when you get back," Hillary said. "Is there anything we can do for you while you're gone? Any cooking we can help with?"

Jane shook her head, stunned. "If you would, just keep an eye on the turkey in the oven."

"Will do," Avis said. "Have a good time!"

By the time Louise got to Sylvia's home, her Cadillac had fish-tailed several times. "I'm not sure we can make it to the stadium," Louise said, "even if the roads are plowed."

"We'll take my car," Sylvia said. "I have front-wheel drive, and it's smaller than your Caddie. We should have an easier time."

The three women transferred the thermoses of hot chocolate and piles of blankets, along with the brand-new Patriot mascot costume and the megaphones, into Sylvia's car and headed for the stadium.

Fortunately there hadn't been enough wind to cause problems with drifts. Judging by the crowd they saw when they got to the stadium, other people hadn't had much trouble getting there either.

"I hope Carole made it all right," Jane said. "Maybe we should have volunteered to pick her up."

"I called her this morning to make sure she had a ride," Sylvia said. "She assured me that her parents were going to bring her."

"Carole?" Louise asked. "Who's Carole?"

Jane and Sylvia looked at one another. It would be a shame for the mystery mascot's identity to get out before the game. "Louise, I—"

"Don't worry," Louise said, smiling. "I don't have the slightest idea what you're talking about. You can tell me about it later."

They parked the car and trudged through the snow melting underfoot on the asphalt. Someone had plowed the parking lot, and when they entered the stadium, they saw that the field had been plowed as well. Huge snow drifts, remnants from the plowing, were piled at the ends and side of the field. The three women went to the Franklin High side of the stadium and walked through the portal to the stands.

"We'd better go find Carole," Sylvia murmured to Jane.

Jane nodded. "Louise, we're heading out now. Can you find someone to sit with?"

Louise scanned the crowd of bundled Franklin High fans. "Yoo-hoo!" someone yelled down from the bleachers.

"I think you found Aunt Ethel," Jane said, grinning.

Louise waved. "Yes, there she is with Lloyd. Good luck, Jane," she said, giving her sister a hug.

"Thanks. We'll need it! Here, have some hot chocolate and blankets," Jane said. She thrust two thermoses of the hot beverage and several blankets into Louise's hands, then hurried away with Sylvia at her side.

Louise climbed the steps to meet Ethel and Lloyd. The two must have gotten there early, because their seats were right on the fifty-yard line.

"Oh good, more blankets!" Ethel said, reaching out to help Louise with her bundle.

"And hot chocolate, courtesy of Jane," Louise added, taking a seat beside her aunt. "Hello, Lloyd." She waved a mittened hand at the mayor, who was seated on Ethel's other side.

"Hello, Louise. Great day for a game. I've got a good feeling about Franklin High."

Louise noticed that he wore a bow tie, as usual, but today he sported the red, white and blue—in honor of Franklin High's colors—that he usually reserved for the Fourth of July. "It's a little chilly today," she said, trying not to laugh.

"Nonsense!" Lloyd boomed. "The sun is out, and it's going to get warmer by halftime, I'm sure. Fred Humbert told me it would, and I trust his weather prognostication better than any of those professional fellows."

"That may be, but my teeth are chattering," Ethel said. "Do you think Jane would mind if we had some of the hot chocolate now?"

"I'm sure that's what she would want," Louise said, unscrewing the top to a large thermos.

Jane and Sylvia found Carole Keith at the bottom of the stadium near the concession stands. She was dressed warmly in sweats and a coat. "Are you going to be able to fit the costume over that?" Sylvia asked.

"I can take all this off. I'm wearing thin thermal underwear underneath," she said. "Mrs. Thrush drew straws, and I'm performing during the second half of the game. Well, I should say *we're* performing during the second half."

"Are you going to watch the first half?" Jane asked.

Carole shook her head. "I'm too nervous. And I'm afraid that if I watch the other mascot perform, I'll lose my courage. I'm going to hang around down here with my friends. If they see me beforehand, too, they'll know I'm at the game but may not make the connection that I'm performing as the mascot."

"All right," Jane said. "Sylvia and I will meet you back down here during halftime, and we can get dressed."

"I have to take the mascot costume to the first person trying out," Sylvia said. "Who is it?"

"Guy Hemstreet, do you know him?"

Sylvia shook her head.

Carole took her arm. "I saw him go this way earlier. Let's see if we can find him."

"I'm going to go sit with Louise," Jane said. "See you ladies later."

"I'll join you up there as soon as I've handed off the costume," Sylvia said over her shoulder as Carole pulled her through the growing crowd of fans.

Jane climbed up the stairs and found the right row. She waved to Lloyd and Ethel and said to Louise, "*Brr*, let me have some of that blanket." She scooted under the cover. "It's a lot colder up here than it is down by the concession stands."

"Must be the heat from all the hot dog and hamburger ovens," Louise said. "Why aren't you with Sylvia?"

Jane reluctantly reached outside the warmth of the covers to pour from the thermos. "She had to give the first mascot the costume. Our candidate won't perform until the second half. Sylvia's going to join us in a minute, though."

"Good thing you brought enough blankets," Louise said.

"Yes, they're keeping us nice and toasty," Ethel said, snuggling with Lloyd.

Jane smiled at Louise.

Sylvia joined them, and they handed her a blanket. "Thank you," she said, her teeth chattering.

"When's that weather supposed to warm up?" Louise asked Lloyd, skeptical.

"Halftime," he said cheerfully. "Mark my words."

Soon the announcer was thundering his welcomes at the opening of the game. For the first time in her life, Jane was reluctant to stand for "The Star-Spangled Banner," and everyone's breath blew out frosty as they sang the national anthem. Then the announcer welcomed the Billings High Billy Goats team, and they ran onto the field in a burst of black and gold. Their mascot, a billy goat, ran behind the team on a leash handled by one of the male Billings High cheerleaders.

"At least the goat is warm," Jane said to Sylvia as they sat down and snuggled back into the blankets. "I wish I had his fur coat."

"Look at their cheerleaders," Sylvia said with a moan. "They have thick fleece warm-ups, mittens, earmuffs..."

Jane grabbed her arm. "Look in the end zone. There's the Franklin High team. Yay!" She clapped her hands. She tried to whistle, but it was too cold.

The announcer's voice couldn't be heard over the roar of the crowd for the Franklin High team. The cheerleaders had set up a large GO PATRIOTS! sign between the goal posts, and the team broke through it and ran onto the field. The auditioning mascot ran behind them, cavorting his way to the sidelines in front of the Franklin High stands. The cheerleaders were not far behind him, clapping their pom-poms and cheering loudly to get the crowd warmed up.

"The mascot costume looks great, Sylvia," Jane said. "That foam-rubber head fits perfectly, and the clothes look good too."

"I'm sure the foam rubber is a good insulator," she said, "but the rest of the costume is just cotton. I hope he puts on a coat."

The cheerleaders performed some strong cheers, including a few that were known as "callbacks," which involved crowd participation. "Hey, hey, it's time to fight," the cheerleaders called. "Everybody yell blue, red, white!"

"Blue, red, white!" the crowd yelled back.

"Hey hey, let's do it again! Everybody yell go, fight, win!"

"Go, fight, win!" Jane and Sylvia yelled along with the rest of the fans in the bleachers. Jane could feel her blood warming up already. When they finally quieted down, Sylvia said, "We can do these cheers, Jane. The squad isn't doing anything special."

"I'm sure they'll save their best for later," Jane replied.

Franklin High kicked off to Billings, and the game began. Sylvia clung to Jane's arm as though the fate of the free world depended on the game's outcome. Jane felt her own heart race, whether from the excitement of the game or her own impending performance, she couldn't say.

The cheerleaders pumped up the crowd while the team warmed up.

Hey, all you Patriot fans, stand up and clap your hands.
Clap! Clap-clap! Clap! Clap-clap! Clap-clap! Clap! Clap!
Now that you've got the beat, stand up and stomp your feet.
Stomp! Stomp-stomp! Stomp! Stomp-stomp! Stomp-stomp! Stomp! Stomp!
Now that you've got the groove, stand up and bust a move!

Stomping and clapping, the crowd went through the same rhythm as before. When they finished, Sylvia turned to Jane. "'Bust a move'? How are we going to compete with that?"

"Remember, we're playing it old school, Sylvia. These cheerleaders are definitely more modern than you and I, but we'll offer fun too."

"I just hope we don't make Carole look bad," Sylvia said.

The first points were scored by Franklin with a field goal. The Franklin stands went wild. They were silent, however, when the Billy Goats answered back with a quick touchdown.

"Don't worry," Lloyd said as the buzzer signaled the end of the first quarter. "The Patriots will fight back and win the game."

"Just like the temperature is going to rise?" Ethel asked grimly. The five of them had drained all the thermoses.

Lloyd nodded. "The temperature's going to rise, and the Patriots are going to win. You'll see."

Sure enough, throughout the second quarter, Franklin fought back and scored another field goal. Then Billings scored again, and Franklin immediately ran back the kickoff for a seventy-yard touchdown. Their try was good. The score was fourteen to thirteen in favor of the Billy Goats.

Jane and Sylvia had a difficult time keeping one eye on the game and one eye on the mascot, Guy Hemstreet. He worked well with the cheerleaders, performing alongside them at times and at others, going off on his own to more isolated Franklin-fan bleachers to pep up the crowd. He moved with the band's music and performed his own stunts, clearly to the crowd's approval.

"He's good," Sylvia said, watching as he performed a standing flip after the cheerleaders had finished a jazz routine.

"A little *too* good," Jane said. "But remember that Carole is a senior, so she's just performing today to try to break out of her shy shell."

"Still, I don't want her to disappoint the crowd," Sylvia said.

She clucked her tongue. "Poor Guy must be freezing. He hasn't even put on a coat the entire time."

"But it's going to warm up by halftime," Jane said, impersonating Lloyd. "Mark my words."

She and Sylvia giggled.

The score was still fourteen-thirteen in favor of Billings when the buzzer signaled the end of the first half. The band had already lined up alongside the field for the halftime show. The Billings High band had done the same, and as visitors, they would perform first.

Jane tapped Louise on the shoulder. "Sylvia and I are heading out now. Would you say a prayer for us?"

Louise smiled. "I already have. You girls will do great. So will your mystery mascot. Sylvia's costume is already a hit."

"Thanks," Sylvia said. She handed Louise the blanket she'd been using, neatly folded. "You know, I think it *does* feel a bit warmer."

"I told you," Lloyd said cheerfully. "Knock 'em dead, ladies."

"Thanks, Lloyd," Jane said.

They met Carole near the concession stands under the bleachers. Her hands were shaking, and Jane took them in her own and rubbed them. "Are you cold?"

"N—nervous," Carole said. "I don't think I want to do this. Maybe Guy can do the second half. I heard he was great."

"I'm going to get the costume from Guy," Sylvia said. "Jane, talk some sense into her."

"Let's move here, out of the way," Jane said. She led Carole to a quiet place behind a concrete column, out of the crowd seeking snacks and stretching their legs during the halftime break. Because Franklin was losing, the mood of the crowd was a bit on the glum side.

"Look at them," Jane said, gesturing at the quiet fans. "They need someone to cheer them up. You've worked hard for this game, Carole. You've got the humor, you've got the moves."

"You're just being nice," Carole said.

"No, I'm not. Sylvia and I would not have worked with you so long or so hard if we didn't believe in your dream. And it *is* obtainable. For one day, don't you want to pretend to be someone other than who you've been all through high school?"

Carole smiled thinly. "It would be nice."

"Exactly." Jane gripped her arms. "Look, after high school, you've got your whole life ahead of you, and you're going places. Think of this as the first step of confidence in your own abilities."

Sylvia came puffing up, lugging the giant foam head and clothes in her arms. "Here we are. Are you ready, Carole?"

The young woman didn't say anything. Jane looked around to make certain no one was watching, and when the coast was clear, she lifted the Patriot head onto Carole's. "I can't even tell it's you," she said. "I don't see shy Carole Keith, book lover, I see the Franklin High Patriot, who will do anything to cheer on the crowd as the team heads for victory." She put out her hand. "I'm in. How about you, Sylvia?"

Sylvia solemnly placed her hand over Jane's. "I'm with you."

"How about you, Patriot?" Jane asked.

Carole waited a moment, then put her hand on Jane and Sylvia's. She made a revving noise behind the giant mask and shook her hand from side to side. Sylvia and Jane shook their hands below hers, then they broke with a loud *yay!*

⌒

Louise removed her blanket, folded it and stacked it on top of the others. The sun seemed to be shining a bit brighter, and she noticed that fans were removing their heaviest outer clothing.

Lloyd smiled at her and nodded.

The Billings High marching band finished their performance, then the Franklin High band took the field. The stands went wild, and everyone rose to cheer.

"Ladies and gentlemen, the Franklin High Patriot band!" the announcer said.

The crowd cheered again, and the band played "The Battle Hymn of the Republic" as they marched onto the field. Stepping smartly and playing their instruments flawlessly, the band segued into another patriotic song, then into snippets from several military tunes. They ended with *The 1812 Overture* and the crowd cheered wildly.

"They have so much talent," Louise murmured, mesmerized by the display and the music. "I didn't realize how good they were this year."

"They won first place in their division in the state marching competition," Lloyd said.

Louise wondered how many of the students would pursue musical careers, but even those who didn't would always know the joy of creating music as a team effort. She applauded enthusiastically along with the others.

The band cleared the field, and everyone fidgeted with impatience for the second half to start. Both teams lined up in the end zones. The Billings team was announced first, and they ran onto the field with confidence.

"And now, ladies and gentlemen, once again, your Franklin High PA-triotsssssss!" the announcer drawled.

The crowd rose to its feet as the team ran onto the field, led by the cheerleaders. Taking up the rear was the mascot and—Louise smiled—Jane and Sylvia. They ran all the way from the end zone to the front of the stands, and Louise knew that all the years of Jane's diligent runs had paid off. She didn't look any more out of breath than the high school cheerleaders.

Sylvia and Jane had removed their coats, and Louise saw that they were wearing old-fashioned white cheerleading skirts that fell below their knees, blue tights and thick red sweaters with a white F on the front.

The mascot took up his position in front of the stands, hands on hips, while everyone clapped. He raised a hand to his ear as if to say he couldn't hear them.

Everyone clapped louder, and Jane and Sylvia looked at each other. Standing side by side, they went into a basic cheer and routine.

> *Two bits, four bits*
> *Six bits, a dollar*
> *All for the Patriots, stand up and holler!*

The crowd clapped politely, but no one rose to their feet.

Louise noticed that the regular Franklin High cheerleaders stood to the side, looking a little confused, but clapping good-naturedly.

Jane and Sylvia huddled together, then they spoke briefly with the mascot. He went to a bag by the cheerleading bench and took out a few clothing items. He quickly replaced his tricorn hat with a black porkpie one. Then he donned what looked like a full-length raccoon coat and waved a red felt pennant with a giant white *F*. He stood alongside Jane and Sylvia, then nodded. They went into an old-fashioned cheer routine to a very old-fashioned cheer.

> *Down by the river*
> *Skit! Skat!*
> *Beat that team and send them back.*
> *With a hidy-hi and a hody-ho.*
> *Truckin'! Truckin'!*
> *Truck some mo!*
> *Our team is red hot!*

While they went through the routine, the mascot waved his banner, doing a little shuffle and raising his hands at the end on "red hot."

Lloyd chuckled. "I remember that cheer from when I was a little kid," he said. "That's from the thirties." He made a megaphone out of his hands and cupped them around his mouth so that Jane and Sylvia could hear him. "Do that one again! I'll help you out!"

Even from the stands, Louise could see Jane's and Sylvia's smiles. Lloyd gestured for others around them to rise also, and soon there were a bunch of fans cheering along with Jane and

Sylvia. The mascot got a little bolder, his movements a little more exaggerated, and everyone was laughing and clapping when the cheer was over. "Do another one!" someone yelled.

Franklin had lost the ball, so Billings had it on their own forty-yard line. Sylvia and Jane linked arms and took up their megaphones.

> *Harass them, harass them!*
> *Make them relinquish the ball!*

The crowd took up the cry, and the band's drummers beat along in rhythm, spicing up the beat with an underscored cadence. The Franklin cheerleaders shrugged, then joined Jane and Sylvia in the cheer. The mascot made exaggerated motions of "harassing" by pushing the air in time with the words. When Billings fumbled, everyone in the Franklin bleachers was on his feet. Jane and Sylvia launched into another old cheer.

> *Victory, Victory, is our cry—*
> *V-I-C-T-O-R-Y*
> *Will we falter and fall right through?*
> *No, we'll fight for the red, white and blue.*
> *Go-o-o-o FRANKLIN!*

The high school cheerleaders executed Herkie jumps—one leg extended straight to the side, with the other bent toward the ground. Jane and Sylvia did a modified Broadway chorus-line kick. The mascot danced around, alternately moon walking and tap dancing.

Ethel laughed and clapped. "Who is the mascot?" she asked Louise.

Louise shrugged and smiled innocently. "That's Jane's big secret, Aunt Ethel."

By the middle of the fourth quarter, all the bleachers were buzzing with the same question as Ethel's. Jane and Sylvia's old-style cheers and low-key routines were a hit, and the mascot's mugging added to the entertainment. The funnier and more clever the Patriot mascot's routine became, the more the crowd wanted to know: Who was hidden by the costume?

Ricka racka boom, ricka racka boom
Ricka racka, ricka racka, ricka racka boom
Sis boom bah, sis boom bah
Franklin, Franklin, rah, rah, rah!

Despite the fun in the stands, the Franklin Patriots were having a difficult time on the field. They had led with a twenty-seven to twenty-one score, but then the Billy Goats scored a touchdown to take a twenty-eight to twenty-seven lead. With half a quarter left in the game, the Patriot fans were optimistic, but the team couldn't push through the Billings defense, and on their next possession, the Billy Goats scored a field goal. The score was thirty-one to twenty-seven in favor of Billings.

"I'm afraid they're not going to win," Ethel whispered to Louise. "There's less than three minutes in the game."

"But Franklin has the ball now, Auntie," Louise said. "All they need is a touchdown to win, then for the defense to hold. There's still hope."

"Yes," Lloyd said, leaning into their conversation. "And the only time the Billy Goats' offense has gotten through is with passes. If the Patriots' defense can shut down Billings' passing game, they'll have a pretty good chance of getting the ball and coming back.

Ethel and Louise linked arms and crossed fingers.

> *1-2-3-4*
> *Who you gonna yell for?*
> *P-A-T-R-I-O-T-S*
> *That's the way you spell it,*
> *Here's the way you yell it:*
> *PATRIOTS! PATRIOTS! PATRIOTS!*

On the next play, the Patriots' quarterback fumbled the ball and Billings recovered. The stands on the other side of the field went wild. The Patriots' offense walked slowly to the bench, heads down, as the defense once again took the field. Ethel and Louise looked at each other sadly. With less than two minutes to go, the game seemed all but clinched. The Franklin High stands were so somber that hardly anyone moved. The high school cheerleaders seemed stunned for a moment, then they huddled with Jane, Sylvia and the mascot. They formed a line, with the mascot in front, and began to cheer.

> *Boom a lacka, boom a lacka, bow wow wow*
> *We need a defense, and we need it NOW*
> *Chicka lacka, chicka lacka, chow chow chow*
> *Get that ball from Billings and—*

At that moment, the Billings quarterback dropped back, then threw the ball. From out of the tangle of players, a Franklin defensive lineman leaped up and intercepted it.

Ethel gripped Louise's arm and jumped up and down, squealing. Lloyd roared with delight. Louise was speechless, and everybody in the stands seemed to be either holding his breath or yelling at maximum capacity.

The defensive tackle charged through the Billings offensive line and ran for the end zone. The Billy Goat quarterback tried to tackle him, missed, and fell on his face. The Franklin player crashed across the goal line and fell in a heap. His teammates instantly jumped on top of him in celebration.

Ethel and Louise hugged, then Ethel turned to Lloyd for another hug. The kick was good! Everyone in the stands went crazy, and the Franklin band played the school's fight song. Too excited to perform a routine, the high school cheerleaders, Jane, Sylvia and the mascot jumped up and down and hugged each other. At last they gathered some semblance of order.

> V-I-C-T-O-R-Y
> *Victory, victory is our cry!*
> V-I-C-T-O-R-Y
> *Victory, victory is our cry!*

There was still a little more than a minute to play in the game, but the Patriots' defense refused to yield even one yard to the shaken Billy Goats. When the buzzer went off, the Patriots had won with a thirty-four to thirty-one score.

The fans cheered with joy, and the entire Patriots team ran onto the field. The players lifted the defensive lineman onto their shoulders and carried him toward the stands.

Louise tried to see who it was but couldn't even make out his uniform number. "Who is that?" Louise asked Lloyd.

"That's Trevor Walker," he said, clapping and whistling with his fingers between his teeth.

The players cheered and applauded toward the stands to show their appreciation, then the band struck the opening notes of the school song. Everyone quieted and sang.

> *Franklin High, dear Franklin High*
> *We'll be true to you*
> *We bring to you our loyalty*
> *Pledged to the red, white and blue*
> *As years go by and memories fade*
> *One thing we'll never rue*
> *That we were part of Franklin High*
> *Because we're Patriots through and through!*

A cheer went up, and Louise felt a chill. She normally did not get sentimental at sporting events, but everyone in the stands, whether an alum of Franklin High or not, seemed to be part of a larger community of something good.

Perhaps because of that, someone started to cheer, "Who's the mascot? Who's the mascot?" Others took up the cry until those on the field joined in as well. Jane and Sylvia stood beside the mascot, who seemed hesitant to reveal his face. At last he nodded, and Sylvia lifted off the Patriot head to reveal Franklin High's biggest bookworm and shyest senior, Carole Keith.

For a moment, there was silence. Then the fans erupted into applause. The players and cheerleaders joined in, and finally Jane and Sylvia bowed in Carole's direction, acknowledging her accomplishment.

Carole looked stunned, but even more so when several of the Franklin High players lifted her onto their shoulders and paraded her and Trevor Walker in a victory march.

Chapter Twenty

After everybody had congratulated Carole for her superb job as the mascot, she explained her intent for the audition. Guy Hemstreet, who had performed in the first half, was delighted to hear that he would be taking over the role of the Patriot full-time next year, as Carole was a graduating senior. They agreed to share the mascot duty for whatever play-off games remained this season.

The Franklin cheerleaders congratulated Carole and also Jane and Sylvia. "The mascot costume was great, Ms. Songer, and you guys were way cool with your cheers," Sophie said.

"Yeah," Candace added. "We're sorry we didn't give you a chance when you tried to show us the routines."

"It was really funny when the mascot had on that crazy raccoon coat alongside you ladies with those long cheerleading skirts," Lashaunda said, laughing.

"Exactly," Jane said. "You girls do what you do best, with your shoulder stands and dance moves. We were just funny because we were unexpected."

"Still," Mai said, "those cheers might work great on a crowd that isn't participating much. Can you teach us a few of those old cheers?"

Sylvia and Jane looked at one another and said in unison, "Any time."

⌒

The roads were much clearer going home than they had been before the game. The mood in the car was much lighter, too, with Sylvia, Jane and Louise singing the Franklin High fight song all the way home. They retrieved Louise's Cadillac at Sylvia's.

"That was the most fun I've had in years," Sylvia said. "I'm glad we got to do it."

"And I'm glad we got to help Carole," Jane said. "But I'm afraid I'm going to be spending all day tomorrow soaking in a tub of hot water. My muscles are killing me."

"Me too, but it was worth it. Are you all set with the Thanksgiving dinner?"

Jane nodded. "That's why I'm putting off the tub soaking for tomorrow. I'll see you later at Grace Chapel."

When Louise and Jane returned to Grace Chapel Inn, they walked through the door just as India, Lois and their cousins, Christal and Misty, were carrying their luggage down the sidewalk. "Where are you going?" Louise asked. "We thought you were staying until tomorrow."

India shook her head. "We would have loved to, but Christal called the airport and found out that they've reopened the runways. Our flights have been rescheduled for later this evening. We can still make it home in time to have Thanksgiving dinner with our families."

"I'm glad," Louise said, "though of course we were looking forward to your company at dinner."

"Wasn't that game a blast?" India said, smiling at Jane. "You and your friend were wonderful! So was that mascot. I told my sister and cousins that even if Franklin High lost, we had a lot of fun watching you ladies and that Patriot."

"Thanks for the vote of confidence," Jane said. "We had a lot of fun, but it was most exciting to see the team win."

India sighed dramatically. "We've had a great time here, ladies. Thanks for everything."

"Yes, it was wonderful, but we're ready to head back to our families now," Christal said.

"We'll be sure to recommend this place to our friends," Misty said.

"Girls, we'd better get going if we want to make our flight," Lois said. "Good-bye, Louise. Good-bye, Jane. Please say good-bye to Alice."

"Good-bye," Jane said as the women headed for their car. Then she glanced at her watch. "Yipes! And how I'm going to manage to get dinner ready at Grace Chapel is going to be another mystery. Better get moving."

Despite the aches and pains from cheerleading, she rushed into the kitchen. There she found Hillary and Avis with the cooked turkey on the table. "It was ready," Hillary said, "so we took it out of the oven about thirty minutes ago."

Louise had followed Jane into the kitchen to see if she could be of service. Jane tried to check the bird without insinuating that

Hillary had removed it prematurely. It seemed to be cooked thoroughly. "Thanks for making sure it didn't burn," she said. "Now I have to pop the tofu turkey—"

"Already done," Avis said. "It's cooking now."

Jane stared at them in wonder. "How did you know what to do?"

"It's easy," Hillary said, holding up a piece of paper. She smiled. "We found your list of things to do on the kitchen table. We wanted to help, since we saw time was running out."

"We also heated up the sweet potatoes, as the instructions said," Avis added. "We found them in the refrigerator."

Jane smiled. "That's Alice's recipe. She made the casserole up yesterday, thank goodness, although I never did find out what her secret ingredient was. And speaking of secrets"—she sat down at the table with the two women— "can you tell us now why you didn't talk for a week?"

"Yes," Louise said, taking the fourth seat at the table. "I am most interested."

Hillary smiled. "Avis and I wanted to take a silent retreat. We wanted to see if we could go an entire week without speaking. We thought it would be too easy if we went to a monastery or on a church retreat, so we chose someplace that wasn't completely isolated but would still be quiet enough for reflection and contemplation."

"But we also didn't want to explain ourselves or rely on paper to communicate our needs," Avis said. "We felt that would be the same as talking."

"Did our other guests bother you?" Louise asked.

Hillary and Avis looked at each other. "They were a bit noisy, but to tell you the truth, they sounded like they were having a lot of fun," Hillary said. "The next time we travel, we're going to invite our friends and have a girls' week like they did."

"We got a chance to say good-bye to them and explain our purpose in coming to Grace Chapel Inn," Avis said. "The funny thing is that they said the next time *they* went off together, they wanted to do what we did instead."

Jane consulted her list of things to do before the dinner. "Well, it looks like you took care of most everything here. Thank you so much. I have just enough time to change and take things over to the church. I hope you can stay for the dinner. The other guests said that the airport had reopened."

"You are still welcome to stay as our guests," Louise said. "Our offer of a free night still stands."

"We'd love to stay," Avis said. "Maybe we can actually have a conversation before we have to leave tomorrow."

With Avis's, Hillary's and Louise's help, Jane ferried all the food to Grace Chapel. Inside the Assembly Room, where the dinner would be held, the decorating committee had already set up tables and a serving area, covering them with paper tablecloths with smiling pilgrims and Native Americans. Sturdy paper plates and plastic utensils marked each place setting. On each table was a cornucopia that the ANGELs had supplied for decoration.

"Vera, your committee did a great job," Jane said when she saw her friend.

"Thanks," Vera said proudly. "It does look nice, doesn't it?"

"I *love* it," Jane said, giving Vera a hug.

"You were wonderful today," Vera said. "And what you did for Carole really boosted her confidence. I saw her after the game, and she was absolutely glowing."

"It was a lot of fun. And dinner will be a lot of fun too," Jane said, eyeing the doorway. People were beginning to stream in, bearing casserole dishes, pies and carafes of hot and cold beverages. "I just wish Alice could be here," she said. "I was hoping she'd be able to make it."

Vera's eyes twinkled. "Look over there."

Standing in the corner and chatting with Avis and Hillary was Alice. She looked up and saw Jane and waved. Jane returned the wave, her heart feeling lighter.

Craig Tracy headed toward her from behind the serving table. "Looks pretty good, doesn't it?" he asked. "Even the tofu turkey." He leaned toward her confidentially. "I made one, too, and, of course, had to sample it," he whispered. "I thought it was quite good."

Jane gazed over the table groaning with food and smiled. "I hope Lorrie likes it. I'm glad to see her here."

Craig frowned. "There's one thing I wish we could have done, though."

"What's that?"

"I wish we could have served more people. There are lots of

people who would have loved to come but don't have transportation or aren't well."

"Shut-ins," Jane said, nodding. She thought for a moment, then smiled. "Do you have your delivery truck here?"

"Yes, I used it to bring the food over," Craig said. "Why?"

"Let's make up plates and take them to some of those folks," Jane said. "Pastor Ken will know who couldn't make it but who would love to be remembered."

Craig smiled. "Let's get to it."

Alice and Louise were sitting together when Jane told them her plan. They thought it was wonderful and agreed to stay at the chapel to make sure that the dinner proceeded as planned. They helped Jane make up plates of food, covering them with plastic wrap, then loading them into Craig's van. By the time Jane and Craig drove away with a lengthy list of names, the dinner inside the Assembly Room was in full swing.

Alice and Louise finally got their food and found places to sit. Louise told Alice all about the football game—particularly about Jane and Sylvia's performance and Carole Keith's. Alice had heard the final score of the game on the radio, and she was pleased that Franklin had won, even though she hadn't been present to see it.

"It wasn't very busy at the hospital after all," she said. "I took the opportunity to catch up on some paperwork and inventory the supply closet. I have to admit that it feels good to sit down."

"I'm proud of you," Louise said, smiling.

"Whatever for?" Alice asked.

"For doing your duty right away and sacrificing the opportunity to go to the game. You could have begged off, but even when it was obvious you weren't really needed, you stayed to help."

Alice smiled. "When I think of sacrifice, I think of Nathan Delhomme and the other veterans. I hope they are having a happy Thanksgiving, wherever they are."

"Louise!" Melanie Brubaker approached their table, carrying an empty plate. "I've wanted to speak to you all night, but you looked busy."

"How are you, Melanie?" Louise asked.

"Notice anything different?" Melanie said, tucking her hair behind her ear.

"You got your hearing aids!" Louise said. "How are they?"

"They're wonderful," Melanie said. "They came in Tuesday, and Mac took me to pick them up before the weather got too bad. I'm still getting used to them, but I'm so glad I got them." She laughed. "It's so strange to be able to hear so clearly. I hadn't realized how much I was missing."

"I am so glad for you," Louise said.

Melanie gave her a hug. "Thanks for helping me. Mac and I also delivered all the goods from the food drive to the Community Pantry. I couldn't have done that, or gotten these hearing aids, without your help. You're a good friend. Oops! I better catch up with Mac and the kids. They're heading for the dessert table without me. Bye!"

Pleased that things had worked out so well for Melanie, Louise turned back to her plate. She took a bite of the sweet potatoes that Alice had made. "These *are* really good. Did Jane ever figure out what the secret ingredient is?"

"Nope." Alice grinned.

Louise took another bite, then swallowed. "You are lucky that it was I and not Jane who saw that Dr Pepper can in the wastebasket," she said.

Alice stared, incredulous, then broke into a smile. "I should have covered my tracks better. She'd never let me hear the end of it if she knew you gave me that recipe years ago."

"Or that it had soda pop as an ingredient."

Alice frowned. "Do you think it's wrong of us to keep it a secret from her?"

"I don't think of it as keeping a secret. I think of it as sparing her culinary sensibilities."

Alice took a forkful of potatoes and swallowed. She smiled at Louise. "I like the way you look at things."

Alice's Mystery Sweet Potatoes
SERVES EIGHT

4 medium sweet potatoes

¼ cup butter

1 cup Dr Pepper soda

⅓ cup sugar

½ teaspoon salt

½ cup chopped pecans

½ cup shredded coconut

Boil potatoes in their jackets for ten minutes. Drain and let stand in cold water until cool enough to handle. Peel by hand, then slice into quarter-inch rounds. Arrange in an eight-by-eight-inch glass baking dish.

In a saucepan, melt butter. Add the Dr Pepper, sugar and salt. Boil for ten minutes. Pour mixture over the potatoes. Sprinkle top with chopped pecans and coconut.

Bake at 375 degrees for thirty minutes, basting once after fifteen minutes.

About the Author

The late Jane Orcutt is the best-selling author of thirteen novels, including *All the Tea in China*. She has been nominated for the RITA award twice. A proud wife and mother of two sons, she lived in Fort Worth, Texas.

Tales from Grace Chapel Inn

Once you visit the charming village of Acorn Hill, you'll never want to leave. Here, the three Howard sisters reunite after their father's death and turn the family home into a bed-and-breakfast. They rekindle old memories, rediscover the bonds of sisterhood, revel in the blessings of friendship and meet many fascinating guests along the way.